LEGACY OF SHADOWS

Keeper's Rebellion

S.J. Winter

Winter Publishing

The characters and events portrayed in this book are fictitious. Any similarity to real persons, living or dead, is coincidental and not intended by the author.

ISBN-13: 979-8-218-24890-1

Cover design by: OliviaProDesign
Library of Congress Control Number: 2018675309
Printed in the United States of America

I am dedicating this book to my loving mother, whose unwavering support and guidance have been my constant source of strength since childhood. Your belief in me has driven my journey, and I am forever grateful for your love and encouragement.

To my dear husband, whose faith in my abilities and dreams never wavered, even when my confidence faltered. Your unwavering support and belief in me have been my anchor throughout this journey.

And to my precious son, whose bright eyes and boundless curiosity inspire me daily. May this book remind us that we can overcome our fears and achieve our dreams with determination and courage. I hope it inspires you to believe in yourself and know you can accomplish anything you want.

With love and gratitude,

S.J. Winter

"You don't have to be great to start, but you have to start to be great."

ZIG ZIGLAR

CONTENTS

CHAPTER ONE

As mourners dispersed along the cemetery's gravel path, Blythe Evans stood alone among fading headstones. The graveyard stretched before her, an eerie sea of granite and marble shrouded in the fading light of dusk. Wisps of fog clung to the ground, lending an ethereal quality to the scene. The ancient trees, their branches gnarled and twisted, seemed to reach out as if trying to console the bereaved.

A sudden wind swept through the cemetery, delivering a fluttering letter to her feet. Blythe picked up the aged envelope, her name penned in familiar handwriting. The seal bore the unmistakable mark of the Magic Council, an authority feared by even the bravest supernaturals. She had avoided their scrutiny for years.

The letter exuded an unsettling energy as if it held a hidden power. Her heart raced, fingers trembling involuntarily.

"Dear Blythe Evans, You are summoned to appear before the Magic Council for an urgent matter at the Council Chambers in the Hall of Mysteries, Brilane, Auroraheim."

The date was a ticking time bomb that threatened her world.

"Your compliance is mandatory, and failure to appear will result in severe consequences. The Council holds authority over the Human and Magic realms."

Blythe's mind raced. The Council was closing in, but Blythe wouldn't surrender. Her father had suffered their judgment, and she refused to be another casualty of their power game.

She clenched the letter, determination mingling with trepidation. She sprinted into the woods, seeking refuge from the crowd near her car.

The tall elms welcomed her, the evening breeze whispered through their leaves, and crickets chorused. Every rustle and murmur seemed to acknowledge her presence. The woods had been her sanctuary, but it had become a battleground of emotions tonight.

Blythe paused, her heart pounding. The confrontation with the Council loomed—an inevitable hurdle avoided for years. She fortified herself with each breath.

A voice shattered the stillness. "Blythe!"

She spun around, heart leaping. Miles Dixon, her former boyfriend and steadfast friend, emerged from the shadows.

"Miles?" Blythe's eyes widened in astonishment. Miles stood before her, his breath uneven from the urgency of his pursuit. "What are you doing here?"

Miles took a moment to steady himself, his blue eyes fixed on her. "I saw you slip away from the funeral," he admitted, his words rushed. "I tried to follow you, but Ben got in my way, and then I lost track of where you went."

Blythe's mind raced, grappling with the revelation that Miles had been tailing her. The weight of his actions and his determination to find her on this moonlit night settled in. Did he know about the summons?

His eyes softened with empathy. "You've been through so much, especially with your uncle's passing. I thought you might need someone to talk to." He paused, "I can't just leave you to deal with this alone." His voice was earnest, determination evident in his eyes. "We've faced countless challenges together."

The mixture of emotions swirling within her held their own internal debate. She contemplated whether to share the letter's contents with Miles and entrust him with the truth of her predicament. His unwavering presence brought forth the temptation to unburden herself. Still, the gravity of the Magic Council's summons held her tongue in check.

Noticing her hesitation, Miles furrowed his brow as concern etched across his features. "Hey... are you okay?"

Blythe drew in a deep breath. "I received a letter," she finally admitted in an uneasy voice, "from the Magic Council. They've summoned me to appear before them."

Miles' eyes widened, the weight of her words sinking in. "The Magic Council? What could they want? And you received this at the funeral?"

Blythe's shoulders slumped. "Yeah. I don't know. It was strange. I felt a slight breeze after the service, and suddenly, the letter was just... there. It was like the wind carried it to me."

Miles looked puzzled, intrigued by the magical means the letter had found her. "That's... unusual."

Her expression darkened as she continued. "The letter doesn't say much, just that it's urgent and mandatory."

Miles' hand instinctively reached out to Blythe's. "You don't have to face this alone. Whatever it is, we'll figure it out together."

Gratitude washed over her. She managed a small smile and hugged him.

Miles chuckled softly. "How about we go back to Fasbridge Manor and plan over a cup of Sorcerer's Sereni-Tea?"

Blythe's expression remained resolute. "No, Miles. I won't set foot in that House until I must pass through the portal to attend the council meeting."

Miles raised his hands in mock surrender, a grin on his lips. "Alright, no magic house for now, but remember, I'm here for you."

Under the moonlit canopy, the weight of the impending council meeting was lightened by the companionship of a friend ready to face the unknown with Blythe.

She lingered a bit longer, gazing at Miles with a soft smile. Their conversation naturally wound down, and she leaned in for one more hug. "Thanks, Miles," she said quietly, gratitude shining in her eyes.

He gently returned her embrace. "Anytime, Blythe. You

know I've got your back."

Blythe and Miles retraced their steps, returning to the cemetery. At the edge of the tree line, Blythe's anxiety eased upon seeing that the mourners had departed, leaving only her car, Miles's, and the gravediggers' truck along the drive.

Before parting ways, they paused, a sense of camaraderie lingering in the air. Blythe turned to Miles, her expression a mixture of gratitude and resolve. "Thank you for being here," she said, her voice steady despite the turmoil within her.

Miles offered a reassuring smile, his eyes reflecting their unspoken bond. "Of course, Blythe. We're in this together," he replied, his words carrying a promise that transcended their present circumstances.

Their unspoken agreement hung in the air, a silent affirmation of their shared path. Blythe's resolve deepened, fortified by knowing she wasn't alone in the challenges ahead. "I'll see you at the House before I face the council," she added.

Miles nodded his expression a blend of encouragement and solidarity. "Count on it. Stay strong, Blythe."

As they turned away from each other and headed to their respective cars, Blythe felt a glimmer of hope. Miles's support was a lifeline, and their rendezvous at the House felt like a beacon of comfort amidst the uncertainty ahead.

Settling into the driver's seat, Blythe glanced at her rearview mirror. Miles's car disappeared into the darkness, yet his presence lingered in her thoughts.

Blythe drove away into the night as moonlight filtered through the trees. Her mind whirled with emotions, consumed by thoughts of the summons and the Magic Council's letter.

She looked forward to arriving at the hotel to gather her thoughts. The road ahead was uncertain, but her determination remained steadfast. With the moon as her guide, she pressed on into the night, leaving the cemetery behind.

Blythe's hands gripped the steering wheel as she drove down the forest road, her nerves on edge and a sense of unease prickling her skin. The narrow road stretched ahead, illuminated only by the car's headlights. She sighed in relief as a sign indicated her hotel's direction. Her momentary calm shattered when movement flickered in the rearview mirror. Blythe's heart raced as she spotted a shadow darting through the adjacent trees.

Instinctively, she pressed the gas pedal to distance herself from whatever presence lurked nearby. Tires hummed on the road as her pulse thudded in her ears. A muffled thud suddenly reverberated through the car, gripping Blythe in panic and causing her steering to grow unsteady.

"Come on, no," she muttered, her grip tightening on the wheel. The car's handling altered, and she fought to keep control. The truth became clear instantly: the ominous thud had signaled a tire blowout.

Blythe's adrenaline surged as she navigated the car to the road's shoulder before silencing the engine. She glanced at her phone and prayed she still had service, but the screen taunted her with a "No Signal" message. Dread pooled in her stomach. She was stranded alone in the dark, unable to call for help.

The woods felt alive, unseen eyes watching. Changing the tire was her only choice. Stepping out of her vehicle and into the chilly night air, her phone's flashlight revealed the shredded tire. Fumbling through her belongings in the trunk, her frustration grew. No spare tire. "Seriously?" she muttered, irritation battling the growing unease. Of course, the one time she needed it, the spare was nowhere to be found.

Blythe slammed the trunk shut, expressing her irritation as her breath quickened. She was alone and stranded, with the forest watching as her feelings of being trapped intensified.

A sudden growl pierced the air behind her. Blythe's heart raced; an instinctive chill ran down her spine. Shadows converged, Blythe's own fear gripping her tighter. Turning, she faced the darkness, her heart pounding as she searched for the source of the sound.

Panic welled as her instinct to flee surfaced. She bolted

towards her car, desperate for the safety of its confines. But when she yanked the door, it refused to open. She was trapped, locked out of her own escape.

Terror gripped her as the growls drew nearer, echoing through the night. Heart pounding, breath quickening, she had no choice but to flee. The forest's darkness seemed to close in, each rustle of leaves a potential threat.

Then, amidst the suffocating blackness, something caught Blythe's attention. Like a distant ember in the night, a faint, ethereal glow flickered through the dense underbrush. It promised safety or danger—she couldn't know. With a racing heart, she veered off, leaving the car behind to plunge into the woods. The faint, persistent glow acted like a distant beacon, guiding her through the shadows.

Time lost its meaning as she pushed forward. Trees loomed like sentinels, branches clawing at the air. The glow pulsed, casting an eerie light over the forest. Blythe stumbled on, driven by an electric mix of curiosity and fear.

As she continued, dread and anticipation tangled in her chest. The glow faded, but the forest's watchful silence remained. The light stayed her focus, guiding her through the unknown. She pressed on with every ounce of determination—her journey through the woods was a relentless pursuit of truth and survival.

Uphill, she spotted old-fashioned street lamps, their glow casting an eerie aura. Her steps faltered, her heart racing. These lamps were strangers in a familiar place. Were they even real? The surroundings pressed closer, the forest's whispers growing louder.

Fear fought with resolve as she approached the lamps. Trees leaned closer, the night alive with unseen watchers. Onward she went, the glow pulling her toward a driveway. The House she had tried to forget loomed beyond, comfort and dread entwined.

The driveway guided her onward, its cobblestones and imperfections illuminated by the phone's light. As she approached the front steps, memories flooded her mind – childhood laughter, secrets shared – yet now, the House bore a new, heavy significance. She steeled herself and, with a deep breath, stepped over the threshold.

Silence met her, but the House's aura was alive, watching as she moved forward. Hesitant in her own past, memories whispered, guiding her steps. Familiar corners felt strange, once-warm rooms now chilled. The pull of the past battled the uncertainty of the present, and Blythe had no choice but to keep moving.

The House resembled an old Victorian mansion in the darkness, its towering spires and ornate architecture casting eerie shadows. The phone's feeble light barely scratched the surface of its grandeur, leaving much to the imagination. The House seemed to absorb the moonlight, giving it an otherworldly presence.

She couldn't help but reflect on her growing up in this place. She remembered how she had yearned to explore beyond the familiar borders that had confined her. Thoughts of Fasbridge Manor lingered in the back of her mind. However, its exact location remained a mystery. The possibility that the perplexing light had led her to the site she had tried to avoid sending a surge of unease through her veins.

Emotions churned beneath the surface, the memories of that place igniting internal turmoil. Images of the manor, the hidden chambers, and the shadows that whispered secrets threatened to overwhelm her. Her heart raced, her steps faltered, and the anxiety that she had kept at bay surged forward. Gathering every ounce of courage, she ascended the front steps, her resolve stronger than her fear.

CHAPTER TWO

Blythe hesitated at the threshold, torn between fleeing and facing the unknown. A low, guttural snarl from behind erased the escape option. "Fine," she muttered and stepped over the threshold. The door closed with a resounding thud, sealing her fate. Her heart raced, emotions swirling within.

The grand entry hall unfolded before her, a haunting blend of dark wood floors adorned with vibrant red, black, and green designed rugs. Cherry wainscoting traced the walls, while faded wallpaper displayed elegant floral motifs, its once vivid colors now muted by time. The coffered ceiling, adorned with intricate patterns, loomed overhead, casting detailed shadows. The carved cherry banister whispered of another era, its craftsmanship a testament to the House's storied history. Blythe's eyes danced across scattered artifacts—an ornate grandfather clock, a tarnished suit of armor, a vase filled with wildflowers. The House's obsession with preserving the past resonated with her, every nook and cranny a testament to a bygone era.

Miles appeared from the side room, his shocking white hair contrasting against aquamarine eyes that emitted an ethereal glow. Rugged charm emanated from him, dressed in black with a simple leather strap necklace.

"Blythe!" he exclaimed, closing the distance with open arms. Guarded enthusiasm met his genuine delight. "You changed your mind," he noted, gripping her hand.

"Not really. The car's got a flat tire and no spare. I need to call AAA," she spoke, focusing her gaze below his chin, guarding herself from the vulnerability she imagined would be in his eyes.

"Flat tire? Talk about rotten luck," he smirked, a mischievous glint in his eyes betraying his composure.

Suspicion crept into her thoughts. "You didn't..."

"Of course not," he grinned, mischief overcoming his attempt at nonchalance.

Heat flushed her cheeks. "How dare you! The shadows in the woods?"

"Wasn't my plan. I just gave it a little nudge," Miles admitted, suppressing a smile.

"Whose plan was it, then?" Arms crossed, she glared up at him.

"Let's just say the House had a hand in it," he held his ground, unyielding to her rising anger.

"The House?" Her frown deepened. "Nice try," Blythe turned her back and walked away.

"No joke, I'm serious!" he protested, following closely as she strode down the hallway.

"There's no point in discussing this. I need the phone, and then I'm out of here," Blythe declared, her steps halting abruptly as Miles swiftly positioned himself in front of her path. His arms extended in a playful, inviting gesture.

"Oh, how I've missed you!" His joy was genuine, and a glimmer of warmth stirred within her despite her resolve. It was a familiar feeling that bound them in the past—a magic that seemed to have cast its spell long ago.

"Miles," she began, her hands clenching and unclenching as a whirlwind of emotions swirled within her. She had been ready to unleash her anger and inflict the same pain she felt upon him. Yet, a change of heart softened her expression, a decision made in the blink of an eye. "You know I care about you, but that was uncalled for. Using magic in the Human World? You're inviting trouble, and not just from me." A small smile tugged at her lips, though her eyes retained a touch of reproach.

"Nah... sometimes bad luck is just that," he grinned.

"Ass," she retorted. It was hard to stay angry when Miles was around. He always had a knack for making her worries dissipate, even if his aversion to schoolwork had made studying together nearly impossible. "How convenient that my car broke down then... fine, I'll stay the night, but I need to replace the tire so I can leave tomorrow."

"I'll lend a hand then," Miles smirked playfully. "But for now, how about following me?" The air seemed to vibrate with possibilities, an unspoken understanding that their reunion might unlock more than she bargained for. Blythe followed him, her anticipation growing as they headed towards the kitchen. She would call AAA and sort out the mess with her flat tire.

The kitchen door swung open, revealing a cozy, vintage interior caught in a time warp. As Blythe stepped inside, her eyes immediately landed on the old rotary phone sitting on the counter, its coiled cord dangling like the relic it is.

"I'm guessing this is what you're looking for," Miles remarked, a hint of satisfaction as he gestured towards the phone.

Blythe nodded, a spark in her eyes. She approached the phone. She picked up the receiver and began dialing AAA, her fingers moving with practiced efficiency.

But as the numbers were dialed and she pressed the receiver to her ear, a silence greeted her instead of the expected dial tone. Confusion wrinkled her brow, and she shot a puzzled glance at Miles.

"What's wrong?" he asked, his curiosity piqued by her reaction.

"The phone... It's not working," Blythe replied, her frustration mounting. She dialed the numbers more forcefully, but the result was the same—an eerie silence on the other end.

Miles leaned against the counter, watching her with sympathy and intrigue. "Seems like this old house has a way of playing tricks."

Blythe sighed in exasperation. "First, the tire, and now this? Seriously, what's next?"

As if in response to her words, the lights above flickered, casting a soft glow over the kitchen. Blythe's gaze shifted towards the ceiling, her eyes narrowing.

"You think this is funny?" Blythe muttered, her voice tinged with annoyance and defiance. "Well, it's not."

The lights flickered again, this time in an almost deliberate pattern resembling a mischievous grin.

Swiftly maneuvering around Miles, she retreated back into the hallway. Approaching the front door, she attempted to open it, but it remained stubbornly unyielding. Frustration welled up as she muttered, "It's not funny..."

"You should know better. If It doesn't want you to leave, you won't be leaving," Miles remarked, leaning casually against the banister.

"It let me leave once... knowing I wasn't coming back," She whispered softly, resting her palm against the door.

"But you did come back, Blythe. You're here now. I'm sure you understand why It doesn't want you to go... It's grieving, too. It needs you here," Miles reasoned.

Blythe could sense the truth in his words, but she also felt there was another reason, something she couldn't quite grasp. She was sure she would uncover it if she stayed a little longer, but she wasn't sure if she wanted to. The constant sting of tears threatened behind her eyes while a heavy weight settled in the pit of her stomach.

"You've always been so sensitive... I know you can feel it," Miles acknowledged, standing still and giving her space.

Blythe turned to him, her eyes locking onto his. She took a deep breath, the words she had been suppressing threatening to burst forth, "There's something you need to know, Miles. Something I should have told you a long time ago."

His brows furrowed in concern, "What is it?"

She hesitated, her chest tightening with the weight of the truth she was about to reveal. "It's about why I left. About my parents... My Uncle, Keeper Fas, told me... He told me that my parents didn't die in an accident."

Miles's expression shifted from concern to curiosity, his attention fully captured by her words. "What do you mean? What happened?"

Blythe's voice quivered as she spoke the words that had haunted her for years, "He said that my father, Demetrius, was killed... Killed by the Council because he had relations with a human, my mother."

Shock rippled across Miles's face, his eyes widening with disbelief. "That's... That's not possible."

Blythe nodded, her throat tight. "I thought so, too. But Keeper Fas told me the truth. He said my father loved a human and they had a child together. Me, and the Council, they... They took him away and killed him."

Miles's shock transformed into a mix of anger and sorrow. "That's... I can't believe they would do that. That's monstrous."

Tears welled up in Blythe's eyes, and she blinked, attempting to hold them back, refusing to let them fall. "I couldn't stay here, Miles. I couldn't be a part of a world that could do something so heartless. So I left, and I never looked back."

Miles stepped closer to her, "Blythe, I'm so sorry. I had no idea."

She managed a weak smile, touched by his genuine compassion. "I wanted to protect you from the pain of knowing. But now you do. And now you know why I can't stay here."

Miles's voice was gentle as he spoke, his words filled with resolve. "Blythe, you don't have to stay if you don't want to. But keep in mind not everything here is heartless. There's goodness, too. And I'm here for you, whatever you choose."

As she gazed into his eyes, Blythe sensed a spark of hope amidst the chaos. With Miles beside her, she believed she could confront any trials that awaited, even the painful truths that had shaped her past and would inevitably shape her future.

CHAPTER THREE

Blythe moved past him, her steps purposeful. He followed her as they ascended the stairs, approaching a gallery of photographs on the walls. The images displayed a lineage of men, their piercing gazes captured in monochromatic frames, the pictures bearing time marks, their edges slightly frayed, and sepia tones faded. As they climbed higher, the drawings and paintings replaced the photographs, but the sense of kinship remained unmistakable.

"It's not a coincidence I received the letter from the council when I did," Blythe said, her words trembling slightly as she examined the portraits. She continued, her gaze locked on the faded faces, "There must be a connection."

Miles nodded thoughtfully, inquiring, "What do you think it's about?"

"The only thing I can think of is that they're concerned about the house's choice, or perhaps whether I used magic in the human world..." Blythe spoke, her fingers absently fidgeting with her shirt's hem. She sighed, feeling drained. "You know I would never..." She paused, her eyes dropping to the floor.

"I have no doubt," Miles assured her, gently lifting her chin to meet her eyes and offering a reassuring smile. He released her chin and reached for her hand, the warmth of his touch comforting. "You know I trust you implicitly, right? Do you think it could choose you?"

"They couldn't be worried about that," Blythe said incredulously, stepping back. "I'm not Keeper Fas' child and was never prepared for the role." She withdrew her hand and continued down the hallway, the flickering lights casting an eerie atmosphere. "You don't think it's about our past relationship?"

"There's no way," Miles shook his head. "We were careful,

and I definitely never told anyone.

Blythe's once-steady stance wavered as if carrying an invisible burden. She hesitated, her brows furrowing, struggling with her unspoken thoughts. Restlessness was evident in her shifting weight and the tension in her jaw. Blythe turned to look at a picture on the wall and eventually confessed, "I left to escape all of this. It's not their decision, nor ours. Ben was always so worried I was trying to get the Keepership. I have never had an interest in that. He didn't teach me how to do the job, and I don't want it."

"He wasn't allowed to teach you," Miles interjected, his concern evident in furrowed brows. "Teaching magic to a half-human is against the law."

Blythe paused, her shoulders sagging, a hint of defiance in her eyes. "Yes, it's against the law." She fidgeted with a stray string on her top. "We will find out what the House decides soon enough."

She turned towards Miles, and he gently took her hand. They exchanged a silent understanding, their unspoken emotions connecting them. "That's why It doesn't want you to leave. It needs you. Your presence has always brought comfort here. Maybe the House hasn't decided yet, and it's easier to decide with you and Ben here."

A bitter, disbelieving laugh escaped Blythe's lips. Her narrowed eyes conveyed bitterness and disappointment. She continued, "Comforting? Not in this House," her words heavy with past experiences.

Blythe withdrew her hand from Miles, her movements cautious as she shifted her focus towards the banister. Leaning slightly, she peered down at the entry to the House below. "You've always been overly optimistic, Miles," she retorted, her frustration evident. Her furrowed brows conveyed her doubts and unspoken emotions. "It couldn't choose me, even if It wanted to. I'm not Keeper Fas' direct descendant."

Miles paused, his eyes locking onto hers, blending sympathy with hope. Unspoken emotions continued to pass between them, strengthening their bond. "Being a blood relative might not be a requirement," he softly countered, grappling with his uncertainties. "The house can make its own rules."

"I can't imagine the council would allow that," Blythe shook her head.

As Blythe leaned back from the banister, a subtle shift in the House's atmosphere coursed through her. The walls seemed to hum softly, a comforting whisper as if the House acknowledged their presence and sensed her inner turmoil.

Miles, too, noticed the change. His eyes narrowed slightly, and he reached for Blythe's hand, a familiar gesture of reassurance from their past.

"I've always believed there's more to this house than what meets the eye," Miles mused, wonder filling his eyes. "It's like it knows us, understands us." His thumb traced a delicate path over the back of her hand, a gesture laden with memories.

"You used to call this place our sanctuary," Blythe said, her gaze locked on their intertwined hands. "A place where we could be ourselves without judgment." She smiled, reminiscing, "Remember all the times in the turret?"

"And it still is," Miles replied with wistfulness. "I've always felt a connection to this house, but it's stronger when you're here." He grinned, adding, "We could always go up to the turret if you wanted."

Blythe playfully punched him in the shoulder, and he laughed.

Their eyes met, a spark of their past romance flickering between them. It was an acknowledgment of their love and a question of whether that love could still exist.

Blythe pulled her hand away, emotions swirling inside her. The House's sentience was undeniable, but the past and her reasons for leaving couldn't be ignored. Memories of their romantic involvement brought both comfort and pain, a reminder of what was and what could never be again.

Miles moved closer until their shoulders brushed against each other. "Secrets never stay hidden for long. He should have told you the truth about your parents. I understand completely."

"I don't think you do," Blythe asserted, frustration bubbling up. She pushed away from the banister and walked down the hallway toward her old room. The first door on her left slowly swung open, puzzling her and Miles. Memories of a bitter argument and the bitterness that had driven her away flooded her mind. But now, the room felt different.

Blythe's hands trembled, her fingers curling into fists. Anger burned in her eyes, and frustration creased her brow. "He lied to me, Miles," she began, her voice filled with suppressed fury.

Miles inquired, "It's bad he didn't tell you the truth about your parents and the Council's archaic laws on interspecies relationships. But he was probably trying to protect you, right?" His brow furrowed, and he rubbed the back of his neck, attempting to console her.

Standing at the doorway, Blythe hesitated, her hand hovering over the doorknob. The scent of the old library wafted from the gap, tempting her senses. It carried the fragrance of aged paper, delicate parchment, and a hint of dust, mingled with the comforting aroma of polished wood from the shelves and furniture. Memories of hours spent with Keeper Fas in the world of magic filled her mind.

She slowly closed the door, seeking solace in its solidity, a barrier against painful memories. "It makes a huge difference, Miles," she turned to him, her eyes unwavering. "In the first version, they died, and no one knew my mother wasn't a witch. I was safe." Her eyes glistened with unshed tears. "But in the second, the truth, the Council knows what I am. Why they haven't killed me yet is a mystery. All I can think is that Dorian had something to do with it... Dorian and this House. He must have convinced the Council that I don't possess magic. Now that he's gone and a new Keeper will be chosen, no one will protect me if they want to get rid of me, and I guarantee you Ben would love to get rid of me."

"The council doesn't kill people for existing, Blythe." Miles shook his head, "And Ben probably doesn't even think about you anymore. He has his own life, and you have yours."

As Blythe's eyes darted to the study door, it creaked open again. Flickering candlelight spilled onto the floor, casting dancing shadows and tempting her to explore hidden secrets.

"The door shouldn't..." Blythe's words trailed off, her hand instinctively reaching for the doorknob. Hesitation held her, her mind spinning with thoughts. With a swift motion, she decided to shut the door firmly, sealing away its mysteries. The House seemed shrouded in deceit, and that chamber held no promise of truth.

"It will open for the Keeper of the house," Miles persisted, his encouraging words tinged with uncertainty, mirroring their complex emotions.

Blythe walked away from the door, putting distance between her and its secrets.

Blythe's thoughts whirled like a tempest within her. Miles paused, reflecting on her words, before addressing the opened door. "Maybe there's something inside that It wants you to find. Maybe it isn't trying to tell you you're the new Keeper? Perhaps Keeper Fas left you something?"

"I don't want anything from Keeper Fas. I won't let the House dictate my actions, Miles," she declared, determination straightening her posture. With a resolute look, she turned away from him, heading toward the last room on the right. "For all those years, I never knew why I was confined to this House, forbidden from venturing into the human and magic worlds." Her fists clenched at her sides, and her shoulders tensed.

Approaching the door, it creaked open, revealing a room bathed in the warm glow of table lamps. The scent of roses wafted, a bittersweet reminder of happier times. Blythe's lips trembled, torn between comfort and pain in the room's embrace.

Miles followed her inside, his eyes filled with concern and disappointment. "Your existence isn't a terrible thing," he said, his brows knitting, his gaze shifting between Blythe and the floor. He chose his words carefully, measuring each phrase. "You know those old laws have kept our secrets safe for a long time." His lips tightened.

Beside the bed, the room's gentle illumination enveloped Blythe. Her gaze remained locked on the photo resting on the nightstand. Loss pierced her heart, a sharp pang she fought to suppress. She closed her eyes, attempting to stave off tears, her face contorting in the struggle to master her turbulent emotions. Leaning against the bedpost, grip tightened, she sought stability amid the turmoil.

"He asked for you before he passed... You didn't reply to my calls or messages," Miles confessed, his voice heavy, revealing unspoken emotions. Anguish surged through Blythe, a painful prick nestled deep within her chest. Her free hand clenched into a fist, nails digging into her palm, seeking an anchor. "He loved you." Blythe's jaw tightened, her eyes narrowing with grief and frustration. She wasn't supposed to grieve for him. Anger was her ally... wasn't it?

"Enough," she implored, shoulders slumping beneath the weight of sorrow, her gaze unwavering on the floor.

Miles persisted, his body tense, brows furrowed in bitterness and resentment. "Don't act like you're the victim!" His lips pressed, a tic forming at his jaw. He drew a controlled breath, chest rising and falling, a whirlpool of emotions in his eyes —years of stifled frustration, unspoken words now demanding release. His words, laden with discontent, mirrored by Blythe's anger. "You didn't have to see him after you left!"

"Get out," Blythe's words burst forth. Eyes blazed with anger and hurt, each word thrust against the air, chest heaving with the power of emotions, heart pounding. Pushing him away, expelling it all, escaping the whirlwind of turmoil.

"He must have had his reasons for keeping secrets. It wasn't fair of you to not let him explain!" Miles snapped back, bitterness in tense gestures and his piercing gaze. "You shut him out like you're shutting me out. I don't know why the Council summoned you, but I hope they, or this House, can help you snap out of this. I had thought you'd outgrown your teenage angst, but clearly, you haven't!"

With those words, he turned and left. The door clicked softly, leaving a lingering tension. Blythe wanted to open it just to slam it shut again and have that satisfaction, but she resisted that urge. Sinking onto the bed's edge, her gaze locked on the photo on the nightstand. Weariness enveloped her like a heavy wave. Her last memory of the night was the smell of roses permeating the air as she cried herself to sleep.

CHAPTER FOUR

Blythe awoke beneath warm covers, disoriented and unable to recall how she got there. Yawning, she sat up, feeling stiffness, realizing she now wore rose silk pajamas, not yesterday's clothes. The House's unpredictability was nothing new. Without dwelling on it, she checked her phone. 3:30 a.m.

Stretching her limbs, Blythe eased out of bed. As her feet touched the familiar warm wooden floor, she paused to appreciate it. Magic. Some people back home had it, but it was expensive and not something she could afford.

Noticing that the House had chosen clothing for her it took her back to her childhood. Somehow, the House always knew what she'd want to wear or what would be most comfortable for the weather that day. Black pants, a crisp white shirt, and a stylish blazer seemed perfectly arranged, evoking elegance and authority. She'd always wondered how the House knew, but Keeper Fas never told her. Blythe decided to enjoy another perk of the House—a bath that never gets cold. After her bath, she dressed and decided it was time to go.

Stepping into the hallway, she was guided by the dimmed hallway lights. The House knew better than to shock people with bright lights at this hour. Her footsteps seemed louder than usual in the quiet House. The door to the library opened as she was passing it. She let out a heavy sigh and decided to go in.

Upon entering the study, the door closed softly behind her. The warm lights and crackling fire greeted her, casting a comforting glow across the room. She glanced around, taking in the shelves laden with books, the cozy armchairs clustered around the fireplace, and the solid wooden table adorned with scattered books and papers. Its timeless charm beckoned her, and the warm firelight kindled a spark of anticipation in her eyes. Her fingers lightly brushed the edge of a nearby bookshelf.

The scent of old books mingled with the crackling fire, creating an atmosphere that enveloped her in a comfortable nostalgia.

As she stood, Blythe's ears caught a faint sound from above—the rhythmic clacking of typewriter keys. Intrigued, she followed the sound to a narrow spiral staircase that led to a balcony above. Ascending the stairs, she found herself before Keeper Fas's desk, a dark wooden Victorian masterpiece. On the desk rested an old black smith-corona typewriter, its vintage charm captivating her. Her gaze fixed on the paper in the typewriter's carriage. It fluttered though no breeze was present.

"Fine, you want me to read this," she challenged, eyeing the paper. "If I do, can I leave if I want? Flash the lights once for yes, twice for no." As if on cue, the lights dimmed and brightened once. "Alright then. I'll read it."

She gingerly picked the page up as if fearing it would burn her.

"Dear Blythe," the letter began, etched in ink upon aged paper. *"If you're reading this, I'm beyond this life. I must assume you haven't read my earlier letters. I've given you space, but now you need the truth. I've kept it too long..."* She paused, putting the letter down, a blend of defiance and uncertainty in her expression. "Really? You want me to read this?" The lights subtly flickered in response, intensifying the accusatory air around her. A resigned sigh escaped her, and she continued reading.

"Your mother and I met during my fifteenth year," the letter continued. *"While exploring the human world, we crossed paths at Stonehenge in England..."*

"Wait... so my father met my mother through Dorian?" Blythe interrupted herself, her mind racing to make sense of the revelation. She resumed reading, emotions coursing through Blythe's veins.

"Meredith, or Mer, caught my attention," the letter recalled a tale from decades ago. *"She was unlike other tourists. I was drawn to her... She had no romantic interest in me initially. Though I pretended indifference, I loved her,"* the letter confessed. Shock coursed through Blythe's veins, anticipation and dread

intertwining. *"We remained pen pals until we crossed again when I was twenty-one. I was engaged to Lila, studying at Cambridge. This is when our affair began."*

Taking a shaky breath, Blythe turned the page, her worst fears looming. Blythe read on, her grip on the letter tightening. Her eyes remained fixed on the words, tracing each letter as if it held the truth. *"I lacked the courage to call off my engagement and married Lila, Benjamin's mother, despite my heart belonging to your mother. When I discovered that Mer was carrying a child—"*

Overwhelmed, Blythe slammed the letter down. Tears welled up as the truth hit her. Questions flooded her mind. "How could you, Dorian?" Blythe whispered, tears falling. The lights flickered, mirroring her shattered trust. A thought struck her. "But why did they mistake Demetrius for my father? How could the Council have made such a mistake?" The page beneath her hand fluttered, urging her to read more. With a deep breath, she collected herself, fingers curling around the letter as she prepared herself.

"—I invited her to stay at the House. You needed to be born with us, just in case. Lila didn't understand; I never revealed your father's identity to her, and she was unhappy. She believed bringing a human into the House was a grave mistake. She feared the breach in secrecy. I had never told Mer I had magic. I didn't break that particular law. I was selfish. The day you were born was the happiest day of my life. Lila adored you as well, in the way many women adore babies. However, she couldn't comprehend when I told Mer she was welcome to stay with you, here, with me, until Mer recovered and decided what she wanted to do. I had hoped that Lila would come to appreciate your mother and agree to let her stay as a friend. Mer knew nothing about my world, and Lila grew tired of hiding in her home. The House, too, found it increasingly difficult to stay restrained and wanted me to let her go. But that would have shattered me, and I couldn't bear it. Your mother sensed the tension and left with you one night shortly after your first birthday. I'm unsure why the House allowed her to take you, perhaps because I had asked to grant her freedom to come and go from the House. I was

devastated."

Blythe's emotions churned. Betrayal, confusion, and loss consumed her. She leaned back, clutching the letter. The House held answers, yet more questions emerged. Her father's actions weighed on her as she grappled with the extent of the deception.

"Not long after, Benjamin was born, as it was expected of me to produce an heir. Over the next two years, I continued pursuing Mer under the pretense of Keeper duties, much to Lila's displeasure. She believed my work should keep me within the House more often. During this pursuit, I received the news of Mer's passing. She had designated me as your next of kin. I brought you back to the House, much to Lila's chagrin. She cared for you, but we already had a two-year-old whom I was supposed to focus on raising and preparing for his future. She couldn't understand why we were raising you. She urged me to find you a human family. But I couldn't bear to let you go. She also didn't know the circumstances of your mother's death or the truth about your father. To her dying day, I never told Lila about my infidelity."

The old black typewriter, Keeper Fas's relic, stood as a silent witness as Blythe grappled with the truth. The fluttering paper echoed its weighty truth. Each word reverberated, a reminder of a shattered past. There was more to read. She couldn't escape it. As she read, the keys had been clattering, typing the rest of Keeper Fas's last testimony. The paper fluttered in the typewriter, and she pulled it out. *"The fact that you possess magic is my fault,"* echoed in her mind. Emotions swirled as she read on, grappling with revelations.

"Even the House couldn't provide answers until after I brought you back. The accident didn't take your life because of your magic. Lila discovered your magical abilities not long after. She demanded an explanation, and I told her that you were my brother, Demetrius's child. She wanted to bring the matter before the Council."

Blythe's stomach tightened. "No..." she whispered.

"This is why you've never felt truly welcome, why I kept the truth from you. The House supported me, preventing Lila from going to the Council. However, she found a way around its influence, and

the Council became aware of your existence."

Blythe's grip on the letter threatened to rip the paper. She tasted the bitterness of betrayal, realizing the layers of secrecy kept from her. *"They hunted my brother, who had no knowledge of your existence, and punished him for my transgressions."* The guilt and remorse in her father's words pierced through her.

Tears flowed as emotions reached a crescendo. Anguish and sorrow mingled with the love she had always held for the father she now saw anew. *"When the Council sent for you, I fought them. I pleaded that it wasn't your fault you existed. I lied to the Council, Lila, and you. We told you your parents had died in a tragic accident. I denied you were my child."* The tangled truth emerged, exposing her father's sacrifice for her sake.

Her heart was heavy, and Blythe struggled to comprehend the enormity of her existence's impact. *"And now you know. If the House chooses you as the next Keeper, it will expose everything, and I fear you will suffer for it."*

The letter's tone shifted. *"I love you, my darling daughter, more than life itself. I hope you'll find happiness and achieve great things."* Love and regret intertwined, leaving Blythe with a bittersweet ache as she confronted her identity's intricacies.

Blythe sat in silence, the letter clutched in trembling hands. The room felt suffocating, as if the air had been sucked out. Tears streamed, dampening the pages. Dorian's revelation had shaken her world to its core.

Years ago, she had confronted Dorian about Demetrius's death, vowing to never return. Now, reading this letter, she understood his silence's weight. He had shielded her from a dangerous truth.

Setting the letter down, Blythe's mind raced. With a deep breath, she addressed the House. "Why didn't you tell me? How did my father communicate with you?"

The typewriter clacked, words materializing on the page. *"As the House, I'm bound by rules. I watched and guided your father to keep you safe. The truth was too dangerous."*

Blythe's frustration and longing surged. She clenched her

fists, nails biting into her palms. "But why? Why keep me in the dark? I deserved to know."

The House's response resonated. *"The truth would endanger you, expose forces beyond your understanding. We chose to protect you."*

Blythe wrestled with her emotions. Understanding her father's intent didn't erase the pain. She had always felt like an outsider in the magical world; now, she knew why.

"The past can't be changed, but the truth is too heavy," she sighed. "I wish I had known before..."

The typewriter clacked the House's silent support. *"Your father aimed to shield you from pain and hardships he knew. His burden was immense. He protected you from our world's reality."*

"And my uncle... Demetrius," Blythe's voice wavered as she talked about him, a shadow of concern in her eyes. She looked distant as if searching for answers in her memories. "What happened to him? Did he suffer because of my existence?" Her words held a mixture of concern and guilt.

The typewriter's words were solemn yet revealing. *"Demetrius faced consequences because of Dorian's actions. He bore punishment for something he didn't do. It was an injustice that your father deeply regretted, and it cast a shadow of guilt over him."*

Tears welled in Blythe's eyes as the weight of the revelation settled upon her. The realization that her mere existence had brought pain to an innocent man weighed heavily on her heart. And the fact that her father could let someone else suffer for his transgressions? It was immoral.

The House's response was gentle and empathetic, its words appearing on the typewriter. *"Your father believed he was protecting you, even if it meant sacrificing his bond with his brother. The past can't be changed, but the future is yours. Your destiny is yours to shape. The legacies of your father and uncle are intertwined,"* the typewriter continued to type out words. *"By embracing your heritage, you'll find the strength to confront whatever the future holds."*

Blythe's emotions surged, gratitude and frustration

mingling within her. The sacrifices made for her were more apparent now, yet the sting of deception still lingered.

"I understand the reasons behind the lies," Blythe's voice trembled slightly, but her determination was unwavering. Though tears still shimmered in her eyes, her resolve shone through. "I want the truth, even if it's a bitter pill."

The House responded with a comforting presence. Its words appeared on the typewriter, offering assurance amid the emotional storm. *"I will guide and protect you, even if the truth is painful. It's your time to be the Keeper and guard the portal between worlds."*

Blythe's mind churned with questions. Frustration and desperation tugged at her as she turned to the typewriter.

Her hands quivered, a whisper escaping her lips in the face of fear and doubt. "Benjamin is the right choice, not me. I wasn't prepared for this! Making me the Keeper puts me in the crosshairs. Is that why the Council wants to meet with me?"

Interrupting her thoughts came an insistent pounding on the door, shattering the stillness. The noise jolted her senses, and an angry voice cut through the silence. Turning to the door, curiosity and concern knitted her brow. "Who's there?" She whispered, her voice quivering with uncertainty and apprehension as if she dreaded the answer but couldn't hold back her query.

The typewriter generated a response on the page. *"Benjamin."*

CHAPTER FIVE

Blythe's heart plummeted, the truth hitting her like a sudden jolt. Her newfound connection with him twisted the situation into uncertainty and fear. Facing Benjamin's reaction wouldn't be limited to dealing with his anger; a whirlwind of resentment and betrayal would churn his emotions. He was supposed to be the next Keeper. What complicated matters even more was that Benjamin didn't know he was her brother. The secret woven into this chaotic tapestry intensified her sense of unease. The news of her selection would strike at the core of his expectations, shattering the foundation of a dream he had carried since childhood.

As she sat in the dimly lit room, surrounded by antique furnishings that whispered of a bygone era, her gaze darted around, seeking an exit. The pounding on the door thundered like a relentless drumbeat, echoing through her senses. "Not now," she whispered urgently, her voice betraying emotional strain. The room's opulence offered no comfort in the face of impending danger.

Panic tightened its grip with each passing second. "He'll tear me apart," she breathed, her fingers striking the typewriter as if to awaken it. Her eyes darted around, searching for assistance in vain.

Then, in response to her desperate plea, a bookcase creaked open, revealing a dimly lit staircase. Without hesitation, she raced down the stairs and to the hidden door, each step echoing her pounding heart. Without second-guessing, she ran into the darkness.

Guided by the dance of shadows cast by the torchlight, she emerged in a chamber drenched in an eerie glow. Cold stone walls exuded an almost spectral ambiance, adding to her sense of displacement. In front of her loomed the portal door. The pantry door stood ajar to her left, while the stairs leading back to the main hallway beckoned to her right.

She ascended the stairs, her movements almost automatic. As she reached the area beneath the main staircase, fragments of Benjamin's heated words reached her ears, accompanied by the calm undertones of Miles attempting to soothe his friend's frustration. Miles must have stayed the night.

The main floor lay cloaked in semi-darkness, the feeble light of the windows casting a ghostly glow. Blythe navigated the dim hallway with purposeful, firm footsteps, her stride a rhythmic counterpoint to the chaos. The front door beckoned like a tantalizing promise—an escape from the encroaching turmoil. Desperation tightened her grip on the doorknob, but it remained immovable.

Above, the voices grew still, and approaching footsteps drew nearer. Frustration surged. "No, not now," Blythe muttered, changing direction, her path leading her to the sitting room—a potential sanctuary from unwanted eyes. Yet, the House had other ideas; a cascade of light filled the room, illuminating her like a lone figure in a spotlight. Frozen and ensnared, she found herself at the mercy of unfolding events. Miles made eye contact and paused, but Ben, in his drunken stupor, passed by, caught up in his rant, oblivious to her presence.

Echoes of crashes and bangs resonated from the kitchen, their discordant symphony drawing her attention like a siren's call. Memories of past clashes surged forth, their emotional reverberations palpable in the air. Her heart raced, torn between the urge to retreat and the ominous weight of the looming confrontation.

Miles approached her, his voice a gentle anchor amid the tempest. "Hey," he greeted softly, his concern evident in his eyes. She sighed, her shoulders slumping beneath the weight of her thoughts.

"What's all that about?" She gestured towards the kitchen, where Benjamin's tumultuous presence resonated loudly.

Miles looked at her, his expression softening with deep concern.

"He couldn't get into the room. Look, I think you need to talk to him. Avoiding it won't make things better. You've got to face him eventually." She met his gaze, defiance, and weariness mingling in her eyes.

"Why bother? Nothing ever changes with him. It's just going to infuriate him to see me." Miles placed a comforting hand on her shoulder.

"I know it's tough, but you never know. You two have been apart for a long time—maybe there's a way to bridge the chasm."

Her frustration lingered, yet his words struck a chord. Dodging confrontation wouldn't solve anything. But the thought of confronting Benjamin, revisiting old pain and anger, was daunting. Miles was an anchor in the chaos by her side, and he met her gaze with empathy and understanding.

"You know, sometimes facing the tempest is the only path to serenity," he shared gently, his words carrying wisdom.

A wry smile curled her lips. "Is that your attempt at motivational speaking?"

He chuckled, a soothing sound amidst the turmoil. "Maybe it is. But seriously, Blythe, you don't have to confront this alone. And who knows, by addressing it directly, you might finally find the closure you've been seeking."

She sighed, torn between the pull of the chaos and the desire for solitude. With a resigned nod, she straightened her posture, resolved to settle this once and for all. Clattering dishes and heated voices seemed to fade as she stepped forward. Miles's presence was a reassuring strength, a reminder that she wasn't navigating this alone.

"He's grieving his own way," Miles mediated gently. Blythe shot him a glance—a mix of exasperation and gratitude. She knew his intent was genuine, yet it did little to make the upcoming confrontation more appealing.

"He has an odd way of showing it," she muttered.

The familiarity of Benjamin's hostility was a stark reminder of why she had left. Her return had been burdensome, and she was already questioning it.

"He might come around eventually," Miles offered optimistically, though even his tone held uncertainty. Blythe wished she could share his optimism, but years of strained relationships didn't evaporate quickly. Her focus returned to the emotional storm in the kitchen.

Miles' touch on her arm halted her retreat. She turned to him, a mix of irritation and weariness.

"Really, Blythe, you can't avoid this forever," he encouraged gently, his gaze searching hers. She knew he was right, which only heightened her frustration.

"Do I have much of a choice?" she replied, resigned. She followed Miles toward the kitchen, her steps conflicted and her emotions running high.

Stepping into the kitchen, she saw Benjamin at the kitchen island, an array of food before him. Her stomach grumbled. She hoped that eating would anchor her amidst the turmoil of family dynamics. She moved to the opposite end of the island and took a seat.

Benjamin's gaze fixed on her, disdain and bitterness evident. "Well, well, the prodigal niece returns," he drawled, dripping sarcasm. "Back from your grand adventures, I see?"

Blythe's jaw clenched, her grip on the glass tightening. Her stare met his, a defiance that masked her turmoil.

Miles intervened.

"How's work, Blythe?" he asked gently, shifting the focus of the conversation. Her gaze shifted to Miles, and for a brief moment, her tension eased. She smiled, thankful for his diversion.

"Busy. Good," she replied, weariness tinging her voice. Benjamin's brows furrowed.

"Busy doing what? Mooching off others' hospitality?" His question took her by surprise.

Blythe kept her answers guarded, wary of revealing too much. "Traveling. Archaeology," she replied, uncertain how to encapsulate her years away.

"Archaeology, huh? Digging in the dirt for trash?"

Benjamin's skepticism was evident.

Blythe's fingers curled beneath the table. "It's about preserving history," she responded evenly.

"Unearthing trash and bones," Benjamin mused condescendingly.

"It's more than that. I've made significant discoveries," Blythe retorted, her voice carrying a note of defiance.

"Cool, Blythe. Learning about the past is intriguing," Miles offered. "Did you catch the Celestial and Ethereal game?"

A spark ignited in Ben's eyes, shifting his focus. "The Celestial Warders were on point!" His enthusiasm carried them into an animated discussion. Blythe's interest waned as they delved into Aerosorb Control and Orb Manipulation. Terms like Pathfinders and Guardians became background noise. Her mind retreated into contemplation.

The council and the Keeper's study once again captured her thoughts. The study stood as a nexus of tension and secrets, entwining her in its mysteries. Her pulse quickened, apprehension and curiosity swirling.

"I can't believe the House won't listen to me!" Benjamin's frustration erupted.

"The study?" Miles inquired.

"It's more than that," Benjamin's reply simmered with fury. "Something here isn't right. The House is showing disrespect!"

The lights flickered, a reminder that the House was listening.

"I'm the Keeper! Access should be mine!" He glared at Blythe. "I don't know why it allowed you in. My father's dead. There's no more leeching off of us for you. You're just a wretched halfling. I can't even fathom how you dare to be here! Your presence at the funeral disgusted me as well. You belong nowhere in this or any other world!"

Darkness descended, disorienting Blythe. She heard a scream and needed light. A warm, golden radiance emerged, dispelling the shadows. Astonished, she realized her dormant magic had answered her call. The orb's glow danced on the walls, her heart racing as her long-suppressed magic emerged, its touch both gentle and resolute.

Benjamin was pressed against the wall, suspended two feet off the ground, a knife poised at his throat. Blythe and Miles stood transfixed, witnesses to the House's intervention.

"Stop," her voice was a whisper, a blend of awe and urgency.

Benjamin was released, falling to the floor with a thud. The knife landed point down next to him. He gasped for breath, his eyes wide with shock and disbelief.

CHAPTER SIX

The lights turned back on, casting a cold, sterile light throughout the room. Blythe closed her fist, extinguishing the ball of light with a controlled gesture. The relief that washed over her was palpable—her dormant magical abilities had responded when she needed them most. Blythe hadn't practiced magic in years, let alone demonstrated it in front of others. The fear of failure had been overwhelming, and she was grateful she had succeeded. However, as quickly as the relief hit her, so did regret. She should have never done that.

Miles furrowed his brow, his eyes fixed on Blythe. Her magical display had left him cautious; she wasn't supposed to know any magic. "It listened to you... but why?" he questioned, curiosity and wariness evident in his voice.

Without wasting another moment, Blythe turned to make her way toward the door. The morning's events had left her drained and overwhelmed; all she wanted was the comfort of solitude. But Ben's anger wasn't quickly quelled.

"Answer the question!" Ben's voice sliced through the air, his anger still simmering. Blythe kept her gaze straight ahead, her steps measured as she continued past him and through the doorway. The cool air that greeted her in the hallway was a slight reprieve, but she knew the confrontation was far from over.

"I don't know, Ben. I'm tired," Blythe's body felt heavy, her head aching with a dull throb. She longed for a moment of quiet, away from the storm of emotions surrounding her. As she made her way down the hallway, she felt the weight of their unresolved issues press on her.

"Wait!" Ben's voice was sharp and commanding, but she didn't stop. She couldn't. Her determination to retreat to the safety of her room outweighed any inclination to engage in further conflict. The events of the morning had brought to the surface the raw tensions that had always existed between them, and she didn't have the energy to spare for another round.

Pressing on despite Ben's protests, she hastened her steps, each footfall reverberating through the hallway. Her thoughts swirled until she came to a decision. Ben deserved to know. It would eventually come out anyway. Her destination shifted, guided by a force that pulled her toward the study. She'd already used magic in front of them. What did she have to lose?

The echoes of her steps were accompanied by the muted symphony of footsteps and voices behind her. The timbre of Miles's voice mingled with Ben's protests, a soothing counterpoint to the hurricane of emotions. His attempts to placate Ben were audible, his words resonating like distant whispers in her ears. Against this backdrop, Ben's invectives erupted like thunderclaps—part curses, part accusations—shaking the air around them as he vented his frustration at the house, Miles, and anyone else within reach.

As she reached the study door, she knew that the moment of reckoning had arrived. She turned the doorknob and entered the room, leaving Ben and Miles stunned behind her. Her eyes fell on the spiral staircase leading to the study's upper floor, where the truth awaited.

She climbed the steps, each feeling like an eternity as her anticipation grew. When she reached the desk, she found the papers she was looking for, the document that held the key to understanding the lies that had shaped her life.

Descending the steps, she held the letter in her hand, her emotions swirling with apprehension and determination. She knew this revelation could change everything and was prepared to face the consequences of unearthing the truth.

She could hear Ben cursing and questioning her about her having used magic and opened the study door. Still, Ben's protests fell on deaf ears as she handed him the letter, her gaze steady as she watched his reactions. As he read, the seconds stretched into an uncomfortable silence, his expression shifting from confusion to disbelief, finally to anger.

The truth had hit him hard, shattering the illusions he

had held onto for so long. The weight of the revelation hung heavily in the air, tension radiating between them all. Miles's gaze shifted between Blythe and Ben, his expression a mix of concern and uncertainty.

When Ben finally looked up from the letter, his anger was evident, his voice a storm waiting to break free. His words were harsh, filled with accusation and pain, reflecting years of resentment.

Blythe wished she could shield herself from his hurtful remarks, but they struck deep, reopening old wounds she had tried to heal. Yet, even as his anger burned, she held onto a sense of calm. She had faced his hostility before, and this time was no different.

"Believe what you want, Ben," she said, her voice steady despite the tumultuous emotions swirling around them. "What's done is done unless you have a way to override the will of the house?" She met his glare with a resolute gaze, unafraid of his anger. She had faced worse in her life, and this confrontation was just another chapter in their complicated history.

"There has to be a reason!" Ben's voice echoed in the space.

Miles opened his mouth, likely intending to intervene, but Blythe's words had already set the tone. She turned away, her gaze focused on the fireplace as the tension in the room seemed to mount. The clock on the mantle ticked away, a constant reminder of the passage of time and the gravity of the situation.

"Why do you think he wrote that?" Ben's disbelieving tone interrupted her thoughts. "It can't be true. You must have done something!"

"It certainly explains why the council didn't come after me," Blythe mumbled, her arms folding tightly across her chest to conceal her trembling hands. "I was certain they would hunt me down..." She turned to stare into the fire. She could hear Ben continuing to curse and blather on with Miles, who was offering a few words here or there, trying to calm him down.

Amid the escalating tension, a sudden change in the atmosphere sent a shiver down Blythe's spine. The air grew charged, and a faint crackling sound filled the room. Her instincts screamed at her to turn around, and as she did, she was met with a shocking sight.

Ben's anger had reached a boiling point, and he had unleashed a surge of magic in his fury. Arcane energy crackled around him, forming tendrils of dark light that snaked through the air. Before anyone could react, the power lashed out, striking against the walls and furniture with explosive force.

Blythe's heart raced as she watched the destructive display, a mixture of fear and disbelief gripping her. The house seemed to quiver in response as if offended by the intrusion of chaotic magic within its walls.

Then, in an instant, the house retaliated. A sudden gust of wind swept through the room, extinguishing the flames in the fireplace and scattering loose papers in its wake. The very foundation of the house seemed to tremble, and a deep, resonating sound echoed through the air.

Before anyone could react, a burst of energy surged outward from the walls and floor, forming an invisible barrier. The barrier surrounded Ben, encasing him in a cocoon of crackling energy. His eyes widened in terror as he struggled against the unseen force, his movements growing increasingly desperate.

Blythe and Miles both rushed forward, their panic driving them to try and break through the barrier. "Ben, stop! You're only making it worse!" Miles shouted, his voice laced with urgency.

But it was too late. The barrier pulsed with energy, and then, with a blinding flash, it erupted. The force of the explosion sent shockwaves through the room, knocking Blythe and Miles off their feet.

As the dust and debris settled, Blythe groaned and pushed herself up, her head spinning from the impact. She turned her gaze to where the barrier had been, her heart sinking as she saw the aftermath.

Ben lay on the floor, his body battered and unconscious. The magic that had consumed him had been too much for the house to bear, and in its defense, it had retaliated with its own power.

Miles scrambled to his feet, rushing to Ben's side. "Ben! Wake up! Are you okay?" he cried out, his voice laced with panic.

Blythe staggered over as well, her mind racing with concern and guilt. She hadn't wanted this. She hadn't expected her revelation to lead to such chaos and danger.

The room was in disarray, the remnants of Ben's magical outburst scattered about. The air was heavy with the acrid smell of burnt wood and lingering arcane energy. The house itself seemed to hum with a mixture of anger and exhaustion.

As Ben stirred, groaning and slowly regaining consciousness, Blythe exchanged a worried glance with Miles. The storm of emotions that had consumed them was now replaced by a tense stillness. The truth was out, but it had come at a price. The rift between them had deepened, and the danger of their situation had escalated.

As Ben's anger simmered and Miles checked him over for broken bones, Blythe's thoughts drifted back to another time. "The house doesn't do anything without a reason..." Blythe's words murmured softly. Her thoughts drifted.

Ten-year-old Blythe lay sprawled on the floor, engrossed in her book, as Dorian settled into an oversized wingback chair. Ben barged in with an injured hand, sniveling as Dorian tried to calm the situation.

"Why would the House slam a door on my hand?!" Ben sniffled, hastily wiping his other hand across his face.

"Well, that depends on what you were doing or going to do," Dorian replied calmly. He reached into his pocket and retrieved a blue healing stone. Dorian had started carrying one whenever he was home. They were good for soothing minor wounds. "The house doesn't do anything without a reason."

"I wasn't doing anything," Ben insisted, his tone defensive. The fire behind him dimmed as if struck by an invisible gust of wind. Ben noticed Blythe for the first time. "What are you looking at?" he

sneered.

CHAPTER SEVEN

Blythe's head throbbed with the sound of her name, the intrusion of Ben's voice shattering her thoughts, snapping her back to the present. The room, with its damaged dark wood paneling and vintage furnishings, seemed to close around them as tension filled the air.

"The council..." Ben muttered, his face furrowing in thought as he slowly sat up with Miles' assistance. His anger still seethed, but there was an air of unease as he cast anxious glances around the room. The House's power swelled as they spoke, effortlessly restoring the damaged objects. Books repaired themselves and floated back to their designated places on the shelves, and the charred wood magically mended itself, seamlessly blending into the intricate patterns of the room's wainscoting.

Amidst the enchanting spectacle, Blythe couldn't help but wonder what secrets the House held, what other magical wonders it could perform. It was as if the House concealed ancient mysteries within its walls, waiting to be unveiled. She wondered if Dorian had even known everything the house could do.

Blythe turned to face him, her eyes locking onto his blazing green gaze—the same green eyes, she mused, that her father had... and her father's father. Her eyes. Ben's rugged features were marked by determination and a hint of unease, accentuated by the flickering firelight.

"What are you talking about?" Miles interjected, looking up from the letter Ben had handed him before the chaos. His aquamarine eyes bore traces of concern.

"I'm going to the Council. This is a mistake. The Council will never allow this half-breed to run a house. It is my birthright, not hers! Surely, they only let her live to appease

Father. But now that he's gone, there's no one left to save you." Ben slowly stood up, limping slightly, and closed the distance between himself and Blythe, their similar heights making his close proximity unnerving. She wanted to step back but found herself pinned against the mantle. So, instead, she lifted her chin and stood her ground.

Miles stepped forward, reaching out to place a calming hand on Ben's arm. "Ben, stop it. She didn't ask for any of this. Maybe talking to the Council isn't the best idea. The house chooses, and we don't know how they'll react when they learn about Blythe."

"You expect me to care?!" Ben shook off Miles's hand and turned to confront him. "She was always his favorite, and now she's stolen my future too. I won't stand by! She's an aberration. I'm surprised they've let her live this long." He glared at Miles. "She's a risk. She knows too much about our world and lives among humans. How can we be certain she hasn't gone there and exposed our secrets?"

"That's why Magical Intelligence has sleeper cells in the human world. They would have taken care of it if she had done anything like that," Miles responded wearily. Blythe couldn't help but recall the letter she had received.

"Ben's right," Blythe interjected.

"What?" Ben sputtered. "You're agreeing with me?" He looked like she had suggested something absurd, like joining a band or singing Kumbaya together. "About what...?"

Miles stared at Blythe with incredulity. "Why would you agree with him on this?! They could kill you! You remember the stories of what happens to those who have lied to the Council." He watched as Blythe pushed past Ben and headed toward the door.

"Or they could strip her of her magic and memories and send her packing into the human world where she belongs," Ben chimed in gleefully, still eying the room cautiously.

Blythe paused and looked back at Miles. "Do they actually do that?"

"I can neither confirm nor deny whether the Council has that power... I'm just a paper pusher. There are plenty of rumors. It's not my job to determine what's true and what's not," Miles shrugged and sighed. "Even if it were, I wouldn't get involved in this. I couldn't play a part in any investigation or prosecution. I'm biased."

"What do you mean you can't? That's a load of nonsense! You work for MI under the Council. Plus, you're my best friend, Miles," Ben's eyes bulged like they might shoot out of their eye sockets. "You should be on my side and help ensure she gets what she deserves. You took an oath... That should override any romantic feelings you have for her!"

Now it was Miles' turn to look annoyed. "Yes, I took an oath," he agreed, folding his arms over his chest and appearing uncomfortable for the first time in their conversation. "But they would never ask that of me... Like I said, I can't be objective in this matter."

"Wait... Do you work for MI? Magical Intelligence? I thought you went to school for Magical Artifacts," Blythe narrowed her eyes at Miles, a tide of fury rising within her. "I thought you spent your days in the archives! Do you really think they will be okay with you being friends with me in your current position? Didn't they look into your background before hiring you?"

"Well... I did attend school for Magical Artifacts during the first semester... but it wasn't as interesting as you had made it out to be, and..." Miles stammered, hands dropping to his pockets. He shuffled his feet. "They did mention something about you during my pre-hire investigation, but I told them we hadn't been in touch in a long time and that we had been children."

"Did they ask you what you thought of illegal halflings?" Ben crossed his arms, glaring at Blythe.

"No. Our personal feelings play no role in our jobs. The law says that having children with someone of another species is prohibited. Still, it doesn't say anything about punishing the offspring." Miles met Ben's eyes. Blythe furrowed her brow, noting the silent conversation that passed between the two of them. She chose to let it go.

"And you just up and changed majors without telling me?" Frustration etched deep lines on Blythe's face, her hands trembling with emotions. "You chose to go work as a spy?" Her eyes searched his, a mix of hurt and anger flashing in her gaze.

"Well... I couldn't tell you... They make us take the oath..." Miles stuttered, looking sheepish again. "Is this really important right now?"

"No, We're not changing the subject," Blythe snapped, pointing an accusing finger at Ben. "He knew what you do?" Her anger intensified.

"Well, he's my best friend," Miles began, but Blythe cut him off.

"When you started University, I was your girlfriend!" Blythe advanced on Miles, poking him in the chest with her finger. "And don't you think I should have known? Especially considering that people in that profession actively seek out people like me?"

"Why didn't you tell her everything, Miles? I thought we were all beyond keeping secrets," Ben interjected, a mischievous grin spreading across his face. Folding his arms, he stepped back, clearly enjoying the conflict unfolding before him. "I'd like to note, though, I've always been honest." Blythe shot him a piercing glare.

"You were already on the verge of leaving, Blythe," Miles responded, his eyes welling with emotion. "You were studying abroad at Oxford, and I felt like I was losing you. I loved you, but you were slipping away. If I told you the truth, you would have left completely. You despise the Council."

"For good reason! How could I not hate them when they don't want people like me to exist? They're bigots and racists! And yet, you chose them over me," Blythe replied, moving away, attempting to create distance between them.

"No," Miles reached out to grip her biceps, his touch laced

with pain and longing. "You don't get to play the victim here. You left me, Blythe. I would have given up everything for you—my scholarship, family, and friends. I would have forsaken my magical heritage just to be with you." Tears welled up in Blythe's eyes, momentarily blinding her from the hurt she had inflicted upon him. She tried to pull away, but his hold remained firm.

Ben interrupted their exchange with dripping sarcasm. "As much as I enjoy this drama between you, it reminds me of the good old days. But let's address the elephant in the room and take her to the Council. After all, you have an oath; she knows what they think of her. And let's not forget that little magic trick she performed in the kitchen." Blythe's stomach dropped, the weight of the situation settling heavily upon her. "The Council did say she couldn't do magic, didn't they?"

Blythe's heart sank, her hope of concealment shattered. She had hoped that he remained oblivious to that particular detail Dorian had imparted on her as a child. "What do you know about the Council's ruling?" she inquired, a touch of unease threading through her words.

"You weren't the only one who eavesdropped in this house," Ben grinned. "Unlike you, I didn't need the house's help to do it."

"I already said I can't get involved..." Miles started, but Blythe couldn't bear it any longer. She placed her hands on his chest and gently pushed him away.

"No. Ben's right. The lies need to stop, regardless of the consequences. Yes... I left, you lied, and now I must correct another man's lies. I shouldn't have done that spell, but it's not like I did it in front of a human... I will face what my father should have faced years ago. You won't have to take me in, Miles. I'll do it myself. They will be lenient since I had no part in this. After all, I didn't choose this. And I hope that somewhere in that black hole where your heart should be, Ben, you can find it in you to let the magic slip-up go as long as I leave the house to you and return to my life." She walked past Miles, dismissing his attempts to stop her again.

"Why shouldn't I tell the Council about your magic? If you're locked up, I get the house and never have to see you again. Win win!" Ben grinned, his eyes gleaming with malice. "You're done for," he sneered, pushing past her and heading toward the door. Miles stepped in Ben's way and glared at him. Ben scowled. "Fine. If you turn yourself in, I won't say anything about that."

Blythe wasn't sure if she believed him, but she moved around them and continued toward the door. As she approached it to leave the study, it slammed shut, the lock sliding into place. She was growing tired of doors locking on her.

"You've got to be kidding me!" Ben snarled, springing forward from his spot in the middle of the room and looking up at the ceiling. "She wants to do the right thing, and you won't let her out?!"

"Apparently, the house doesn't agree with you two," Miles could not hide the smugness in his demeanor.

"Okay... if you don't want me to go to the council, what do you propose?" Blythe asked as she sank into the chair next to the fireplace. The weight of her emotions was becoming overwhelming. Miles moved to sit in the other chair by the fire, seeming resigned and seeing no point in rushing to block the door when the house had already done it for him.

"This is complete nonsense," Ben snarled, positioning himself before the fireplace. The clicking sound of keys drew their attention to the loft. Blythe hurried across the room and ascended the spiral steps. She slowed as she reached the top and noticed a page sticking from the typewriter. From a distance, it appeared blank, but she was sure she had heard the keys being pressed. She cautiously walked across the floor and pulled the page free from the typewriter. It wasn't blank at all. A single word was written on the sheet.

"Wait."

CHAPTER EIGHT

After heated arguments, they decided against reporting Blythe to the authorities. The tension in the room was palpable as voices grew hoarse, emotions running high. Eventually, the House unlocked the door, allowing them to leave. Benjamin stormed out, muttering curses, his fiery temper unabated. On the other hand, Miles rushed off to work, his promise to investigate Blythe's summons further etched on his determined face.

Alone in the library, Blythe settled into a chair by the fire, drained and uncertain. The flames danced in the fireplace, casting flickering shadows that mimed the turbulence in her thoughts. Returning to bed seemed futile; her flight was now impossible. Lost in thought, she clutched a cup of tea the house had provided. The House kept it warm, as always.

"You know the Council summoned me?" Blythe murmured, gazing into the fireplace's flames, her voice tinged with apprehension and frustration.

No response came from the House, but Blythe persisted and resigned. "If I must attend the Council, you must let me go. It's the only way to avoid complications."

Silence lingered, heavy and oppressive. Blythe sighed, placing her teacup on a nearby table. She stood up and declared, "I'll wait then. This partnership feels one-sided."

As she paced, seeking help from the House, a book on a high shelf caught her eye. It trembled and landed at her feet. Blythe raised an eyebrow, picked up the book, and untied the leather strap. Inside, she found pages filled with intricate runes, only readable with her right eye closed. The runes appeared blurred and unintelligible when she tried to read them with both eyes open.

Intrigued by this strange phenomenon, Blythe

experimented. She closed her right eye and examined the runes with her left. They came into sharp focus, revealing a hidden script that seemed to dance with ancient magic. Blythe's heart quickened as she realized that this book held secrets meant only for her, a Keeper with a unique connection to the magical world.

The book, titled "Grimoire of Ancients," had beautiful drawings of magical creatures, plants, and artifacts, some with descriptions in an elegant script she didn't know. Blythe was captivated by the book's contents, lost in the mysteries of the magical world.

Suddenly, the House shook violently, interrupting her thoughts. Ben's voice came from the hallway, telling her to answer the portal.

Reluctantly, Blythe followed Ben down to the basement. She felt overwhelmed and unprepared for her role as the Keeper. Doubts filled her mind, but she hid her vulnerability from Ben.

In the basement, Blythe faced the portal door. Its ancient wood seemed to hold the secrets of centuries, etched with runes and symbols that hinted at its mystic nature. Ben's impatience grew as he mocked her for not knowing how to open it. He explained the task's complexity, intensifying her uncertainty.

But Blythe remained determined to prove him wrong. With resolve, she approached the door, her fingertips lightly tracing the intricate carvings that adorned it. Frustration and uncertainty hung in the air as she sought guidance, with the House dropping hints, subtle as whispers in the wind.

With a grumble, she requested, "Help me out, will you?" To her surprise, she found the Grimoire of Ancients nudging her foot. She picked it up, realizing its secrets were meant for her as the Keeper. Within the book, she discovered a rune called "Peeper" and drew it on the door. A window materialized, allowing her to see through to the other side. She spotted a man in a trench coat through her eyes but couldn't decide whether to admit him.

She made up her mind.

She turned the handle, and the door swung open.

The man on the landing's lips parted in a genuine smile, his pearly white teeth contrasting with his dark complexion. Blythe sensed his pride in his appearance. He looked athletic and confidently stepped into the cramped basement, his black loafers landing softly.

"Well, Ms. Evans, I presume?" Quentin said, his voice smooth as silk.

"Who the hell are you?" Ben asked, his eyes narrowed in suspicion.

Maintaining his focus on Blythe, he spoke again, gracefully tipping his hat. "My name is Quentin Hendrix, at your service." He locked his gaze on Blythe's as he removed the cap from his neatly shaved head, tucking it into his trench coat. "I'm a lawyer, here to assist and represent you," he continued, offering her a reassuring smile.

Blythe couldn't help but feel a strange flutter in her chest as Quentin's captivating smile met her gaze. His presence made her heart race, and she couldn't quite put her finger on it.

Ben's anger boiled over as he confronted Quentin. "You're going to defend her? Do you even know what she is? Impure. It's a crime for her to exist, and defending her against the Council is futile. She's destined to lose," he scoffed, folding his arms defiantly.

Quentin remained unfazed, studying Ben for a moment. "Impure?" He briefly puzzled over the term but didn't dwell on it. "Well, I'm offering my counsel as her defender. Let's get to work," he replied calmly, his eyes returning to Blythe. He smiled gently, a glimmer of reassurance in his eyes, and walked past Ben, heading for the stairs.

Blythe followed Quentin, feeling somewhat defeated but intrigued by the alluring presence of this inscrutable man who had suddenly entered her life.

"So... why did Miles send you here?" she asked as they entered the main hallway, her eyes trained on him.

Now visible in the hallway's light, his eyes bore a deep purple hue reminiscent of grapes she had seen in an Italian vineyard during her summer visit. The memory stirred pleasant feelings—sun-warmed shoulders, carefree days. It contrasted sharply with her current state of mind, snapping her back to reality. She searched for knowledge to comprehend this enigmatic man. His eyes triggered a sense of familiarity she couldn't quite place.

"He mentioned that you received a summoning note," his smile returned, adding warmth to his features. "He thought I could assist you in your meeting with them."

Blythe frowned, her skepticism growing. "How can you possibly help me? I'm just an ordinary person caught in the crosshairs of an extraordinary mess."

Quentin's smile widened slightly, a hint of mischief dancing in his eyes. "Ah, my dear Blythe, there's no such thing as an ordinary person. Everyone has a story, a hidden strength. You simply need someone to help you uncover it."

Blythe hesitated, her distrust warring with a glimmer of hope. She wanted to believe him, to trust that there was someone out there who could help her navigate this treacherous path. With a sigh, she finally relented, sinking into the armchair opposite him.

"Fine," she conceded. "But I have one condition."

Quentin leaned back, a small smile tugging at the corner of his lips. "And what would that be?"

"You have to prove to me that you're on my side," her gaze remained steady, her posture unwavering. "No more playful banter or cryptic comments. I need to know that you're truly here to defend and fight for me. Can you do that?"

"You're quite paranoid, aren't you?" he remarked with a slight chuckle. "But I can't blame you. The circumstances surrounding your summoning and the Council's interest in you can easily make anyone wary. Trust, however, is a two-way street. I also need to trust you will trust me despite any reservations."

Quentin leaned forward, his eyes locking onto hers with sincerity. "But, I understand your reluctance to trust me completely. And I won't ask you to blindly put your faith in me. But I ask for a chance to prove that I'm on your side and can help you navigate this situation with the Council. Will you give me that chance?"

Blythe hesitated, her mind filled with doubts and reservations. But deep down, she knew she couldn't face the Council alone. She needed someone who understood the intricacies of magical law and had experience dealing with their bureaucracy. Silence filled the room as they locked eyes, each sizing the other up, searching for hidden motives or vulnerabilities. The tension between them dissipated, replaced by a glimmer of understanding. Blythe paused for a moment, contemplating Quentin's words. She recognized the truth in his assessment and realized that her suspicion might have clouded her judgment. Reluctantly, she nodded. "Fine, Quentin. I'll give you a chance. But don't expect blind loyalty. You must prove to me that you're truly on my side."

A knowing smile curved Quentin's lips, and he extended a hand towards her. "Deal. I will do everything possible to protect you and ensure a fair outcome. We're in this together now."

In its usual manner, the House had provided refreshments on the coffee table between them. Quentin offered to pour her a cup of tea, but she shook her head in refusal. He poured himself a cup, adding a spoonful of sugar and a dash of cream, before helping himself to a cookie and sitting back on the couch. With his trench coat removed, Blythe could now see the shape of his muscular arms more clearly. He was indeed as imposing as he appeared.

Quentin retrieved a brown notebook and a stylish black pen from his briefcase, ready to address the matter.

"I haven't done anything wrong, so I'm sure they just want to talk and resolve things," Blythe dismissed nonchalantly, trying to maintain a sense of composure amidst her growing unease.

"Well... that's certainly one possibility," Quentin responded, gesturing towards the chair next to the tea cart.

"Please, let's have a conversation over tea. No pressure at all. I'd feel more at ease if I knew you were fully informed about what you'll be facing." He smirked before adding, "Don't worry, this is pro bono, as the human lawyers would say."

Leaning forward slightly, he rested his folded hands on the notebook. Blythe remained silent, granting him permission to proceed. "Have you ever been to the other side of the portal door?"

She pondered the question, finding it peculiar. What did that have to do with anything? "No."

Quentin's gaze remained fixed on her, his expression growing more serious. "You see, Blythe, your mixed parentage—witch and human blood—has always been a contentious matter within the Council. For some reason, they strongly believe that human blood is the worst to be mixed with." He paused, eyebrows furrowing and lips pressing into a straight line. His gaze softened, and his shoulders slumped slightly. "That's likely the reason behind your confinement to this side of the portal. They fear the unpredictable consequences of such a combination. It's unfair, I know, but it's the reality we're dealing with."

Her knowledge of the magical world was limited to fragments she had overheard and the books she had clandestinely acquired from the library, thanks to Dorian's occasional leniency. In hindsight, she realized he must have been aware of her secret book raids. He likely knew far more about her than he had let on.

"Did you ever wonder why they restricted or deemed you a risk?" Quentin's brows furrowed slightly, his eyes studying her with genuine curiosity.

Blythe's expression hardened, her frustration mounting. "Yes, I've wondered. It never made sense to me. Other magical beings freely travel between worlds without restrictions. Why should I be any different?"

Quentin's eyes softened, and he leaned back in his chair. "I understand your frustration, Blythe. It's unjust, and I agree with you. I've had my fair share of run-ins with the Council. Not everyone in the magical world agrees with their archaic views. I've seen the damage their narrow-mindedness can cause. I believe in justice, and I believe in fighting for what's right."

As they discussed her situation and the Council's prejudice, Blythe couldn't help but feel a glimmer of hope. Quentin's genuine concern for her and his thoughts about the unjust laws struck a chord within her.

From the recesses of his briefcase, Quentin produced a trove of essential documents, carefully spreading them across the coffee table. There were volumes of case law, precedents, and scrolls detailing magical decrees. His thoroughness was impressive, and Blythe couldn't help but feel a glimmer of hope.

With newfound determination, they began to delve into the intricacies of magical law, their pens scribbling notes and the hours passing unnoticed. As they delved deeper into the complexities of the case, Blythe couldn't help but feel that, despite their rocky start, she might have found an ally in Quentin. He was willing to challenge the oppressive Council and fight for justice.

CHAPTER NINE

The following day, Blythe's mind buzzed with worries, consumed by her conversation from the day before. Quentin's words echoed in her thoughts as she pondered his plans for the trial. Her uncertainty about trusting him, his capability to fulfill his promise, and the Council's intentions weighed heavily on her. Blythe's lack of knowledge about her father's world gnawed at her sanity, the uncertainty becoming unbearable. Yet, as she wrestled with these questions, a sense of destiny beckoned her. It was as if the magical world had opened a door, inviting her into a realm of unforeseen possibilities.

Frustrated, Blythe decided to take matters into her own hands and venture through the portal alone. Yet, she felt it was only fair to inform Quentin of her decision if he arrived unexpectedly. She would leave him a note.

After taking care of her morning toiletries, she approached a full-length mirror. Blythe pondered her appearance and decided to let her hair fall freely around her shoulders, projecting confidence.

Blythe opened the doors of her magical wardrobe. Within seconds, it presented her with a comfortable pair of jeans and a modern blouse, exuding style and comfort. She was ready to face the Council.

Completing her preparations, Blythe took a final glance in the mirror. Determination shone in her eyes. She put on her coat after gathering essential items in a bag, including the Grimoire of Ancients. She grabbed an umbrella provided by the wardrobe.

With purpose in her stride, she left her room and went to the basement, where the portal awaited her. The time had come for her to enter the magical world, face the Council, and forge her destiny. No matter the outcome, she would remain true to herself and embrace the magic within her.

Blythe cautiously approached the portal door. She

whispered to herself, "Well... here goes nothing," as she opened the doorknob. Stepping into the portal was a disorienting experience, akin to being spun around fast and pushed forward. When her vision cleared, she stood on a covered porch looking out into a light rain shower.

To her astonishment, the magical world's front mirrored the human world front with uncanny precision. However, she noticed a small barn that didn't exist in the human realm. As she pondered this anomaly, flapping wings interrupted her thoughts.

Looking up, she beheld a majestic winged reptile descending from the sky toward her. Instinctively, she retreated a few steps.

A sound broke through Blythe's apprehension from atop the reptile, causing her fear to momentarily subside. "Hello there!" His unexpected greeting left her puzzled yet intrigued as she tried to make sense of the situation unfolding before her.

The giant beast ceased circling and gradually descended to the ground, its massive body resembling the size of a Buick. Its brown-golden hue glistened under the sunlight that pierced through the rain clouds, illuminating its shimmering golden scales.

As the creature gracefully touched down, Blythe's eyes were drawn to a figure perched on top of it—Quentin.

"What are you doing here?" Blythe couldn't help but take a step backward, her gaze fixed on Quentin as he dismounted the beast with remarkable grace. The creature folded its wings and began sniffing the ground, seemingly disinterested in the presence of both Blythe and Quentin.

"It's good to see you too." Quentin's signature irritating smile adorned his face as he sauntered toward her, exuding an air of nonchalance.

"Sorry, your arrival just took me by surprise. Why are you here, Quentin?" Blythe demanded, her grip on the umbrella shifting to her other hand.

"I came to meet with you and finalize our plans and see

if you were up to leaving a day early..." Quentin's eyes briefly flickered toward Blythe's messenger bag, acknowledging her preparedness. "Although it seems you've decided to venture out alone?"

"I can find my own way," Blythe resumed her walk. She passed Quentin but soon realized the beast had blocked her path on the driveway.

"Don't worry, Ellira won't harm you," Quentin stepped beside her. "I'm sure you can make it to town yourself, but then what? Do you know where the Council convenes? And I truly hope you don't plan on meeting them dressed like that. They are quite old-fashioned... They might have a heart attack if they see a woman wearing pants." A playful glint danced in his eyes as he spoke.

"You're joking, right?" Blythe turned to face Quentin, a mix of surprise and incredulity on her face. "They actually have a problem with women wearing pants?"

"I wish I were kidding." Quentin's hands disappeared into the pockets of his trench coat, a mischievous glint in his eyes. "I enjoy seeing a woman in a nice pair of well-fitted pants."

"Fine, I'll change when I get there. I'm sure I can find out where the Council meets... it can't be that difficult, can it?" Blythe resumed walking, giving Ellira a cautious wide berth as she passed. "I'm sure someone in town would be willing to give me directions."

"But when you ask, they'll realize you're not from around here, Blythe. That will raise suspicions and invite unwanted questions. Once someone figures out you're an outsider, they'll likely turn you in to the Sentries," Quentin swiftly caught up to her with his long strides, now walking beside her. "It would be safer if you allowed Ellira and me to give you a ride. I'd be happy to show you around on the way if you'd like."

Blythe paused, her gaze shifting back to Ellira, contemplating Quentin's words. Perhaps there was merit in his suggestion. Keeping a low profile seemed like the wisest course of action.

"Alternatively, you could simply tell me where to go and how to get there, and then I wouldn't have to ask anyone any questions," she countered, lifting her chin. Quentin chuckled.

"Okay, we could do it that way. But do you really intend to walk the entire way? It will take you so long that you'll undoubtedly be late. That wouldn't make a good first impression."

"I was actually going to check inside," Blythe gestured towards the barn, "to see if there was a bike or something I could use." She frowned as Quentin chuckled. She wished Quentin would stop laughing at her. It wasn't amusing, and she found his laughter rather unkind.

"You could do that. But have you ever traveled by magical means?" Quentin watched her with amusement.

"What do you think?" Blythe shot him a glare.

"Well, it's not as simple as hopping on and going. Traveling magically without proper knowledge can be dangerous, and you could seriously hurt yourself," Quentin explained. Blythe rolled her eyes in response, then turned on her heel and returned to the barn.

"Please, Blythe."

"I'll figure it out," she huffed, yanking open the barn door and stepping inside, closing her umbrella. Glancing around, she took in the dim lighting filtering through the windows. Her eyes landed on several rolled-up rugs, brooms, push scooters, and a collection of bicycles. Approaching the bikes, she carefully inspected them, searching for one that suited her height.

As Blythe searched, Quentin remained by the door, his expression mixed with concern and amusement. "You could simply accept the ride, you know."

"And give you the satisfaction? Not a chance," she mumbled, finally settling on a bike and wheeling it towards the door. Quentin stepped aside, observing her intently as she swung her leg over the seat, calming herself and gripping the handlebar with determination. She could feel his eyes on her, adding a touch of pressure as she prepared to push off.

Placing one foot on a pedal, she propelled herself forward, intending to switch to the other pedal. But to her surprise, the bike shot forward like a rocket, far faster than any she had ever ridden. The speed was too much for her to handle. Her feet couldn't keep up, and she quickly lost control of the slick ground.

The bike veered off the path, careening through the grass, hurtling straight towards a towering tree. Blythe reacted instinctively, throwing herself off the bike, desperately attempting to avoid a collision. She tumbled and rolled across the muddy ground, the impact knocking the breath out of her and leaving her disoriented. Through the haze, she heard a crash and Quentin's shouting.

Lying on her back, she gazed up at the sky, raindrops falling on her face and tracing a wet path down her skin.

"Blythe!" Quentin's footsteps squelched in the wet earth as he hurried over, his face appearing over hers. "Are you okay? Say something."

Gradually, her breath returned, and she remained still momentarily, taking stock of her pain. Though she was sore, the injuries didn't seem too severe. Slowly, she pushed herself up with her elbows, sitting upright. Quentin's hand rested on her back, offering support.

"Are you okay?" he repeated, worry etched into his face. Blythe rubbed a tender spot on her side where she must have collided with something other than the ground.

"I'm fine," she grumbled, her pride slightly wounded.

Quentin's face looked like he was holding back a chuckle. He tilted his head, studying her face intently as if trying to read her thoughts or ensure she hadn't lost her senses. Blythe glanced over and noticed the crumpled heap of the bicycle lying at the base of a towering oak tree. The thought of crashing into it made her cringe inwardly. Reluctantly, she acknowledged that Quentin had been right. It pained her to admit it to herself, and she certainly wasn't about to disclose it to him.

"You know, Blythe," Quentin began, his voice soft and contemplative, "I understand your need to handle everything independently. The desire to prove that you're above stereotypes, that you're not weak or incapable because you're half-human."

Blythe looked at him, "You get that?"

He nodded, his eyes distant as he spoke. "In a way, yes. You see, I have my worries too. I'm concerned that people often suspect me of manipulating their emotions or actions simply because I'm Fae." Quentin sighed, his gaze dropping to the ground. "Our kind of magic is closely tied to nature, and we possess a unique ability to be exceptionally persuasive, which some use for dishonest purposes. So, I try to demonstrate to others that I'm not tampering with their thoughts or choices, leaving them to make decisions of their own free will."

Blythe's eyes widened with realization, her gaze fixed on his. "That's why your eyes are purple," she said, her voice filled with understanding. "You're Fae."

Quentin nodded, a mixture of relief and vulnerability in his expression. "Yes, I am. But I've always tried to hide it, blend in, and prove that I'm not what they might expect."

"You know, it's kind of funny that you're a lawyer," Blythe thought out loud. Quentin looked at her, one eyebrow-raising. She smiled mischievously, "I would think that you'd win a lot of cases if you did use your power."

He grinned, "If only I could. They protect the hearing rooms against such things, I'm afraid."

"Alright, Quentin," she took his hand and allowed him to assist her to her feet. As soon as she stood, feeling steady, she released his hand. "Let's go." Blythe cautiously approached the majestic beast. "But first... what is Ellira?"

"She's a dragon. A rare one, in fact—a Golden Draak. They're known for the magnificent sheen of their scales, which are highly sought after on the black market. They also lay golden eggs, which have considerable value to the unscrupulous," Quentin explained, moving past her and gently placing his hand on Ellira's snout. The dragon closed her eyes and nudged against his hand, emitting a deep rumble from her chest. Blythe retrieved her fallen umbrella and followed Quentin. "She's been with me for years. How we met is quite an intriguing story I'd love to share with you over dinner sometime." Quentin smiled warmly at Blythe and extended his hand towards her. "But for now, let me help you mount, and we can set off."

Blythe hesitated, fidgeting her hands as she eyed Ellira. "Is it safe... to ride her?" Her lower lip trembled, memories of the bike accident dampening her enthusiasm for magical travel.

Quentin reached out, his reassuring smile putting her at ease. "Absolutely!" He took her umbrella, pointing to the clearing sky. The rain had ceased, and sunlight pierced through the dissipating clouds. Folding the umbrella, he tucked it away in his trench coat, where it vanished. She would have marveled at that if she'd forgotten where she was.

Heart pounding, Blythe followed Quentin to Ellira's side, her breath quickening. She stumbled and bumped into Ellira's hind leg, catching the dragon's curious gaze. Quentin steadied her before mounting Ellira and extending a helping hand. Blythe took a leap of faith, placing her trust in him as she took his hand. His touch sent a warmth through her that she tried to ignore.

With a gentle pull, Quentin effortlessly lifted her onto Ellira's back. Blythe settled behind him, her fingers interlaced in front of his chest. Quentin's back radiated warmth against her as he gripped the ridges of Ellira's neck. The dragon extended her wings, and they soared into the sky in a powerful leap.

As they ascended, Blythe's stomach dropped, and she squeezed her eyes shut, tightening her grip on him. She pressed her face and body closer to him, trying to suppress her fear. Quentin's laughter urged her to open her eyes and lift her head, revealing a breathtaking panorama below.

Patchwork farmlands and miniature houses unfolded like a quilt. They flew over towns resembling toy train sets, and Quentin pointed out landmarks, sharing intriguing facts. Blythe found solace in Quentin's warmth amidst the chilly winds and discovered unexpected comfort in Ellira's presence.

Quentin's voice rose above the wind, mentioning the

sighting of a reclusive Phoenix, a harbinger of fortune. Blythe watched the majestic bird with awe.

"You know, some say that seeing a Phoenix flying when you're thinking of someone special is a sign of a budding romance." She felt the chuckle as warmth spread through her cheeks.

As they glided through the air, time seemed to fade away. Blythe gradually loosened her grip on Quentin, finding solace in the rush of wind and the rhythmic beat of Ellira's wings.

Approaching their destination, a mix of anticipation and nervousness fluttered within Blythe's heart. Riding a dragon had been exhilarating, but entering an entirely new world thrilled and intimidated her.

Quentin looked back, excitement and reassurance dancing in his eyes. "We're almost there, Blythe," he shouted above the wind. "Just a little longer."

CHAPTER TEN

Quentin skillfully maneuvered Ellira towards a concealed rooftop landing pad nestled amidst the towering city buildings.

"Keep your head down, Blythe. We wouldn't want to catch the attention of the Sentries," Quentin glanced behind them. Blythe ducked her head while trying to peek at what he was looking at. She couldn't see anything.

As they descended, the whooshing sound of Ellira's wings filled the air, and Blythe's ears popped in response. They touched down with a graceful, almost silent precision. Blythe couldn't help but marvel at the unique modes of transportation in the city. Broomsticks and umbrellas hovered above the bustling figures against the painted canvas of the sky.

Amidst her quiet observations, Quentin's laughter rang out, causing Blythe's heart to flutter involuntarily. "You can let go now, kitten," he said gently. "Unless of course you want to keep holding me?" Blythe's pulse quickened, and she withdrew her hands, a mix of confusion and denial crossing her face.

"You have some nerve..." She crossed her arms, irritation, and vulnerability covering her features.

He gracefully dismounted and extended a hand towards her, attempting to bridge the emotional distance. She brushed his hand away, intent on proving she didn't need his help. Blythe clumsily dismounted, and Quentin reached out to steady her. She hastily pulled away.

Her heart battled against the rising tide of affection as they surveyed the breathtaking cityscape. The towering buildings and spires exuded a mystical ambiance, suffused with the gentle glow of the sun. Quentin joined her, his gaze still drawn to the sky where Ellira had vanished moments ago.

Intrigued by his fascination, Blythe couldn't help but

inquire, "What has caught your attention up there?"

Quentin's eyes met hers, revealing a mix of introspection and determination. "I was simply admiring the view and reflecting. There is so much for you to discover about our world, Blythe if you choose to embrace it... if we manage to convince the Council."

Blythe wrestled with her thoughts between uncertainty and a burgeoning desire for belonging. "You're right... If I want to find my place, I'm still grappling with whether I truly do. But for now, until the council meeting, I'll give it a chance," she sighed, redirecting her gaze from the sky to meet Quentin's earnest eyes.

As the moment settled, she recalled the question that had eluded her earlier. "Speaking of which, can you tell me about the Sentries?"

Quentin's gaze softened, "How about we go inside to talk about them?"

"Better yet, let's take a stroll and explore the city," Blythe proposed, heading towards what she presumed was the door leading to the building's interior and the bustling streets beyond.

However, Quentin swiftly intercepted her path, his expression clouded with hesitation. "That's not a good idea."

She studied his face intently, her arms crossing protectively. "Why not?"

Quentin shifted his weight, avoiding her gaze. "What if someone recognizes you, Blythe? You're not entirely unknown."

Blythe's brow furrowed, her gaze fixed on him. "Who would recognize me?" she questioned, skepticism edging her tone. "Surely the Fas family isn't wandering around."

"No... but there are others..." Quentin trailed off, the weight of his words hanging in the air.

Blythe narrowed the gap between them, their faces mere inches apart. Her gaze bore into his eyes, searching for honesty. "Tell me the truth, Quentin," she demanded, her voice a hushed but insistent plea.

Quentin exhaled, reluctantly meeting her gaze. "There

are individuals from the Magical Intelligence who are aware of your existence, of what you are," he confessed. "I've gathered information about your situation. Trust me." He reached out and took her by the hand, "Now we really must get inside." He led her toward the door, her protests falling on deaf ears.

"Hey!" Blythe resisted, attempting to free her hand from his grasp. "You promised me the truth, Quentin!"

"We can't discuss it out here. Trust me," Quentin insisted, his hold unyielding. They traversed a short hallway until they reached an old-fashioned elevator.

Blythe's eyes widened, her breath quickening as she struggled against his grasp. "Let go! You're scaring me!" Her voice quivered with fear as she pleaded, her fingers clawing at his hand, desperately trying to break free. However, Quentin's grip remained unyielding.

"I'm truly sorry for this," Quentin apologized, a slight frown marring his features. "I wish we could explore the city together without these concerns. But right now, your safety is my utmost priority, and you'll be safest inside my apartment. Then we can talk." In a disorienting instant, the elevator doors opened. After a short ride, Quentin finally released his grip on her hand, and they exited the elevator. Blythe instinctively turned to open the metal grate, but it stubbornly refused to budge. Mimicking Quentin's actions, she pressed her hand against it, hoping for a response, but to no avail.

"You're not on the lease, kitten. It won't open for you," Quentin remarked, his tone tinged with amusement.

Blythe growled in frustration, whirling around to face him. She closed the distance between them, shoving him with all her might, but he barely budged, taking a small step back as if to appease her. It was clear that her efforts had little effect on him. "Don't call me that!" she snapped, crossing her arms and giving him an exasperated glare.

Quentin's smile faded, replaced by an expression of pity as he regarded her. "Blythe, I truly am sorry," his tone gentled as he spoke. He caught her hands before she could pull them away. "If we had stayed up there to talk, the Magical Intelligence or the Sentries would have inevitably caught wind of it." Blythe dismissed the unfamiliar term "Sentries." She attempted to free her hands and step back, prompting Quentin to release his grip.

"What happened to telling me the truth, Quentin?" Blythe demanded, crossing her arms and fixing him with a glare.

"I'm going to," Quentin replied, removing his hat and walking past her toward a sizeable wrought-iron coat rack by the door. He hung up his hat and trench coat before returning to face her, his steps nearly silent on the worn wooden floor. "I intended to talk to you once we got here. We can't be too careful."

Surveying her surroundings, Blythe looked for escape routes. The industrial space featured a central sitting area with glass windows offering a city view. An L-shaped couch with aqua and ocean blue sections, two armless purple cushioned seats, and a glass-topped tree trunk coffee table adorned the room. To her right, iron stairs led to a loft, while below, a spotless kitchen enclosed by steel-framed windows contrasted with exposed brick and concrete. Quentin watched her closely; for now, she resigned to staying put.

"Well?" Blythe pressed, her impatience evident as she hoped for some answers.

"Right..." Quentin motioned towards the couch, inviting her to join him. Ignoring the offer, she remained rooted to her spot. "Sentries are Valkyries employed by the Council as a military force to apprehend criminals," he explained.

"Valkyries?" Blythe furrowed her brows, recalling the Norse mythology. "You mean the female spirits who collect the souls of fallen warriors and guide them to Valhalla?"

"Exactly," Quentin affirmed, meeting her gaze. "Most of the mythologies humans have aren't really myths. They stem from a time when the portals between worlds were unguarded, allowing magical creatures to freely travel while humans remained on their side. Their stories about what came from our world were enough to keep them away."

Blythe absorbed his words, a mix of fascination and

disbelief coursing through her. Quentin continued. "So, the Houses and Keepers were established to control this, as humans were preyed upon by darker creatures. The Council was formed to maintain peace, assigning Keepers to watch over the portals. They manipulated what humans knew through the secret control of Magical Intelligence, ensuring they wouldn't search for the portals."

Curiosity sparked within Blythe, and she leaned forward, her eyes narrowing. "But what would happen if humans went through the portals? Why were they kept away?"

Quentin leaned back on the couch, tapping his fingers on his knee as he contemplated her question. "It's a dangerous proposition, Blythe," he explained, his brow furrowing. "The realms beyond the portals harbor creatures and magic that humans aren't equipped to handle. They could easily fall victim to the darker beings that lurk there."

Processing his words, Blythe furrowed her brow, lightly drumming her fingers on her thigh. "So, the Council and the Keepers kept the portals closed to protect humans from these dangers?"

"Exactly," Quentin nodded, hands folding in his lap. "Maintaining a separation between our worlds was crucial for the safety of humans and the balance of our realm. Opening the portals could unleash chaos, bringing harm to both sides."

With countless questions swirling in her mind, Blythe knew there would be time for answers later. For now, she focused on the present situation and the man before her. Shifting her weight, she leaned slightly to one side and asked, "So, what is my role in all of this? Why am I here?"

Quentin's gaze softened as he reached out, gently taking her hand, offering a reassuring squeeze. "Blythe, you are a unique being. A bridge between worlds. It's crucial we keep you hidden to ensure your safety."

His expression turned grave as he continued, "The truth is, the Council doesn't want you to exist. They see you as a threat, an anomaly that disrupts the delicate balance they've established. They've gone to great lengths to suppress any knowledge or evidence of your existence."

Blythe's heart sank, her grip on her bag tightening for comfort. "But why? What have I done to be considered a threat?"

Quentin's grip on her hand tightened, empathy filling his eyes. "It's not about what you've done, Blythe. It's about what you represent. Your existence challenges their control over the portals and their monopoly on magic. They fear that if the truth were to come out, it would undermine their authority and potentially lead to a shift in power."

Quentin released her hand, leaving the room filled with a heavy silence. He rose to get lunch pulled together.

Quentin seemed to understand her urgency as he elaborated, "The truth is, Blythe, I believe in equality. I think true peace can only be achieved through it, but obviously not everyone agrees." He began arranging food on the table, delicate porcelain plates clinking softly.

"Equality?" Blythe questioned, her curiosity piqued.

Quentin sighed, the weight of the world evident in his voice. "There have been protests, meetings, and petitions, but the Council doesn't exactly tolerate opposition."

"Have been?" Blythe inquired, prodding for more information.

A bitter smile touched Quentin's lips as he turned to face her, a glint of defiance in his eyes. "But there are those who have managed to get close to the Council, brave souls who gather intel to ensure the truth is revealed."

Blythe's curiosity prompted her to seek further clarification, her heart pounding with newfound purpose.

"The Council is ruthless and will stop at nothing to protect their secrets," Quentin cautioned, his voice laced with frustration. "I don't want to see anything happen to you."

A determined fire burned within her as she clenched her fists. "I won't stop, Quentin. I need to know the truth about why the Council is after me and how to get them to leave me alone."

Quentin nodded solemnly, his eyes holding her gaze with

unwavering determination. "Then we'll find the truth together, Blythe. But remember, we must tread carefully. We must get you through this hearing unharmed."

Blythe nodded in agreement, and their conversation turned to preparations for the impending hearing, the room filled with the scent of their shared determination.

CHAPTER ELEVEN

After lunch, a sharp knock echoed through the room, startling Blythe from her thoughts. Quentin excused himself and returned with an ornate box, its contents stoking her curiosity. The room was quaint yet cozy, with sunlight filtering through the lace curtains and casting a warm glow on the antique furniture.

"I asked a friend to bring these clothes for your upcoming summons," he explained, nodding toward the box. The apartment bore traces of a well-traveled life, with souvenirs from various places adorning the shelves.

With eager anticipation, Blythe opened it to reveal a collection of finely crafted garments—dresses, blouses, and skirts adorned with delicate embellishments, all in muted colors. Each piece seemed to tell a story, hinting at the world outside the apartment.

"Freshen up and try these on," Quentin suggested, guiding her to the loft bathroom. The bathroom was clean and modern, its gleaming tiles contrasting with the vintage charm of the apartment.

Blythe wasted no time shedding her muddy clothes and luxuriated in the warm water, cleansing away her earlier ordeal. She emerged, choosing a dress that resonated with her newfound confidence. The dress was a soft lavender shade, its fabric silky against her skin.

Quentin's voice floated up to the loft as she approached the mirror, breaking the momentary silence. "You look beautiful," he complimented with a warm smile. Blythe's cheeks flushed with a mixture of embarrassment and appreciation.

Her emotions swirled a blend of gratitude, uncertainty, and determination. "Well, it's a beautiful dress. I appreciate your thoughtfulness." She moved to join him downstairs.

Just then, the apartment door swung open, revealing Miles. "Blythe?" he exclaimed, his eyes widening in astonishment. The room seemed to hold its breath as everyone's attention shifted to the new arrival. "You look stunning!"

Blythe smiled appreciatively, touched by his genuine admiration. The room's decor, a fusion of vintage and modern styles, provided a backdrop to this unexpected reunion. "Thank you, Miles."

His presence provided a comforting anchor amidst the uncertainty of their journey. "You deserve to feel beautiful, Blythe," Miles continued. "That dress suits you perfectly."

Gratitude swelled, and she whispered, "Thank you, Miles."

Miles moved to the kitchen, a playful smile on his lips. "That dress will turn heads when you walk into that council chamber. It's certainly caught mine."

Despite the moment's charm, a pressing question weighed on Blythe's mind. "Miles, I've been wondering about something." She paused, hesitating briefly before continuing. "Are you involved with the Magical Intelligence, investigating me, perhaps?"

The room tensed as Blythe confronted Miles. He appeared taken aback but quickly shook his head. The apartment's atmosphere shifted from warmth and nostalgia to tension and unease. "No, Blythe. I'm not investigating you for MI," he assured her earnestly. "You can trust me on that."

Blythe, arms crossed, still held reservations. "It just seems too coincidental, Miles. You encouraged me to come here, the house entrapped me, and then there's that letter..."

Miles stepped closer, his voice filled with empathy. The vintage clock on the wall ticked softly, marking the passage of time. "I understand your suspicions, especially given our history, but I promise you, Blythe, I have no involvement in any investigation against you. I want to help, not hinder."

Scrutinizing his face for any signs of deceit, Blythe sighed, her tension easing slightly after a moment. "I want to believe you, Miles. I want to trust that you're on my side," she confessed, her words tinged with cautious hope. "I'm feeling as if I'm terrible at telling if someone's lying to me."

Miles reached out, his hand gently resting on her arm. The apartment's new-world charm seemed to embrace them in this moment of vulnerability. "Blythe, I can't undo the past mistakes, but I'm here for you now. Let's leave behind the suspicions and focus on unraveling the mysteries together. We can be a team again."

Their eyes locked, and Blythe found a flicker of trust rekindling within her. "Alright, Miles. Let's give it a shot," she agreed, cautiously optimistic.

Blythe hadn't noticed that Quentin had left the room but realized once he returned. "Your travel clothes are clean now. If you want to be more comfortable, save that for tomorrow."

Blythe thanked him, and she headed upstairs to change, leaving Miles and Quentin to their own discussion.

She exited the bathroom to hear Quentin and Miles's raised voices below. Miles and Quentin had re-settled in the living room. Blythe ducked out of sight, hesitant to intrude on their conversation.

Miles expressed concern about the potential consequences of the upcoming trial for Blythe. Quentin leaned back in his chair, his brows furrowed. The apartment's vintage furniture bore witness to this heated conversation.

"I understand your concern, Miles," Quentin began, his voice measured, "but I don't think it's as straightforward as that. I've doubted the Council's true intentions for a while now."

Miles leaned forward, his eyes wide with apprehension. "What do you mean? What are they really doing?" The apartment's atmosphere grew charged with uncertainty.

Quentin sighed, running a hand through his hair. "I wish I knew for certain, but I've noticed patterns and inconsistencies in their decisions. It's almost as if they have a hidden agenda, something more nefarious. They're not just banishing people; there's something else going on."

Miles leaned in closer, his voice a conspiratorial whisper.

"But what could it be? And what happens to those who are banished? Are they left powerless, cut off from everything they've ever known?" The apartment's vintage charm echoed their shared concerns. "Or is there a worse punishment? I'm afraid in MI, they don't tell us these things. What if you lose this case, Quentin?"

Quentin nodded, his expression grave. "That's what I'm afraid of. Miles, I've never lost a case like this, but the stakes seem higher this time. If I can't convince the Council to see reason and they decide to strip Blythe of her magic, I fear the consequences for her could be dire."

Miles sighed heavily, his worry palpable. "I just can't bear the thought of her losing everything, Quentin. We need to find a way to protect her to ensure she gets a fair chance. If only we knew the Council's true intentions, we could devise a plan."

Quentin leaned forward, determination etched on his face. "I won't rest until I uncover the truth, Miles. I'll dig deeper and gather more information. We can't let them take away everything Blythe holds dear. I'll fight tooth and nail to ensure justice is served."

Miles began pacing back and forth, his hands occupied by a restless blue orb that he manipulated and spun. On the other hand, Quentin appeared at ease, reclining on the couch with his tie loosened and vest unbuttoned.

Miles raised a valid point, concern etched on his face. "Q, if the Council finds out you brought her here early, you could face the same consequences as her."

Quentin's movements grew fidgety, his hands shifting between his pockets. Blythe sensed his anxiety, watching his restless behavior. The apartment seemed to close in on them.

"She was invited. We simply commenced her journey earlier than expected," Quentin replied, his tone filled with determination as he put on his trench coat. "Don't worry so much, Dixon. I've done this before."

Miles muttered softly, his worry lingering as he watched Quentin place his hat on his head. "Yeah... that's what worries me."

"I'll keep her safe, Miles. You have my word."

Blythe decided it was time to come out. She started down the stairs, and Miles stood up when she reached the bottom.

"Well, I think it's time I should head back to work," Miles interjected, his feet shifting uncomfortably. The apartment's vintage clock seemed to count down the moments of their conversation.

"Oh, okay," she replied, suddenly awkward in the room. Should she address what she had overheard? She decided against it. "I guess I'll see you at the trial?"

"I won't be at the trial," Miles responded with a tinge of sadness. Blythe paused, her gaze fixed on him.

"Oh... okay, so I'll see you after?" she asked, a hint of disappointment crossing her expression. She wasn't entirely sure why his absence at the trial affected her in such a way.

"Yes, of course. After," Miles replied, his smile returning as if trying to regain his confidence. "Okay, I'll be off then!"

Blythe bid a belated goodbye as Miles left, her mind still grappling with mixed emotions. The vintage charm of the apartment held the echoes of their conversation as if it, too, had witnessed the complexities of their relationships.

CHAPTER TWELVE

Blythe had planned to spend the remainder of her day engrossed in books from Quentin's library. She aimed to gain a deeper understanding of this world and demonstrate her ability to fit in. She settled comfortably on a window seat, surrounded by a sea of books. Quentin had left for an important client meeting, granting her the solitude she needed for uninterrupted learning.

Though the allure of the sunlight streaming through the expansive windows beckoned, Blythe resisted its temptation. Instead, she delved into one of Quentin's law books, hoping to acquaint herself with the fundamental magical laws to avoid inadvertent violations. Pages filled with flying traffic regulations and penalties for flying under the influence met her gaze. She shifted her attention to the newspaper for a more engaging read.

One headline in particular caught her eye: "VALKYRIE MURDERER STILL AT LARGE." Beneath it, a vividly drawn image of an enraged red-haired woman stared out from the page. The article revealed that Hera Eyundal, a former Sentry student, faced charges of murdering two mages. Quentin's earlier hints about underlying tensions and resistance within this magical world returned to her thoughts, and she resolved to discuss this with him upon his return.

The newspaper contained typical news topics, such as finances, trade, and natural disasters. Still, the image of Hera Eyundal and the crime continued to occupy Blythe's thoughts. She contemplated the existence of spells that could amplify the lethality of weapons. She pondered what could drive someone to commit such a heinous act. The label "former Sentry student" raised further questions about Hera's background. Had she failed to complete her training? Her curiosity deepened.

While preparing lasagna, Quentin returned from his meeting. The tantalizing aroma drew his attention. He mentioned that he had news to share during their meal. They settled at the table, plates filled with food and glasses of wine in hand. Curious and eager for Quentin's update, Blythe prompted him to share.

"So, what's the news?" Blythe inquired, leaning forward with anticipation.

Quentin chuckled, admitting that the aroma had momentarily sidetracked him. "Benjamin has managed to escape the House. But don't worry, I doubt he has anything to tell the council that they don't already know."

Blythe, however, couldn't help but question the potential consequences. "Are you sure about that?"

With a deep breath, Blythe decided to voice her concerns. "Quentin, I appreciate your optimism, but I can't help but feel anxious about this summons. With Ben now loose to talk to whoever he wants. I feel like that makes it worse, you know?"

Quentin paused, placing his fork down and gazing at her with understanding. "I get it, Blythe. That's normal. But remember, we're in this together. I'll be there by your side, supporting you every step of the way. Like I said, he couldn't have anything else to share with them."

Blythe decided to let it go and they returned to their meal, savoring each bite as they mentally steeled themselves for the challenges on the horizon.

The following day began with Blythe and Quentin's journey to the hearing. Upon arriving at their destination, Quentin pointed out the Hall of Mysteries, where the council convened. Blythe was awestruck by the grandeur of the Hall, which exceeded her expectations. It resembled more of a majestic castle than a legal institution, with its pristine white exterior adorned with green trim and its regal gray roofing, pavilions, towers, and dormers. The central clock tower loomed tall, dominating the skyline. Blythe stood across the street, feeling a mixture of awe and nervousness in the presence of this imposing structure.

Quentin stood beside her, recognizing her momentary hesitation. "It's quite imposing, isn't it?" he remarked with amusement. "I remember being terrified the first time I had to enter. They certainly don't shy away from grandeur and intimidation. But we'll be just fine." He gestured, signaling their next move. "Shall we?"

As they stood there, waiting their turn to cross the street, Blythe watched a cyclist effortlessly ride backward while flipping through a book. The street bustled with activity, even though flying was the preferred mode of transportation. Blythe observed a woman accompanied by ten identically dressed children following her like a row of ducklings. Soon after, a family glided past on a large carpet, occupying the same space the children had just vacated. These magical quirks added charm to the otherwise ordinary daily life scene, reminding Blythe of the unique world she had entered.

Following Quentin's lead, they crossed the street toward the grand marble steps leading to the main entrance. Two imposing figures flanked the door, armored guards with swords at their sides, their foreheads adorned by silver headpieces bearing an inscrutable symbol. One had long, braided blonde hair, the other a brunette with a similar braid. The doors swung open, revealing a dimly lit interior that felt like entering another world.

Quentin addressed her, breaking the silence. "Those, Kitten, are Valkyrie. Don't let them intimidate you. They won't act unless provoked. Just follow me."

Blythe swallowed her unease as they entered. Elaborate paintings framed in dark wood trim adorned the walls and ceiling, and the marbled floor blended white, gray, and gold. They walked down the hallway, her eyes briefly capturing murals depicting scenes of robed figures pursuing centaurs, dwarves, and fairies and another of merpeople listening to robed leaders in the ocean. These paintings revealed the power dynamics and biases in the magical realm, leaving her unsettled.

People bustled around, each absorbed in their pursuits, some hurrying, others leisurely. Conversations filled the air, a mix of hushed tones and animated chatter. Occasionally, women dressed similarly to the guards stationed outside passed by, their swords visibly strapped to their hips, radiating an air of readiness.

Anxiety surged within Blythe, prompting her to clutch Quentin's arm, her voice trembling. "Is it too late to run for it?" she whispered urgently.

Quentin chuckled, his expression warm and reassuring. "No need to worry. Everything will be fine. Now, this way." He guided her down a seemingly endless hallway until they stopped before a pair of intricately carved doors. Two more Valkyrie stood guard, stepping forward to block their path.

The doors loomed before them, a masterpiece of magical craftsmanship and artistry. Made from dark, ancient wood, they bore intricate carvings of symbols, runes, and patterns, narrating the magical realm's history. The arched tops resembled mythical creature wings, while the lower portion showcased sculpted vines and leaves dotted with gemstones that sparkled like stars, giving the doors an ethereal quality.

In the center of each door, a circular emblem in shimmering gold depicted unity and balance. Mythical creatures encircled a wise phoenix, its wings spread protectively. Elements of earth, air, fire, and water surrounded the phoenix, symbolizing the harmony of magical forces. Ancient runes engraved around the emblem acted as protective spells, guarding the room from ill-intentioned magic.

The doorknobs were masterpieces, one resembling a silver griffin with piercing eyes, the other a gold dragon clutching a sparkling gem. They seemed like guardians, granting or denying access based on intentions.

As Blythe and Quentin approached, the doors seemed to pulse with energy, acknowledging their presence. The carvings seemed to come alive, telling tales of ancient wisdom and powerful enchantments. A faint hum, barely audible, emanated from the doors, adding to the aura of mystique that surrounded them.

"State your names and the purpose of your visit," one of the Valkyrie demanded. Her lips pressed tightly together, giving the impression that a wrong answer would result in instant impalement.

"Good morning!" Quentin greeted cheerfully, clasping his hands on his briefcase's handle. "My name is Quentin Hendrix, and this is Blythe Evans. She has been summoned to appear before the council." A heavy silence hung in the air, the tension palpable. Blythe's heart pounded in her chest as she wondered if they were at the wrong door, fearing their response might have been inappropriate for this particular location. She regretted her choice of outfit, feeling a sudden warmth and noticing her palms growing clammy. The worry of her makeup smudging due to perspiration added to her unease.

"Wait here," the other Valkyrie finally spoke, turning and disappearing through the door. Time stretched on endlessly as Blythe faced the intimidating Valkyrie, struggling to suppress her restlessness. Glancing at Quentin, she noticed his calm demeanor, as if he were contemplating dinner in the elevator of his apartment building. Just as her nervous bladder threatened to demand the location of a restroom, the door swung open, and the Valkyrie reemerged.

"You may enter now."

The air around the doors felt charged with magic, and as the Valkyrie guards stepped aside, the doors creaked open with a sense of anticipation. The room beyond beckoned like a hidden world of secrets and wisdom, and a warm golden light spilled out from within, casting intricate patterns of light and shadow across the corridor.

The doors' craftsmanship was a testament to the magical prowess and artistry of the ancient beings who had created them. They exuded an air of reverence and authority, commanding respect from all who approached.

Quentin placed a reassuring hand on her back. "Okay, kitten. Let's do this." With a gentle nudge, he urged her forward, and they ventured through the doors.

As Blythe and Quentin stepped through the doors, they knew they were about to enter a realm of profound significance, where their destiny would be decided, and the magic that bound their world together would weave its intricate tapestry.

CHAPTER THIRTEEN

As the heavy wooden doors clanged shut behind them, Blythe's heart raced, pounding with anxiety. The chamber they now stood in was unlike any she had seen before. Its walls were adorned with intricate tapestries depicting scenes from ancient magical battles, their threads shimmering with a subtle enchantment. The ceiling towered above, vanishing into the shadowy depths where ancient spells' hushed secrets seemed to linger. Blythe discreetly wiped her clammy palms on her skirt, failing to quell her nerves. The hope of finding solace within these walls had faded, replaced by an oppressive sensation akin to suffocating in a confined space. It felt like being thrust on to an unfamiliar battlefield, armed only with her wits.

In a hushed tone, Blythe leaned closer to Quentin, her voice trembling as she confessed, "Quentin... I'm not sure I can handle this." The dimly lit hallway they had traversed offered little comfort, with a faint light beckoning from the distant end. Despite their past differences, she felt a surge of gratitude for his presence beside her.

Quentin's reassuring smile radiated his usual confidence. "I believe in you, Blythe," he whispered back. "And remember, you have me." He winked and flashed a smirk, igniting a flicker of courage, even if she wished she possessed half his self-assuredness.

Rolling her eyes at his attempt to bolster her spirits, Blythe inhaled deeply, drawing upon her inner strength. She took a determined step forward, heading towards the beckoning light at the end of the hallway, Quentin following closely behind. The weight of the impending trial pressed heavily on her, but she had resolved to confront it head-on.

Upon entering the chamber, Blythe was momentarily blinded by the searing light that engulfed her vision. She blinked, adjusting to the overwhelming brightness. As her sight gradually cleared, she stood in an amphitheater adorned with intricate cherry wood carvings. The white and black marble floors showcased a prominent 'W' in a striking black flame design at its center, hinting at the room's versatility for hosting various events based on the numerous seats that filled it.

The resonant voice filled the chamber from all directions. "Blythe Evans, daughter of Dorian Fas," it proclaimed. Blythe turned her gaze to six men clad in black robes, accompanied by a man in a deep crimson robe seated in their midst. It was the man in red who spoke. "You have been summoned before the council to answer for your crimes. You stand accused of exposing the human world to the magic realm."

Blythe's stomach plummeted, her breath catching in her throat. How had she unknowingly exposed magic to humans? When? Wait, he'd called her the daughter of Dorian. How did they know? The man in the red robe continued, his wrinkled face and hooked nose exuding disdain and authority as he looked down at her.

"Also, you are charged with pursuing knowledge of the magic realm despite explicit prohibition. As a half-human, you have no entitlement to this knowledge," he continued. Blythe felt sick, struggling to comprehend the gravity of the situation. Why wasn't Quentin speaking up? Shouldn't he object, as lawyers do?

Without granting her an opportunity to respond, the man in the red robe accused her of engaging in romantic relations with a wizard and assuming the role of Keeper of House Fas, both forbidden acts.

Blythe's head spun, silently cursing Quentin for not adequately preparing her. She hadn't anticipated such an array of charges and felt ill-equipped to defend herself. How had he not known what the charges were? Back home, a lawyer would have obtained precise details of the accusations and ensured their client was well-prepared.

Before Blythe could utter a word, Quentin stepped forward. "Supreme Wizard," he nodded at the man in red.

"Council of Wizards, I am grateful you granted us an audience. My name is—"

"We know who you are, Mr. Hendrix," the man to the right of the one in red interjected, sporting a caveman-like appearance with flowing dark hair and a prominent brow. "Please, speak for your client or let her speak. We don't require theatrics." A few of the council members snickered. Blythe had a sinking feeling that despite Quentin's confidence in his ability to sway them, they were not his admirers, and the situation might be more complex than he had anticipated.

Quentin remained composed, his briefcase resting on the table, drawing Blythe's attention to its presence. As he circled the table, he directed his gaze towards the council. Blythe hurriedly sat, hoping to steady her nerves before the impending discussion. Quentin took charge, addressing the first charge leveled against Blythe.

"Regarding the house assignment," Quentin began, his demeanor relaxed as his words flowed effortlessly into the room. "The House holds the authority to choose its Keeper. Due to Ms. Evans' direct relation to Keeper Fas, she naturally became a candidate for the role. Currently, there exists no provision to refuse this position. However, if there is an alternative solution, Ms. Evans is willing to step down." His eyes scanned the council for any objections, finding none. He proceeded to address the following accusation.

"As for the alleged romantic relations with a wizard, it remains purely based on hearsay. There is no substantial evidence to support this charge, and we request its immediate dismissal," Quentin began to delve into further details, but a council member on the far left interrupted.

"We have a witness to substantiate this claim," Blythe's heart momentarily stopped. How could there be a witness? She believed that Miles would never betray her. Then, she remembered that Benjamin had escaped the House. She cursed herself for forgetting that detail. He probably ran to the council to spill everything he knew, like the tattle-tale he always had been.

"Bring forth Mr. Benjamin Fas," the man in the red robe commanded, his voice echoing through the room. Blythe turned, her gaze falling upon Benjamin as he strode into the chamber, accompanied by a tall, lanky man in a dark suit and tie. Benjamin moved with unwavering confidence, his strides purposeful and assured. Dressed immaculately in a smart gray suit, Ben and the skinny man reached the center of the room, acknowledging the council with a respectful bow.

"Supreme Wizard, esteemed members of the Council of Wizards, I express my gratitude for summoning me to speak before you today," Benjamin began, his posture conveying respect, his unwavering gaze locking onto theirs. He introduced his legal counsel, Mr. Edlin Freyorn, who stood beside him, ready to navigate any potential complications. Benjamin's body language melded formality with self-assuredness, speaking volumes.

"I can attest to having witnessed Ms. Evans and Mr. Dixon engaging in intimate relations on multiple occasions," Benjamin stated matter-of-factly. Blythe's heart sank at his words. She felt her shoulders slump and bit her lower lip to steady its trembling. She focused on her breathing, trying to quell the rising panic. Memories flooded back, and she knew it wasn't as scandalous as Benjamin portrayed. Their first innocent kiss, shared on Blythe's 16th birthday in the widow's peak, was far from the X-rated tale he was spinning. He elaborated, making their innocent moment sound far more explicit than reality. They'd shared one kiss, one tender peck, and then she'd noticed Ben watching them, and they'd chased him away. He didn't mention anything else unless he had succeeded in spying on them other times.

As Benjamin continued addressing the council, Blythe felt shock and indignation surge within her. Her fists clenched in her lap as she listened to him fabricate stories of her and Miles engaging in secret romantic encounters. Her cheeks flushed with embarrassment and frustration, and she squirmed uncomfortably in her seat, unable to call out the lies without evidence to counter his claims.

In the dimly lit chamber, Benjamin's confident gestures and dramatic flair accompanied each fictional encounter he described. He gestured with sweeping hand movements, wearing a smug expression as he wove his deceptive narrative. Blythe exchanged anxious glances with Quentin, silently seeking support and reassurance. They both knew they had to follow the council's rules, even if those rules seemed inherently biased.

The Supreme Wizard leaned forward, his stern gaze fixed on Benjamin as he listened to the young man's increasingly outlandish tales. Other council members scribbled notes and exchanged disapproving glances among themselves. Blythe's heart sank as she realized the impact of Benjamin's false accusations on their perception of her.

Under the weight of these baseless allegations, Blythe fidgeted in her seat, her eyes darting around the room, searching for any sign that the council saw through Benjamin's lies. Quentin, seated beside her, offered a reassuring hand on her back, urging her to maintain her composure despite the turmoil within her.

Finally, Benjamin concluded his baseless accusations, and the man in the red robe turned his attention to Blythe. "Ms. Evans, do you have anything to say in response to these allegations?" he inquired sternly.

Taking a deep breath to steady herself, Blythe lifted her head and looked directly at the council. "I categorically deny any romantic involvement with Mr. Dixon," she asserted firmly. She hoped her determination would convey her innocence despite Ben's false stories. She and Miles had shared multiple rendezvous, but they were not as scandalous as Benjamin portrayed. She prayed they couldn't see through her lie, as they seemed to believe his lies.

The council members exchanged skeptical glances, their faces betraying doubt as they considered Blythe's claims. Her heart raced, knowing that without evidence, her word alone might not prove her innocence.

Quentin stepped forward, his tone authoritative and eloquent. "If it pleases the council, we are willing to provide any evidence necessary to refute these baseless claims," he offered, his hands spreading wide, his head inclining in deference to them. "Including testimony from Mr. Miles Dixon himself."

The Supreme Wizard nodded, his expression revealing nothing. "Your offer shall be considered, Mr. Hendrix. The council will deliberate on this matter and decide in due time. Should these accusations prove credible, we will summon Mr. Dixon to account for his actions." Blythe's stomach churned. Would Miles be subjected to this ordeal as well?

As the council members huddled, Blythe's mind raced with thoughts of how to clear her name. She hoped the truth would prevail but could only endure the false accusations and trust their ability to present a strong defense.

The Supreme Wizard nodded in agreement, joined by several council members who concurred. Blythe couldn't help but speculate on their silent decision, fearing they might have hastily condemned her. She wondered if they'd already cast her as the deceitful one deserving punishment.

"Thank you for your testimony, Mr. Fas," the Supreme Wizard acknowledged with a nod of appreciation.

However, before they could depart, Edlin stepped forward, securing permission with a slight bow. "May I have a moment, Supreme Wizard?" he began. "Regarding the Keeper of the House position, it warrants special consideration. Benjamin Fas, the rightful heir of Dorian and Lila Fas, was meticulously groomed for this role without the knowledge of any half-sibling. There is no precedent for such a challenge to this position in our houses. Benjamin is the lawful heir, and we firmly believe this mistake should be rectified. While the House holds ancient wisdom, it may have erred in this instance," Edlin leaned in to whisper something to Benjamin, who nodded in agreement, a sly smile curving his lips.

"We will factor your statement into our deliberations. You

may now depart," replied the man in the red robe. Benjamin strolled past Blythe, a smug smile directed at her, before leaving the room with his lawyer. Blythe couldn't help but feel hurt and bewildered, questioning how he escaped the House. She had believed the House would be on her side, but something didn't add up. It allowed Ben to leave, even though he wanted to turn her in. She had been sure the House wouldn't let him go.

"Mr. Hendrix, please continue," instructed the man in the middle, his arms folded over his chest, his bushy brows furrowed, and his eyes squinting over his wire-rim glasses. Quentin remained unfazed, his composure providing solace to Blythe, who hoped he had a hidden strategy.

"Thank you, Supreme Wizard," Quentin said, clasping his hands behind his back. He addressed the council members confidently, shoulders back and chin held high, making direct eye contact as he spoke. "Regarding Blythe's access to magical knowledge and connection to our realm, Keeper Fas unknowingly permitted her access to forbidden books. She had no reason to believe his actions were illegal, especially since she was a child. His blatant ignoring of the laws cannot be her fault.

"Additionally, the claim of her exposing our realm to humans is false. Blythe attended Oxford, a human institution, and pursued studies in Archaeology and Anthropology, specifically to mitigate any potential risks of exposure from the past. Her involvement has led to a significant decrease in magical findings and the need for memory erasure and relocation in her area of study," Quentin revealed, causing the council members to exchange whispers and engage in hushed discussions.

While Quentin addressed the council, their members engaged in hushed discussions, their expressions revealing the weight of his arguments sinking in. With newfound awareness of Quentin's prior knowledge regarding the charges, Blythe silently decided to confront his omission later, focusing now on the critical proceedings at hand.

"Thank you for your words, Mr. Hendrix," the Supreme

Wizard acknowledged. "We will give them due consideration. Ms. Evans, do you have anything you would like to share with the council?"

Blythe swallowed nervously, recalling Quentin's advice to stick to their rehearsed plan. Taking a deep breath, she rose from her seat, displaying a mixture of nervousness and determination in her body language. Her hands trembled slightly, but she clasped them together to steady herself.

"Thank you, Supreme Wizard and esteemed members of the Council of Wizards, for allowing me to speak today. I have lived my life caught between two worlds—the human world of my mother and the magical realm of my father," she paused, her eyes glistening with unshed tears, her voice quivering with emotion. "I distanced myself from the House during my time in college, with no desire to return or involve myself in the magical realm. I acknowledge that, due to my lineage, I am not a true Witch. I deeply regret my father's transgressions, as he made mistakes. I sincerely hope to assist in righting these wrongs. Thank you." Blythe sat down, feeling weak and overwhelmed, considering it the most arduous day of her life.

"Thank you. Ms. Evans and Mr. Hendrix, please wait in the adjacent room while we deliberate." The collective gaze of the council remained fixated on them, making Blythe feel like a zoo animal under scrutiny. Quentin stood, gathered his belongings, and gently guided Blythe to follow him out of the chamber.

"Don't," he whispered softly, restraining her as she attempted to approach Benjamin in the side room, his grip firm on her arm as he guided her away. They settled into seats as far away from Benjamin as possible, with Quentin strategically positioning himself between them. "We cannot discuss anything substantial in this environment. I can't fathom how you must be feeling, but don't worry, you did exceptionally well," he reassured her, his glance darting towards the Valkyrie, cautioning against further conversation.

Resting her head against the wall, Blythe closed her eyes, seeking solace in a moment of meditation. She focused on regulating her breathing to calm her racing heart and regain a sense of normalcy. Despite her initial doubts, the practice had a calming effect and allowed time to pass peacefully.

CHAPTER FOURTEEN

"The council requests Ms. Evans' presence," a woman's voice abruptly interrupted Blythe's thoughts, causing her to startle. She and Quentin promptly rose to their feet, bracing themselves for whatever lay ahead.

"I am Ms. Evans' representative," Quentin asserted. The Valkyrie stood in his way, gripping her sword firmly as she locked eyes with him. "But I can wait here for her." Blythe exchanged an anxious glance with Quentin.

"Quentin... I can't..." she began to protest, but he held her forearms firmly, his eyes conveying his confidence.

"You can, and you will. Don't worry," he reassured her with a supportive smile. Then, gently turning her around, he encouraged her toward the door. Blythe looked fleetingly at Benjamin, who seemed to enjoy himself thoroughly. However, Quentin's worried expression caught her attention, revealing a rare, genuine concern. She swallowed and proceeded through the door.

The room had transformed, its opulence fading under the dim lighting, creating an eerie atmosphere that hinted at the gravity of the situation. The council chamber, adorned with ornate carvings and ancient tapestries, loomed around them, emphasizing the weight of the impending judgment. The solemn expressions on the council members' faces contrasted with their richly decorated surroundings.

Alone in the room's center, Blythe stood as the door closed behind her, facing the solemn men in their robes. The room had darkened, devoid of the table and chairs that had been there before. It felt as though she were about to confront the harbingers of doom themselves. The council chamber's elaborate carvings and ancient tapestries created an eerie atmosphere, emphasizing the weight of the impending judgment.

"We have reached a decision on all the charges brought against you," the Supreme Wizard announced, raising a paper from the table before him. Adjusting his spectacles perched on his hooked nose, he scanned the page.

"Blythe Evans, daughter of Dorian Fas, you have been found guilty of exposing the human world to the realm of magic," the Supreme Wizard declared, his words hanging heavily in the air. Panic surged within her. How could they reach such a verdict without substantiating their claims? The council chamber's atmosphere grew even more stifling, as if the air had become tense. "You are also found guilty of learning about the magic realm and practicing magic." This couldn't be happening. For the first time since she met him, she longed for Quentin's reassuring presence. "Furthermore, you are found guilty of engaging in a romantic relationship with a wizard.

"Additionally, you are guilty of assuming the Keeper of House Fas role. You will be immediately escorted to a cell for final sentencing." Blythe's mouth went dry, disbelief washing over her. How could they find her guilty without presenting any evidence?

Two Valkyrie emerged from the shadows, their presence sending tears welling up in her eyes. The council chamber's dim lighting cast long shadows on the ornate carvings, creating an eerie backdrop to her unjust verdict. She fought against them, refusing to let the tears fall. This couldn't be real.

"No..." Blythe pleaded softly, her eyes wide with desperation, her voice trembling as the Valkyrie closed in on her. She glanced between the Wizard's council and the imposing figures of the Valkyrie, her heart racing with fear. "I don't understand... There was no evidence presented against me... I don't understand!" Each Valkyrie took hold of her arms, their grip unyielding as they dragged her across the room towards the left side.

"You are an aberration," the Supreme Wizard boomed, his words resonating with authority. "My predecessor made a grave mistake by allowing you to live this long. We shall rectify this error." He retook his seat, conversing with another council member as if a young woman were not being forcibly dragged away, her cries of despair falling on deaf ears.

"Please!" Blythe cried out, her words strangled by sobs as she struggled against the Valkyrie's unrelenting hold. The sounds escaping her lips were unrecognizable, a raw expression of anguish. Before she knew it, she was pulled through the doorway, leaving behind the opulent room for a dark, damp, stone hallway that undoubtedly led to her bleak cell.

"Walk," one of the Valkyrie ordered, their grip tightening as they forced Blythe to her feet. The pain in her arms, the coldness of the stone floor, and the discomfort of her surroundings accentuated the harsh reality of her unjust conviction. Where was Quentin? Would she ever lay eyes on him again? And Miles... she regretted not saying a proper goodbye. Would she be allowed visitors? Could she find some form of recourse against these charges? This couldn't be the end. There had to be a glimmer of hope, some possibility of appeals or justice.

The journey through the dimly lit hallway and down a winding spiral staircase barely registered in Blythe's overwhelmed mind. Before she knew it, she was unceremoniously thrown to the ground inside a small, windowless cell. Pushing herself up, her eyes stung with tears as she watched the door slam shut and lock behind her. The Valkyrie walked away without a second glance, leaving her to face her despair alone.

Tears streamed down her face, mingling with the dirt on her cheeks. Crawling to the back corner of the cell, she wrapped her arms around her knees, seeking solace in the cold embrace of isolation. The cell's stark simplicity, with its rough stone floors and walls, provided a stark contrast to the opulence of the council chamber. Feeling the stiffness from sitting on the floor, she rose to her feet and approached the cell door.

"Hello?" Blythe called out, her voice echoing through the

silence, her brows furrowed in concern. She strained her ears, hoping for a response, but only a profound silence engulfed her. "Is anyone there?" she repeated, a flicker of hope dancing in her eyes.

"Seriously? Some of us are trying to sleep," a voice responded, laced with irritation. The woman behind the voice was clearly annoyed. "It was bad enough listening to all that blubbering. Sheesh."

"I'm sorry... I just wanted to ask a question," Blythe replied softly, leaning against the cell bars, resting her head on them.

"You must be new here, girly. No one working here cares or will answer your questions," the woman retorted wryly. "Get used to being ignored and keeping quiet."

"Okay, then..." Blythe whispered, resigning herself to the reality of her situation. She moved away from the bars, finding solace in the bed's simplicity. Sitting down, she stared at the opposite wall, her mind swirling with questions. How had she ended up in this predicament? What steps could she take now? The silence in the cell became suffocating, and she couldn't discern whether it was day or night. The faint glow of a single light bulb above her and the distant hallway lights provided the only illumination. Bending down, she untied her black shoes and lay back on the bed, her gaze fixed on the ceiling. "This is quite a predicament," she muttered before closing her eyes, seeking rest without any other viable course of action.

CHAPTER FIFTEEN

In her turbulent dreamscape, Blythe's fragile state crumbled under the council's collective rejection. She should have just run. Turned and never looked back.

The dreamscape was a surreal realm, filled with shifting shadows and ethereal forms. It was as if she floated in a void with no solid ground beneath her. Strange, ghostly figures whispered and swirled around her, their forms ever-changing.

Dorian, her father, materialized as an ethereal presence, his stern countenance casting a shadow. Blythe whispered his name, her voice quivering. "Dorian, father, I tried my best."

His gaze bore into her with disappointment. "You are a mistake, Blythe," he declared. "I should have never given you the magical amulet. Your existence has brought disgrace."

Tears welled in her eyes. "I love you, Father. I'd give up magic just to be free."

Dorian transformed into Miles, his features twisted with anger. "You were a mistake," he spat. "You've ruined me. It's all your fault!"

Blythe reached out to him, voice trembling. "No, Miles, please! I love you. We can find a way to set things right."

But Quentin emerged before she could bridge the gap, bitterness in his eyes. "I should have never bothered. You're beyond redemption."

Her heart shattered. "No, Quentin, please. I need you."

Quentin turned his back on her and walked away. The dream crumbled.

Amidst the darkness, a gentle voice reached out to Blythe. Seraphina, her mother, appeared in a radiant glow. She embraced Blythe.

"My precious daughter," Seraphina's eyes brimmed with love. "Believe in yourself, for you can rise above their judgments."

Blythe clung to her mother's words, renewed with purpose as the dream faded.

Upon awakening in her cold and desolate cell, tears streamed down Blythe's face, the remnants of the dream still lingering in her heart. Yet, she clung to the sliver of hope. Seraphina's empowering words were etched into her mind as a guiding light amidst the darkness surrounding her.

"Blythe?" Startled, she jolted upright, having dozed off again after what felt like hours of staring at the ceiling. Two figures, Quentin and Miles, stood just beyond her cell door.

Quentin spoke first, his voice filled with concern and tenderness. Relief flooded her, and she hurried to her feet, racing towards the door. A glimmer of hope rekindled within her.

"Quentin told me everything," Miles began, reaching out to grasp her hands through the bars. Their fingers brushed lightly, a delicate connection amidst the harsh surroundings. His touch sent a shiver of warmth through her.

"We're going to find a way to fix this, Blythe. I promise."

"How?" Her voice trembled, choked by the welling tears.

"Not now," Quentin's impatience was evident, but Miles's gaze remained locked on her.

"Listen, Blythe," Miles interjected. He reached for her hand, but she hesitated before allowing their fingers to graze, a fleeting touch that ignited a spark within her. "We can't linger here for long... but I promise we'll find a way to secure your freedom. You can trust me."

With a reassuring nod, he turned away just as a Valkyrie approached. Miles tugged at her arm, urging her closer to the cold metal bars. Without thinking, she allowed him to pull her into a comforting, through-the-bars embrace, a fleeting moment of solace amidst the confines of their circumstances. The world around them blurred, and they briefly found comfort in each other's arms.

"I'm here for you, Blythe, always," he whispered, his breath warm against her skin as their foreheads drew near, creating an almost imperceptible connection. His implicit devotion hung like a delicate promise, left unspoken yet profoundly felt.

She allowed her eyelids to flutter shut, a wave of unspoken emotions enveloping them both, the depth of their feelings echoing silently in the charged atmosphere.

With those words, he broke the connection and moved away, following Quentin's lead. As he passed the resolute Valkyrie, his gaze remained fixed forward, deliberately avoiding meeting their eyes, and he disappeared down the hallway.

Despite her best efforts, Blythe found no respite in her surroundings. She had reluctantly reclined on the uncomfortable "bed" after Miles and Quentin's departure. Then, a Valkyrie with long braided purple hair emerged, bearing a tray of food. Clad in the same attire as her fellow guards, she exhibited an apparent disdain for conversation. Blythe, however, couldn't resist the urge to inquire about the length of her confinement. Yet, her questions were met with unyielding silence.

"Well... I suppose this isn't exactly a fine dining establishment," she murmured wryly, carrying the tray to the makeshift bed.

As she progressed with her meal, the purple-haired Valkyrie reappeared, accompanied by a red-headed counterpart. Blythe set aside her food and rose, obediently approaching the open cell door. The red-headed woman promptly shackled her wrists, connecting them to the chains around her ankles. Blythe couldn't help but question the necessity of such restraints; after all, she was neither a violent criminal nor an escape risk. Yet, it seemed that dramatics were the order of the day in this wretched place.

Led through a labyrinthine network of hallways, Blythe struggled to maintain her balance under the heavy shackles impeding her every step. Whenever she faltered, the women accompanying her responded with forceful jerks, dragging her back up and propelling her forward. Surprisingly, the return journey to the council chamber felt shorter than the initial trip. As they drew nearer, the murmur of voices grew louder, signaling a distinct contrast from her previous encounter. The chamber itself teemed with an eclectic mix of witches, wizards, fae, dwarves, and even a man adorned with strands of seaweed in his hair—a clear indicator of his merfolk heritage. The crowd's murmurs gradually faded upon her entrance, leaving only the echoing clatter of her chains.

Guided to the center of the room, Blythe's ankle shackles were firmly fastened to a previously unnoticed ring embedded in the floor. Steeling herself, she took a deep breath, surveying the gathering before her. A momentary silence enveloped the chamber, broken only by the hushed whispers that soon swelled anew. Their gazes, filled with judgment and scrutiny, made it abundantly clear that she was the topic of their discussions. Briefly, she pondered what her House would do to them if they dared to judge her while within its confines. Oh, how she longed for the comfort of that House now.

Her searching eyes eventually settled on two familiar faces—Miles and Quentin—standing side by side, their concern for her unmistakable despite their feeble attempts to conceal it. The sight of them threatened to unravel her composure, tears pricking at the corners of her eyes. She willed them away, refusing to display vulnerability in front of this callous assembly. So, she averted her gaze, directing her attention to a point just below the council dais, deliberately avoiding any direct eye contact.

The room descended into an eerie stillness, the only audible sound being the rhythm of her own pounding heart thumping loudly in her ears. She silently hoped for a swift and painless ordeal. However, a nagging intuition whispered that such a merciful outcome was unlikely. Why offer her an easy escape when they could revel in her suffering? It was clear that this place hungered for entertainment, as evidenced by the gathering crowd that awaited the unfolding spectacle.

"Blythe Evans," the Supreme Wizard's voice echoed

through the chamber, chilling her to the bone. He clearly relished this role. "You stand before the council, convicted of crimes against the realm. You have been found guilty of exposing magic to humans, practicing magic as a half-human unnatural being, engaging in a relationship with a wizard, and wrongfully acting as the Keeper of House Fas." Whispers and gasps swept through the crowd, their animosity palpable.

Blythe glanced at Miles and Quentin. Miles looked horrified while Quentin radiated anger. He stood beside the shirtless man, deep in conversation. When Quentin noticed her gaze, he smiled reassuringly, attempting to project normalcy. But Blythe wasn't fooled. She knew the situation was dire.

"We, the Wizard's Council, have reached a decision after careful deliberation," the Supreme Wizard announced, reveling in the suspense. It was clear the audience enjoyed this spectacle. Suggestions for her sentencing were shouted from the crowd: death, lifetime imprisonment, even slavery.

Blythe turned to Miles, Quentin, and the merman, who were deep in an argument. She couldn't fathom why they argued when her fate hung in the balance.

The Supreme Wizard addressed the crowd, his back turned to Blythe. "Blythe Evans, the daughter of Dorian Fas, stands convicted of grave transgressions against our laws and the sanctity of our magical heritage. Her existence as a half-human unnatural being challenges our society's very fabric. We can't ignore the consequences of her actions, as they threaten our magical order."

Blythe scanned the crowd, seeing smug and gleeful faces, including Benjamin's. Tears welled up, stung by his hatred. She tried to block out the Supreme Wizard's words, but they echoed in her mind.

"While her lineage is complex, precisely this dual heritage requires us to make an example of her. We can't allow half-breed offspring to flaunt our laws without consequences. Doing so would render our laws meaningless and disrupt the harmony we've fought for.

"Ms. Evans's transgressions extend beyond exposing magic or practicing it; they reach the depths of her relationships. Her involvement with a wizard and false assumption of the Keeper role underlines her defiance of our traditions.

"Our path is one of responsibility and discipline. As guardians of the magical realm, we must protect it from threats. Blythe must bear the burden of her actions—a living example of what befalls those who defy our laws.

"I don't relish this sentencing, but our duty demands it. Let this be a warning to those considering forbidden unions —a stark reminder of our commitment to safeguarding our heritage.

"We, the Wizard's Council, must stand united to protect the sanctity of our realm. This sentencing reinforces our dedication to our principles and resolve to uphold the magical order.

"May the world witness our decision today, a lasting reminder of our commitment to protect our realm. May our actions pave the way for a future where harmony and order prevail, ensuring the sanctity of our magical heritage."

"After careful deliberation," the crowd hushed, their anticipation palpable as they awaited the sentencing pronouncement. "You shall serve 20 years in the mines for each charge, and we will confiscate your amulet," the decree echoed through the chamber. Whispers swelled once more, repeating the weight of the grim sentence. Yet, the pronouncement continued, extending its doomy grip on Blythe. A sense of dread filled her heart. Without her amulet, what would become of her magic?

He was still talking, but his words fell on deaf ears. Blythe's gaze remained fixed as a council member descended from the dais toward her. With a few uttered words, he reached out and forcefully tore her necklace away. In an instant, it felt as though her very essence had been stripped from her, leaving an unsettling void where her magic once thrived.

The amulet clattered to the ground, its significance

echoing in the distant words of the council member. The irrevocable loss washed over her, and a cold, gnawing dread settled in. What would become of her magic without the amulet? It had guided and empowered her throughout her life, an integral part of her identity. Now, she found herself adrift, severed from the wellspring of her strength.

Fear and vulnerability surged within Blythe as she grappled with the harsh reality of her situation. The council's judgment had not only condemned her to servitude but had also torn apart the very essence of her being. She had lost her freedom and a fundamental part of herself. Uncertain and despair threatened to consume her in the face of this profound loss.

A sense of dread washed over Blythe as she comprehended the enormity of the verdict—20 years for each charge, amounting to 80 years of servitude to the realm. Confusion and desperation clouded her thoughts, instinctively driving her to seek answers from Quentin. However, he and Miles began maneuvering through the throng, seemingly leaving her behind.

The two Valkyries who had accompanied her reappeared and swiftly released her from the floor restraints.

"No, Miles!" she called out, but her voice was drowned amidst the jubilant clamor of the audience. She made another desperate attempt, shouting for Quentin, yet her pleas went unnoticed. As her cries fell upon deaf ears, they forcefully dragged her out of the chamber.

She continued calling for Quentin and Miles, desperately grasping for a lifeline amidst the sea of faces. The only other person who caught her attention who wasn't celebrating was a shirtless man standing beside Quentin, surprisingly adorned with a discontented expression amid the celebratory atmosphere. Shaking his head, he observed her being hauled away. Meeting her gaze, he offered a nod before turning away. The doors closed behind her, muffling the euphoric sounds of revelry and leaving her isolated in uncertainty.

CHAPTER SIXTEEN

The Valkyrie guards' iron grips tightened around Blythe's bound arms, propelling her through a dimly lit, winding corridor. Flickering torches painted eerie shadows on rough stone walls, heightening her anxiety. Questions swirled in her mind. Where were they taking her? What lay ahead in the darkness? The uncertainty clawed at her, leaving her defenseless against their control over her fate. Each step propelled her further to an unknown future. Fear and anxiety coursed through her veins.

The corridor stretched endlessly ahead. The Valkyrie guards maintained an unyielding silence, betraying no hint of their motives. The walls seemed to close in on her, and the air grew heavier with each step.

They exited through an inconspicuous back door into a secluded courtyard, its charm muted by the waning daylight. Blythe had lost all sense of time. Was it still the same day or already the next? Undeterred, the guards guided her toward a solitary structure lurking in the shadows. Tall trees enclosed the courtyard, their leaves rustling gently in the evening breeze. At the same time, a distant owl's hoot added to the eerie ambiance.

A small box lay before her, hardly more than a crate. Panic surged as she resisted, attempting to break free, but her struggles proved feeble against their superior strength. They effortlessly placed her inside, unmoved by her pleas.

The box was a claustrophobic embrace, barely accommodating her bound limbs, leaving her feeling captive and vulnerable. Panic surged as the lid slammed shut, enclosing her in oppressive darkness. Blythe's breathing escalated as she wrestled to rein in her fear.

The box stirred into motion, the grating and shuffling noises signaling another round of transportation. Blythe's vision was useless, the swaying movement inducing nausea.

Trapped, enveloped by darkness, Blythe grappled with suffocation.

With swift efficiency, the Valkyrie guards lifted Blythe from the confining crate. They led her through a labyrinthine tower that loomed ominously in the darkness. Her heart raced as they descended into a foreboding dungeon, its stone walls bearing the weight of countless forgotten secrets. They locked her in a dimly lit cell, and she crawled to the cold, damp wall, the oppressive sense of isolation settling over her like a shroud.

Time slipped away as she pondered her predicament. Minutes stretched into endless stretches, distorting her perception of reality. The cramped space and dwindling air supply provoked desperate gasps for breath.

Doubts and fears gnawed at her resolve. Why had she been subjected to such treatment, and what destiny awaited her? Was this dungeon to be her lifelong abode, a place forgotten by the world above?

Time slipped through her fingers as she cried out, her pleas echoing faintly. She yearned for a savior—to kindle a spark of hope within the gloom.

Yet, deep within her, a glimmer of resilience persisted. Blythe knew surrendering to despair wasn't an option. The imperative of her strength became unmistakable. She anchored herself in the belief that brighter days could yet unfold. She clung to memories of brighter days—laughter, kinship, and love interwoven with those she cherished. These memories infused her with strength.

And so, she huddled in the dungeon's corner, grappling internally to quell her tears. She vowed, "I will find a way out of this. I'm not going to let this be my end."

A sudden sound cleaved the air, tendrils of trepidation snaking down her spine. It was a deep, entrancing voice laden with malevolence. "Good. You're useless to us dead," it intoned.

Before she could react, a hand clamped over her mouth, a cloth pressed to her lips and nostrils. An unfamiliar, pungent aroma emanated from the fabric, inducing panic. She struggled against her captor's grip, but her strength waned rapidly.

The cloth's fumes infiltrated her senses, inducing dizziness. A feeling of unwelcome heaviness overcame her body. Darkness encroached, her struggles succumbing.

The world dissolved into oblivion while the cloth pressed against her face. Consciousness ebbed away, ensnaring her in unconsciousness. The eerie echo of that sinister voice whispered of a fate graver than death. Then, all plunged into darkness.

From above, a deep, plummy voice resounded, asking, "Is this the girl?"

"I suppose so. She was in the cell we were directed to," came a more soothing and melodious response.

Gradually, consciousness returned to Blythe, leaving her enshrouded in grogginess and confusion. The events leading to her current predicament felt hazy and disjointed. As she blinked, trying to clear the haze clouding her vision, she became aware of the pervasive darkness. The overcast night concealed any potential moonlight that could have offered clarity. Though she couldn't discern their forms, she sensed their proximity.

"Well... did anyone go get the General?" the first figure pressed.

"Yes, I sent Xander to inform him," the second confirmed.

"Good," the first figure responded. Blythe weighed her options, debating whether to remind them of her presence or feign lifelessness. She took a quick glance around.

The surroundings remained unfamiliar, lacking distinctive shapes or landmarks. The air was cool and damp, and the soft rustling of leaves and occasional owl hoots reached Blythe's ears from a distance. Evidently, she was outdoors, yet the shroud of darkness prevented her from gauging her location relative to civilization.

As her senses slowly returned, fear and uncertainty washed over her. Vulnerability and exposure gripped her, intensified by her solitude in the darkness. The threat of panic hovered, yet she understood the importance of maintaining composure and focus. Determined, she decided she had to escape the grasp of these unfamiliar figures.

Blythe tried to move to orient herself, but her body betrayed her with weakness and unsteadiness. The uneven ground beneath her feet confirmed that she was outdoors. Frustration and fear welled up, threatening tears, but she steeled herself against their advance. She understood the need to press forward, to seek an escape from this dark and desolate realm.

"There he is," an unidentified voice announced. Uncertain of the identity of this "he," Blythe froze.

"What are the two of you doing just standing there? Help her up!" a commanding voice ordered. She heard hurried movements, and soon, the two figures rushed to her side. Their strong hands lifted Blythe into a sitting position. But before she could assess their numbers, a blinding light engulfed her surroundings.

Sheltering her eyes from the sudden brilliance, Blythe squinted until her vision adjusted. Amid the luminance, she seized the moment to draw in a breath of refreshing air tinged with the aroma of wood and bonfires. Gradually, she opened her eyes, revealing a clearing. Gazing upward, she took in the expanse of the dark sky adorned with countless twinkling stars. With a gradual scoot backward, she inadvertently bumped against a solid object, a massive tree trunk. As she focused her gaze ahead, she strained to distinguish the faces of the figures standing before her. Flanking the central figure were two individuals—one slender and diminutive, the other short and stout.

"Well... she's prettier than I thought she would be," remarked the willowy figure to the left, his voice tinged with a hint of mischief. Even though Blythe detected their male voices, their faces eluded her view.

"Really? That's your assessment of her? Very helpful," retorted the short, burly one, arms crossed.

"Silence, both of you," commanded the figure in the middle. Stepping forward, he squatted down in front of Blythe.

Now, his features became more apparent, and a shock of recognition surged through her.

"But... you're dead," she gasped, blinking in disbelief, attempting to correct the impossible sight. The two behind the figure burst into stifled laughter. They quieted when the man shot them a look. He turned his attention back to her.

"So I've heard," the man smirked, his black hair, pale skin, and green eyes resembling her father's. Yet, on closer inspection, subtle differences emerged—his face bore a faint scar from temple to chin, and his build appeared leaner and more muscular than her father, Dorian. He held a resemblance, yet he was not her father.

"You're not..." Blythe's eyes widened.

"Dorian, no." He stood, extending a hand to assist her to her feet. She tentatively placed her hand in his, but her weak muscles protested, causing her to withdraw and lean against the tree for support. "But I am, apparently, a relative of yours," he grinned, folding his arms across his chest. "Your uncle, to be exact."

"I thought... I thought you were sent to the mines as punishment for what Dorian—my father—did," she gently rubbed her arms, chafed raw from her struggles against the box earlier. "Or, did he have another brother?"

"We have a lot to talk about, Blythe." He turned and began walking, motioning for her to follow. Cautiously, she stepped forward, mindful of roots that could trip her.

"Xander, please see about finding more suitable attire for our guest." Blythe peered in the direction he had looked. Still, only a fleeting shadow met her gaze before disappearing too swiftly to reveal details. Her eyes wandered as she followed her uncle, realizing they were in a camp. Large tents encircled crackling fires, some occupied by huddled figures while others stood vacant.

"Most here call me General Fas. You can call me Uncle or Uncle Demetrius if you'd like." Guiding her into a tent, he held the flap open, prompting her to enter. She hesitated, then reasoned that if he intended to harm her, he wouldn't have bothered to arrange new clothes for her. "You and I share something in common."

"What's that?" she asked, taking in the tent's interior. It had the typical setup with poles, but there was enough space for a table and chairs at its center. A dark red rug covered the ground, and a cot sat beside a wooden box in the corner. A lantern hung from the tent's apex, casting a warm glow.

"We were both targeted by the council because of Dorian," Demetrius explained, pulling out a chair and sitting down. Blythe was startled by a gust of wind, and suddenly, a tall figure materialized next to Demetrius, holding a stack of clothing and a pair of hiking boots. The figure wore a long black cloak with the hood concealing their face in shadows.

"Thank you, Xander," Demetrius acknowledged before the figure disappeared with another gust of wind. Blythe wanted to inquire about Xander but was preempted by Demetrius.

"Xander is a vampire. Socializing isn't his forte." He stood up. "You must be tired. A bath has been prepared for you in your tent, along with some food and sleeping clothes. I'm sure you have many questions, but it's late, and there will be time later to ask whatever you'd like."

"Okay... but can I ask at least one thing?" Blythe requested as Demetrius handed her the pile of clothing and led her out of the tent.

"If you must," he replied, guiding her to the tent adjacent to his own. Blythe quickened her pace to keep up.

"Where are Miles and Quentin? Were they involved in whatever this was? Why did you knock me out?" She followed him into the neighboring tent.

"That was three questions. Miles and Quentin will join us when they can, but they can't arrive together or too soon, or the Council could track them here," Demetrius explained, placing the clothing on the cot in her tent. This tent was smaller, with a large wooden tub instead of a table. A small table beside the cot was adorned with a food tray—bread, steaming chicken, potatoes, and green beans. A pitcher of water and a glass completed the setup. Another stack of clothing lay on the bed. "I apologize for the way we retrieved you. It was faster this way. Your rescuers didn't have time to answer your questions or explain where you were going. Our methods may be abrupt, but they are effective. Now, freshen up, eat, and rest." He turned without further ado, leaving Blythe with many unanswered questions.

Blythe paced within the tent, grappling with what she should do. She could comply and go along with their peculiar plan or retreat back home.

"Well... I might as well get clean and eat something," she mused. Blythe bathed swiftly, immersing herself in the warm water and washing away the grime of her confinement. After drying off, she changed into the provided undergarments, jeans, and sweater. She put on the socks and hiking boots, then took a piece of chicken from the tray, eating it contemplatively.

Her mind buzzed with uncertainty. What should she do? Blythe moved to the entrance of her tent, peering outside. The central fire burned in the clearing, but no one was around it. Light emanated from the giant tent, with shadows of figures within. One silhouette was pacing and gesturing. She cautiously ventured further, ensuring no one was nearby, then retreated into the tent. Blythe wrapped the remaining food in the blanket on the cot, donned the cape she found, and returned to the entrance. Finding the clearing devoid of people, she slipped out and swiftly went to the other side of the tent. She hurriedly departed the clearing, disappearing into the dense thicket of trees.

Amid the overcast darkness, Blythe sought refuge behind a tree, waiting for her eyes to adjust. The faint moonlight cast a sliver of visibility, allowing her to navigate the woods without stumbling. Yet, the shadows veiled potential dangers, demanding her utmost vigilance. Uncertainty about the reasons behind her rescue festered within her, sowing doubt in her willingness to trust those who had taken her captive.

With determination fueling her steps, Blythe advanced cautiously, her senses heightened by the nocturnal stillness. Each footfall resonated loudly in the darkness, amplifying her fear of discovery. Her heart raced with each rustle of leaves and distant animal cry. Her escape was a desperate gamble, a leap into the unknown.

Blythe's thoughts whirled in disarray as she ventured into the forest. Her uncle's cryptic words, the elusive figures who had taken her, and the uncertainty of her safety swirled in her mind. The world around her seemed alien and unfamiliar, enveloped in darkness and hushed by the night.

Hours passed, and exhaustion began to gnaw at her resolve. Blythe's steps grew slower, her movements less confident. She needed rest, but she dared not stop for long. She leaned against a tree, seeking momentary respite from the relentless pursuit of escape.

The night air was comfortable, laden with the earthy scent of leaves and soil. Blythe's breaths gradually steadied, her heartbeat echoing in the quietude. She contemplated her choices, weighing the peril of her surroundings against the unknown future that awaited her among her captors.

Amid her contemplation, a faint rustling nearby roused her from her reverie. Tension gripped her as she strained to discern the source of the disturbance. A sense of vulnerability settled upon her as she realized that, even in the heart of the forest, she was not alone.

The sound drew nearer, and Blythe's heart pounded in her chest. She knew she couldn't remain hidden forever. Her escape had only begun, and the darkness held secrets she had yet to uncover.

CHAPTER SEVENTEEN

Darkness closed in around Blythe, heightening her vulnerability in this unfamiliar place. She stumbled repeatedly, driven by a fierce determination to escape. Growls and snarls of hidden creatures echoed maliciously, spurring her forward. Branches and twigs snapping around her.

The creatures' growls urged her to navigate the labyrinthine landscape with reckless abandon. Panic welled within her, but she fought to maintain composure.

Suddenly, she tumbled to the ground, searing pain shooting through her ankle. Gasping for breath, she desperately sought refuge.

Desperation surged, compelling her to her feet. But before she could flee, a powerful grip seized her waist, lifting her off the ground. Her scream was silenced as a cold hand clamped over her mouth. The pursuing creatures' growls echoed through the area, and her captor hissed, repelling them.

Caught and powerless, Blythe struggled in her captor's hold, her mind racing for an escape plan. The shroud of darkness concealed her surroundings, leaving her uncertain about where she was or where to go.

Just as suddenly as they had appeared, her captor released her, and she was dropped to the ground. Her heart raced as she scanned her surroundings, searching for the person who had intervened. However, the dimly lit landscape offered no clues, underscoring her profound isolation.

A voice broke the silence behind her, startling her. She spun around to face a cloaked figure, their features obscured in the shadows.

"Excuse me?" she retorted, instinctively stepping back. Uncertainty flooded her mind as she questioned the stranger's intentions. The voice triggered her memory—it was the same voice from earlier.

"I said there's no excuse for such thoughtless behavior," annoyance oozed in their tone. "If I had my way, those creatures could have made a meal of you," they continued, their voice cold and low. "But I wouldn't wish the guilt they'd feel afterward. What kind of reckless person roams these lands at night?"

"I wasn't just wandering aimlessly. I had no idea there were dangerous creatures here," Blythe explained.

"Unawareness doesn't excuse recklessness," the figure hissed. "Return to safety. I won't save you again." With that, they vanished, leaving her bewildered.

As she grappled with the encounter, the growls of approaching creatures reached her ears like dire warnings. Clearly the creatures had waited for the figure to leave. Panic surged as she realized that outrunning them with her injured ankle was futile. Just as despair began to set in, the figure reappeared from the shadows, positioning themselves between her and the imminent danger.

With unwavering determination, they confronted the snarling creatures. An overwhelming aura of power radiated from them as they raised their hands. The animals hesitated, sensing the presence's formidable strength and danger.

In a mesmerizing display of agility and finesse, the figure evaded the creatures' lunges, effortlessly sidestepping their razor-sharp claws with supernatural grace. Their movements flowed like a dance, redirecting the attacks without harm, demonstrating a profound understanding of the creatures' instincts. She was able to get a better look at the creatures. They were massive wolves.

Tension thickened in the air. Fueled by a primal force, the figure unleashed a power surge, sending the creatures tumbling backward, wounded but alive. The wolves whined and one turned and ran, closely followed by the others.

In silence, the figure turned to Blythe. The crimson glow in their eyes softened, a glimmer of concern piercing their stoic demeanor. Struggling against the limited illumination, Blythe strained to discern their features. Yet, their face remained concealed, intensifying her curiosity.

"Get up," came their low voice. A sense of familiarity tugged at Blythe's senses.

Transfixed by the spectacle, Blythe sat, overwhelmed by admiration for this mystifying figure who had rescued her. Why would someone who so obviously hated her save her?

His concealed face left her to speculate as to who he was. His voice and mannerisms oozed with disdain towards her. "Here," he offered his hand to her to assist her standing, his tone laced with begrudging assistance.

Caught between apprehension and curiosity, Blythe cautiously accepted his hand, relying on his support as they returned to safety. The adrenaline still pulsed through her veins, and the mysterious figure who had intervened without causing harm to the creatures continued to captivate her. Her ankle throbbed painfully as they walked.

As they reached safety, Demetrius approached with a lantern to guide their way. Upon seeing Blythe, relief washed over his face. A mixture of gratitude and concern etched on his features, he sincerely addressed the man, "Thank you for bringing her back, Xander. We owe you a debt of gratitude." Xander. The Vampire. Of course. Blythe felt stupid for not realizing who it was.

The man nodded, his demeanor steady and inscrutable. "I merely acted as you would wish," he replied coolly. He vanished into the shadows without further words, leaving Blythe and Demetrius alone. He once again escorted her back to her tent.

"This time, try not to wander off," he scolded. "Good night."

Blythe felt like a child being scolded for having snuck out after curfew. She decided not to argue, and instead, with a throbbing ankle, she hobbled back into the warmth of her temporary shelter.

CHAPTER EIGHTEEN

The following day, Blythe awoke with a pounding headache, an aching jaw, and her injured ankle still throbbing. She lay on the cot, staring at the tent's roof as sunlight filtered through, casting intricate shadows. Questions swirled in her mind about her presence here and her potential escape from these strangers.

Outside, cheerful male voices reached her ears. Despite the temperature drop overnight, she resisted the warmth of the blankets and got up. She ignored her sore ankle and wore a cozy gray knit sweater, jeans, socks, and sturdy hiking boots.

Emerging from her tent, she spotted four men congregated around the smoldering remains of the previous night's fire: a short, stocky man in a plaid shirt sharpening an ax; a slender woman, initially mistaken for a man, tended to a camping stove with tightly braided red hair and pointed ears; and a third man with curly dark hair and a beard sat with Demetrius, deep in conversation. They seemed engrossed in the discussion, and no one else had noticed her. She took a moment to get her bearings.

The camp sat within a densely wooded area with a hint of saltwater in the air. Tall oaks stood like towering giants, their branches reaching upward, casting dappled sunlight on the forest floor. Various tents of different sizes and colors were scattered around the clearing. Rebels moved with purpose, engaged in conversations, and shared laughter. The camp buzzed with activity.

Demetrius's impatient voice broke through her thoughts as he gestured for her to join them. She approached and settled beside him.

The stocky man later revealed to be named Griffin, was in the middle of a playful, over-the-top story about his uncle's adventures in a battle against three men in a bar whom he may or may not have drunkenly challenged to a fistfight over the color of cabbage. Demetrius joined in the banter, and Blythe's attention shifted to the woman at the stove.

Noticing her gaze, Demetrius spoke. "So, how's breakfast coming along, Hera?"

"It's coming." Hera looked up. "Would you like something to eat, Blythe?" she asked quietly.

Blythe's eyes fell on her intricately designed cuff bracelet, and Hera's question didn't immediately register with her.

"What?" Blythe realized she had lost her thoughts and missed the question.

"I'll take that as a yes," Hera commented, her actions quick and efficient as she loaded a tin plate with eggs, bacon, and toast. Balancing the dish, she walked over to Blythe, extending the offering. Blythe expressed her gratitude, genuinely touched by the small act of generosity.

Griffin couldn't resist a playful jab, "Thank the stars Hera's a better fighter than a cook, or we'd be in a world of trouble!"

Blythe chuckled at Griffin's jest while Hera responded with a good-natured grin. Demetrius reassured Blythe with a comforting smile, "Don't mind them. Griffin likes to tease Hera. If he keeps it up, he may be on the receiving end of her battle skills.

They ate silently, lost in thought as minutes stretched on. Blythe's unease simmered, interrupted when Demetrius spoke up.

"I've asked our healers to join us for breakfast. They'll tend to your ankle soon." His gaze drifted to her untied boot.

"Thank you," Blythe hesitated before continuing, "I'd like to return to the human world if possible. I'm not an escaped convict there. I won't face forced labor or werewolf attacks back home. If you can guide me to another portal, I'll leave."

Blythe wiped her hands on her pants, her anxiety creeping in. She didn't know these people well enough to trust them entirely. They had made her a fugitive, and she feared they might pose a threat if she didn't cooperate. She felt powerless in this unfamiliar world.

"Go back? Why?" Demetrius sounded genuinely puzzled as if he couldn't understand why someone would want to leave.

"I have a life," Blythe reiterated firmly, crossing her arms and fixing her gaze on Demetrius. "A life I'm not willing to lose."

"But that's not an option," Demetrius stated matter-of-factly, setting his fork aside. "Especially not with your injured ankle."

"What do you mean it's not an option?" Blythe's irritation flared, her confusion evident in her narrowed gaze.

"The council's reach is broader than you realize," Demetrius explained, his tone carrying a weight of seriousness. "Now that you're hiding from them, they'll ensure you have no life to return to. When they say their reach also goes into the human realm, they mean it."

"What do you mean?" Blythe inquired, her frustration momentarily subsiding in favor of curiosity.

Griffin and Octo returned with buckets of water, shifting the group's attention as they poured the water into a pot.

"They won't just make you a fugitive here but also in the human world," Hera added, skillfully preparing plates of food for the rest of the beings in camp. "Their spies hold influential positions there, and their reach is extensive." She then addressed the large, shirtless man who had recently joined them. "Here you are, Octo," she said, offering him a plate. Octo, an imposing figure Blythe thought must have been over six and a half feet tall, had deep, shimmering skin, jet-black hair cascading down his back, and sea-green eyes.

"They've even infiltrated the merpeople ranks," Octo said, pausing to take a big bite of bacon. "To regain control, we must ensure they remain ignorant of our actions and manipulate the narrative in our favor."

"You're a merman?" Blythe's gaze fixed on Octo, her curiosity piqued by his reference to merpeople. It suddenly clicked in her memory - Octo was the shirtless man she had seen with Quentin and Miles at her sentencing.

"That's one way of putting it," Octo responded casually, directing his attention to his meal. "I witnessed your sentencing. Your boyfriends, whatever you call them, they're an interesting pair."

"They're not my boyfriends," Blythe clarified, her expression shifting to a mix of irritation and exasperation.

"Good. Romance complicates matters," Demetrius chuckled, momentarily lightening the atmosphere.

"And if ye think about it," Griffin interjected, brushing aside the side conversation, "Ye'll find the portals a tough rock to crack, lass. They're well-guarded by them Lizard folk, and rightly so. No way they want any ol' witch or wizard stumbling upon 'em."

Blythe's brow furrowed as she tried to comprehend the situation. "Lizard people?"

"Yes," Hera confirmed, "they have an alliance with the council and are paid to secure the portals. They don't bother other creatures as long as they steer clear."

“Aye,” Griffin agreed. “Me Uncle Bromlin, he did venture into them Mireglow Fen Bogs, he did. But he never did return, poor soul.”

"Maybe he got lost," Octo suggested, speculating.

"Aye, that's right," Griffin added, "he was a seasoned dwarf warrior, he was. Always came back with tales to tell. But not that time."

Demetrius added firmly, "It's true. I barely escaped the Dark World through a portal. If not for Hera's mother and the banished Warlocks, I'd be trapped there like countless others banished by the council."

Blythe's skepticism gave way to curiosity. "I thought you were sent to the mines? What is the Dark World?"

"Before the council's rise to power, it served as a realm of exile for all dark creatures banished by the ancient leaders," Demetrius explained, his eyes reflecting solemnity. "The Council lies and tells everyone that prisoners are sent to labor mines when they're banished to the Dark World to suffer as prey to or fight for their survival against the evil that lives there."

"Why were the Warlocks banished?" Blythe inquired.

"This council member convinced everyone that Warlocks were committing crimes with their dark magic," Demetrius revealed. "Warlocks and Eyra, Hera's mother, aided me when I was there, and I vowed to help the Warlocks escape."

"How can you trust they won't turn against you?" Blythe's confusion grew.

"Tell her already, Demetrius," A woman dressed in Valkyrie armor interrupted with a raised eyebrow. She had joined them at some point in the conversation, and Blythe was surprised she hadn't noticed her. She bore a striking resemblance to Hera. She smiled at Blythe, "I'm Eyra, by the way."

"What we mentioned about the council banishing people to the Dark World is accurate. They framed individuals they deemed 'inferior' to appease the dark creatures to keep the actual criminals there. The dark creatures demanded more victims to play their part in guarding their side of the portals. Most who were banished there were not actually evil at all. We represent the last hope for equality and freedom for them and the rest of us," Demetrius moved to the other side of the fire and turned to face Blythe. Griffin joined him, assisting in tidying up the cooking supplies. Hera grabbed a plate of bacon and took a piece to eat.

Blythe shook her head, "I'm really not interested in being a part of all of this."

"Interested or not, you're in it now," Eyra looked at her with sympathy. "You won't be able to return to your life until the Council is dealt with."

"And you're a key to our success," Demetrius added. "We have a plan."

Blythe couldn't fathom what lay ahead, her mind grappling with the enormity of their cause. "It better be a good one."

CHAPTER NINETEEN

Later that day, the camp came to life with activity. Blythe found herself at the wash station, scrubbing breakfast remnants from dishes while the camp's dynamics hummed around her.

Demetrius, Eyra, and Octo huddled within Demetrius's tent, engrossed in hushed strategic discussions. Nearby, Hera and Griffin were diligently sharpening weapons, their focus unwavering. Blythe couldn't help but feel like an outsider, yearning to glimpse their plan. When she'd attempted to inquire, they assured her that her role would be revealed when the details solidified.

Amidst the clattering of plates, as she piled them into a basket, ready to carry them to the nearby river for cleaning, a petite woman and an equally diminutive man entered the camp. Aenwyn and Nreman introduced themselves as healers, their voices warm and apologetic for their tardiness. Intrigued by the newcomers, Blythe invited them into her tent, their presence a welcomed distraction from her persistent curiosity.

Nreman unpacked an assortment of ingredients from his bag. At the same time, Aenwyn approached Blythe with a gentle request to remove her boot and sock. Blythe complied, eager to see what they had in store.

With a practiced eye, Aenwyn carefully examined Blythe's ankle, now displaying an unattractive hue of purple and blue. A concerned expression crossed her face as she diagnosed it as a severe sprain.

"Blythe, you've sprained your ankle," Aenwyn touched Blythe's ankle gently. "But fret not, I have just the remedy – Thandori paste. It should help alleviate the pain and expedite the healing process."

"Does anyone have a healing stone? My father, Dorian,

would often use that to heal sprains and minor cuts and bruises," Blythe inquired hopefully.

"Unfortunately, no," Nreman replied with a furrowed brow. He was Aenwyn's younger brother, a dedicated apprentice in the field of medicine. "We must be cautious about using magic and possessing magical items that might draw the council's attention." Nreman busied himself assembling the necessary components for the paste; his actions were swift and methodical.

As Blythe felt gratitude and curiosity bubbling within her, she couldn't help but speak up. "Thank you both. How does this Thandori paste work?"

Aenwyn's kind smile reflected years of experience. "Thandori paste is a concoction of healing herbs and magical elements renowned for their soothing properties. When applied to the affected area, it reduces inflammation and speeds up the recovery. I am teaching Nreman the art of field medicine, and passing down the recipes that have been in our family for generations."

Nreman, his hands deftly blending the ingredients, added enthusiastically, "Aenwyn has been a wonderful teacher, and I'm eager to put my skills to good use. Tandoori paste has shown remarkable results in our past cases."

Observing the siblings work together, a sense of appreciation washed over Blythe. Individuals like Aenwyn and Nreman dedicated themselves to healing and solace for those in need. It served as a reminder that even in the darkest times, pockets of light and hope still existed.

As Blythe surveyed the camp, filled with people from diverse backgrounds united by a common goal, she couldn't help but feel a spark of optimism. Though outnumbered and facing formidable odds, they were resolute in pursuing a future where equality prevailed and the oppressive rule of the council would be dismantled.

Her gaze returned to Aenwyn as she patiently guided Nreman through the necessary ingredients. Taking advantage of the moment, Blythe seized the opportunity to study their appearances. Aenwyn and Nreman, despite their small stature, bore the distinct features of adults. Aenwyn's short hair showcased vibrant hues of pink and purple, accentuating her elegant pointed ears. She wore a whimsical hat crafted from flowers and leaves, complementing her one-shoulder leaf dress and flower belt. Nreman sported a similar hairstyle with blue and white tones, topped by a leaf cap. His attire consisted of leaf pants and a shirt adorned with a bramble and berry belt. Blythe's curiosity was piqued by their choice of clothing, as well as their lack of footwear.

After carefully pounding the mixed ingredients into a smooth paste, Aenwyn and Nreman applied it gently to Blythe's ankle, ensuring complete coverage before skillfully wrapping it with cloth and twine. A soothing warmth immediately enveloped her injured ankle, gradually alleviating the pain. Blythe expressed her heartfelt gratitude for their assistance.

"Thank you," Blythe conveyed her appreciation as she gingerly slipped her sock and boot back on, a sense of relief washing over her. The welcome respite from the throbbing pain starkly contrasted with her previous discomfort.

Aenwyn and Nreman spoke in unison, their voices reminiscent of the twins from The Shining. "It's no problem!" they chimed, cheerful tones echoing. Aenwyn encouraged Blythe to seek them out for any future medical needs. With a swift departure mirroring their arrival, they disappeared, leaving Blythe alone with the remaining dishes.

Eager to finish her work, Blythe approached Hera, inquiring about the designated area for washing dishes. Hera promptly directed her toward the nearby river, cautioning her about the strong current during this time of year. Grateful for the guidance, Blythe made her way to the riverbank, finding solace in the soothing sound of the flowing water.

With diligence, Blythe began washing the breakfast dishes, the cool river water running over her hands as she meticulously cleaned each plate and utensil. Placing the cleaned items in the basket she had brought, she savored the tranquility of her surroundings, with the soft murmur of the flowing river creating a serene backdrop for her thoughts.

A couple passed by as she relaxed on the riverbank, lost in the calming ambiance. Blythe's instincts alerted her that they were not ordinary wanderers. Demetrius had previously informed her about the camp's meticulous border patrols and protective runes. Their constant vigilance reminded them of the looming threats they faced, intensifying Blythe's awareness of their precarious situation.

Lost in contemplation, Blythe was startled by Quentin's voice behind her. Her heart raced, and she quickly rose to her feet, momentarily forgetting her injured ankle. The pain was a sharp reminder, causing her to wince as she turned to face Quentin, who stood uphill from her. Dressed in jeans, a green shirt, hiking boots, and a brown fedora, he exuded a warmth that frustrated and comforted her. Uncertain of her emotions, she maintained a cautious distance with the river flowing behind her.

"Quentin," she uttered, her eyes reflecting a blend of uncertainty and relief, as if unsure how to navigate the complex emotions his arrival had stirred. He closed the gap between them, encroaching slightly on her personal space, eliciting a flutter in her stomach.

"You certainly rock the female lumberjack look," Quentin remarked with a hint of admiration. "If there were a calendar for women of the woods, you'd definitely be Miss February." He reached out to brush a stray strand of hair from her face, a gesture that stirred conflicting feelings within her.

"You're absurd," she retorted, swatting his hand away and turning her gaze aside, intending to disengage from the conversation. She stepped back, recognizing that maintaining some distance allowed her to think more clearly.

Quentin's brows furrowed slightly, a glimmer of hurt flashing as he responded, "It's not very kind to say that to the person who brought you your belongings." Blythe sensed a hint of disappointment in his demeanor as he held out her bag to her, his gesture a mix of resignation and lingering concern.

"Thank you." She slung the strap across her chest, acknowledging his assistance, and gestured towards the camp, signaling her intention to depart. "I would have appreciated a bit of a heads up on how that trial would go."

"Honestly, I couldn't foresee how everything would unfold," Quentin explained, matching her stride. Removing his hat, he observed her with his penetrating gaze, causing her to feel exposed and vulnerable. "Our laws don't dictate that the Council tell us the charges in advance. It's really an unfair advantage on their part."

"What if you had known?" Blythe asked, her eyebrows furrowing slightly and a glint of curiosity in her eyes.

"If it wouldn't have jeopardized your safety, I would have told you," he replied before she could interject. "Not because I doubt your abilities. On the contrary, that's precisely why I've brought what you'll need to learn how to wield your magic effectively. You should be able to protect yourself." A faint smile tugged at the corners of his lips. "The book you had is in the bag."

Blythe felt his words like a stab in her heart. "But Quentin, they took my amulet. I don't have my magic anymore. The Grimoire will be useless to me without it."

"Are you sure of that?" Quentin tilted his head slightly.

"Pretty sure," though the way he said that was making her doubt herself.

"I'm thinking you should probably ask your Uncle," he said with a smile. "I've heard rumors but wouldn't want to give you incorrect information."

"Thanks," she responded, appreciative of his consideration and suggestion. "Speaking of my Uncle, did you know he was alive?"

Quentin looked uncomfortable, "Yes, but for his safety and the safety of the mission, I couldn't tell you that." Blythe thought about it a moment and nodded, accepting his response.

His smile softened as he closed the distance between them

once again. "How are you holding up?" They started walking back to camp, and he offered to take the basket from her, though she declined the assistance.

She sighed, her shoulders slumping with a tinge of weariness as if carrying a burden that extended beyond her words and the basket she carried. "Honestly, I'm overwhelmed." She carefully set the basket near the breakfast area as they reached the camp. "Where's Miles? Demetrius mentioned he'd be here soon."

"He'll be here. We have a strategy meeting tonight. Miles always adds a spark to the discussions. His unwavering optimism is endearing. He believes in the possibility of effecting change from within... He thinks we can peacefully restore the council to its former glory."

"And you don't?" Blythe crossed her arms, uncertain how to navigate her conflicting thoughts and emotions.

"It's a pleasant notion, but we're all too aware of how the council and their ilk think and operate. There never was true glory. It was all subtly and not so subtly hidden racism. Also, they won't relinquish their power without a fight. Democracy is truly dead in this realm."

"So, you plan to confront them?"

"My role is to provide information about innocent people who require rescue and any other valuable insights I gather throughout the day." Quentin placed his hat back on his head, slipping his hands into his pockets. "And, moving forward, perhaps some battle if it comes to it."

"Blythe," Hera interjected, observing their conversation with a watchful gaze. "Supplies belong in that tent." She gestured towards a nearby tent. Blythe lifted the basket and made her way in that direction.

"So, you've assisted others like me?" Blythe inquired as they approached the tent.

"Never anyone quite like you," Quentin admitted, holding the tent flap open for her with a mischievous wink. She rolled her eyes in response. "Strictly speaking, you're the only one they've tasked me with assisting."

"What about the others you haven't helped?" Blythe's curiosity was piqued as she set the basket down and stepped out of the tent, Quentin trailing behind her.

"They keep things pretty 'need-to-know' around here," Quentin replied mysteriously.

"Does the council suspect you because you represented me?" Blythe's concern tinted her tone as she observed Quentin closely for any signs of trouble.

"They shouldn't. I was having drinks with a council member's son when you were freed," Quentin reassured her with a smile. "You know, we should go for a drink or dinner once this is over. Maybe try some Italian or Thai cuisine together. I've researched human world food, and it could be fun."

"Quentin..." Blythe shook her head, taken aback by his audacity.

"Hey, just asking you out. We'll have to celebrate when this is done," Quentin persisted, undeterred by her initial reaction.

Their conversation was interrupted by raised voices from Demetrius's tent, causing both Blythe and Quentin to turn their attention towards the commotion.

"No," Demetrius's voice carried across the clearing, followed by muffled arguing.

"Wouldn't it be interesting to be a fly on the side of that tent?" Quentin mused, standing beside Blythe as they both attempted to eavesdrop.

Blythe glanced at Quentin. "Sitting around and waiting isn't my style. Aside from the trial, I feel like that's all I've been doing." She shot him a sidelong glance. "What do you think they're planning? Any guesses?"

"I'm not one for guessing games, but I can think of other ways to pass the time than speculating," Quentin suggested, stepping in front of her and invading her personal space. She swallowed nervously, taking a step back.

"Quentin..." Blythe started, but he raised his hands, understanding her unspoken words.

"I should've known after that moment in the jail," Quentin admitted, stepping away.

"What do you mean by that?" Her brows furrowed as she tried to understand.

"It's okay, Blythe. You and Miles have history," Quentin replied, a smile on his lips. Yet, she sensed insincerity beneath, despite his attempt to hide it.

"That wasn't what you thought it was," she felt the need to clarify. "That's all in the past. I don't want to revisit it. I was scared I'd never see Miles or you again. I didn't expect..." Blythe trailed off, struggling to put her emotions into words.

"And you shouldn't, especially with matters of the heart. But don't worry, kitten. I'm okay," Quentin reassured her, his voice carrying a hint of hurt. Blythe's heart sank as she watched him go, regret washing over her. "I think it's time to check in with the boss." He adjusted his hat, tipped it toward her, and approached the tent, where the intense discussion continued. Unsure of her own feelings, Quentin's departure made her wonder if she should've been more honest. Should she have taken the chance to express her growing affection? Did she even have growing feelings for him? Maybe Demetrius was right. Romance would just create unnecessary complications.

Blythe half-started to follow Quentin, her steps faltering before she stopped. Conflicting emotions battled within her, and uncertainty gnawed at her resolve. The magnetic pull she felt toward him was undeniable. Yet, the lingering presence of Miles and their complex relationship couldn't be ignored. Caught in an emotional crossroads, she watched Quentin's retreating figure, her heart heavy with indecision.

CHAPTER TWENTY

Blythe's gaze remained fixed on the tent that had swallowed Quentin a moment ago. Questions buzzed in her mind, curiosity mingling with uncertainty. Emerging from the shadows, a figure caught her eye – a teenage boy striding purposefully, determination etched across his features, interwoven with a touch of something she couldn't recognize.

"Hey there," he called out. "You Blythe?"

Turning toward him, Blythe's interest piqued. "Yeah, that's me."

Coming to a stop a short distance away, he met her gaze head-on with a slightly unsettling intensity. "I owe you an apology," he began, his words tinged with remorse and candor. "For last night. Our human side takes a backseat when the full moon rises, and the instincts kick in."

Understanding flooded over Blythe as she caught up with what he was saying.

"You're one of the werewolves," she realized.

With a nod, he continued, "I'm Bertolf. Sorry for not introducing myself earlier."

Empathy welled up within her, "Thank you, Bertolf. I appreciate your apology, but I should apologize for my ignorance and for going out there during the full moon. I had no idea."

Bertolf shook his head, "Don't worry about it." He shuffled his feet and looked around momentarily before continuing, "Anyway... thanks, Blythe. And if you ever need assistance from me or the pack, don't hesitate to ask."

"I'll keep that in mind," she smiled.

"Thank you," he repeated, a boyish grin crossing his features. With a nod, he pivoted and retraced his steps toward the camp's edge, where his fellow werewolves waited. Blythe's gaze followed him, encompassing the huddled group, their collective gaze locked on Bertolf.

As he rejoined his packmates, he blended in effortlessly, receiving a pat from one member and ruffled hair from another. It made her think of how normal siblings must interact. Though, are there ever really any normal siblings? She for sure didn't know. Bertolf turned towards her and waved. She couldn't help but chuckle. For being so large, he was obviously still very young. She waved back.

Alone again in the quiet camp, Blythe confronted her lingering doubts about her magic, which had bothered her since her conversation with Quentin about her amulet. Ever since her amulet had been taken, she had felt a nagging emptiness. She desperately hoped Quentin was right.

With determination and a touch of anxiety, she headed into the nearby woods, careful not to attract any unwanted attention, especially from those within the tent. Blythe needed to try to use her magic first before running to her Uncle for help. Maybe Quentin was right - she tended to want to do everything herself. It may wind up being her Achilles heel.

She reached into her bag and pulled out the Grimoire of Ancients. Turning to the page with the "peeper" rune she had done before, she closed her right eye and traced its intricate lines onto a tree. She positioned the rune on the tree to face Demetrius's tent. Hope swelled within her, but it was accompanied by a nagging worry. Could her magic still work without her amulet as a conduit?

The forest was silent except for the soft leaves rustling and distant camp noises. Blythe closed her eyes, took a deep breath, and concentrated on the rune. She reached deep for her magic, seeking that flame, but there was nothing. She kept trying.

For a moment, nothing seemed to happen, and doubt crept in. But then, after what felt like an eternity, Blythe found the tiniest flicker of magic deep within her. It felt different, somehow. Almost primal. She focused harder on it, urging it to grow like blowing on an ember to start a fire. A subtle shimmer of magic filled the air, causing the rune to faintly glow. Blythe's eyes flew open, and a mix of amazement and relief washed over her. Her magic had responded, though it was weaker than before. It was like a small light in the darkness, giving her hope. She didn't stop to consider why and instead pressed on.

As her focus settled on the rune, an unexpected voice pierced the air, causing her to start and glance around, half-expecting Quentin to emerge. Yet, it became clear that the conversation within the tent was audible to her as if she were standing amidst them. She leaned forward, peering through as the window opened where the rune had once been. Curiosity gripped her, and she listened intently, every word reaching her ears. She watched the meeting as if watching Television. She could see Demetrius, Eyra, Griffin, Hera, Octo, and Quentin gathered inside.

"We should wait," Eyra's voice carried a sense of urgency, its tone reaching Blythe's ears even from the tent's exterior.

"We can't," Demetrius responded. His expression shifted, a blend of concern and determination crossing his features as he engaged with Eyra. "How much time do we have?"

"Not more than a few days," Eyra resembled a trapped animal as if she wanted to pace but couldn't. Her response held a grave undercurrent, churning Blythe's spine.

Demetrius's voice sliced through the air, bearing a note of triumph. "A few days is perfect," he smiled broadly. "That's probably the best news since we heard that Blythe had returned to the House."

They knew about her coming to the House? Had Miles told them? Quentin?

Quentin, seizing a chance to contribute, added, "On a different note, the Council intends to make a major announcement tomorrow regarding new regulations. Should I go?"

"Stay low, Quentin," Demetrius shook his head. "I think you should keep your distance from them for now."

Eyra stepped in, her voice offering a solution, "I'll attend.

It'd raise suspicions if I were absent during a pivotal declaration about new regulations. I need to be informed, considering my Valkyrie will implement them. I will leave tonight."

"Agreed—Octo, you too," Demetrius's directive held authority. Octo muffled his response, a disgruntled note apparent. "I would like both of you back as soon as possible to let us know what happened."

As the conversation pressed on, Blythe wrestled with her course of action. To reveal herself, demand answers, or continue lurking in the shadows for vital intelligence? This was probably the only way she would get any real answers. She wanted to know the good news, but it didn't seem like they were returning to that topic. Conflicting emotions tugged at her, the weight of her unspoken feelings for Quentin adding another layer of complexity. Was he being honest with her? This would be an excellent way to find out. She could ask him about the conversation later.

Amid her inner debate, Blythe's attention returned to another voice – Hera addressing Demetrius. Captivated, she strained to catch their dialogue.

"Demetrius, what's her role in our struggle?" Hera's blend of curiosity and concern resonated with Blythe.

His response held authority, a plan unfolding, "You'll be her battle mentor, Hera. I'll personally guide her in mastering her magic. We need her to take us to the human realm."

"Blythe was concerned about having lost her magic," Quentin said. "It might be a good idea to talk to her about that," Quentin speaking about her concerns struck something within her. She should be careful how much she shares her own thoughts for now. It might not help her to have everything she said shared with the entire rebel crew.

Another thought struck her like a lightning bolt. Battle training and harnessing her magic were essential to protect herself from the Council and whatever else she might face going forward. It also dawned on her that her involvement was presumed and taken for granted. She hadn't really agreed to anything. A swell of uncertainty coursed through her. The knowledge they offered might serve her beyond this moment, but how much did they expect her to help? Refocusing on the unfolding conversation, she delved deeper into their plans.

She had missed what Demetrius said but caught Quentin's response. "Why train her? What do you want her to do?" Quentin's brows creased.

Before Blythe could catch the answer, a rustle in the bushes behind her jolted her, causing her to pivot and stumble over a root. In a split second, Miles reached out, his arm wrapping around her waist to steady her. Recovering her balance, Blythe's emotions mingled, and she attempted to pull away, a swirl of conflicted feelings inside her.

"You scared me, Miles!" Blythe's whisper was a mixture of relief and frustration, her gaze fixed on him. Miles responded with a soft chuckle, his hold remaining steady.

"Sorry, love. I didn't mean to startle you," he had a warmth in his eyes as he released her. "Impressive trick there," nodding towards the fading rune on the tree. "Nice to see your magic isn't gone and is being put to more than just light tricks."

"Why didn't you tell me about this?" Blythe inquired, her eyes locked onto Miles, seeking transparency in this world shrouded in secrecy.

"I wanted to, really," Miles confessed, his gaze cautious. "I would have told you at the House if we had real privacy. You're not the only one who knows these tricks. Ben could have been listening to our conversations. And just to clarify, I didn't make sure you went to the House the other day. If it were up to me, you would have been far away from all of this."

"You said you and the House did..." Blythe's words trailed off as the truth settled in, her brow furrowing. How much more had they kept from her? "Miles, tell me the truth."

Miles sighed, "It was Demetrius's idea, not the House or I and honestly, Quentin didn't agree either. I had to make something up because I couldn't tell you that he was alive without giving away information that would be dangerous in the wrong hands. I didn't know why he wanted you to come, but considering your summons and the Council closing in, I agreed to keep you close and ensure you were safe." Miles looked down briefly before looking back up at her, "Demetrius keeps his plans closely guarded. He only told me because I was supposed to be there and ensure you stayed... We didn't anticipate the House taking over that role," Miles clarified, his voice carrying a mix of frustration and regret.

"Miles, how can I trust you?" Blythe's voice dropped to a bitter whisper, her doubts tainting the air between them. "You could have found a way to tell me. I'm tired of all this," her gesture encompassed their surroundings and situation. "It's too much."

"What do you want from me, Blythe?" Miles's voice held a note of desperation, his gaze locked onto hers. "Do you think any of this is easy for me? I didn't want to be some kind of spy for an anti-government group." He shook his head, his inner turmoil evident. "All I ever wanted was a job in Magical Intelligence in the human world, ensuring the secrecy of this world... and maybe, in the process, winning you back."

Blythe's emotions swirled, uncertainty and weariness vying for dominance. Had he gotten a job in MI, would she have returned with him? But no, he couldn't have worked in MI and had a relationship with her. They never would have allowed it. They both would have faced her sentence.

Miles grinned, bridging the gap between them, his expression earnest. "I would follow you anywhere," he declared. Blythe rolled her eyes, a faint smile touching her lips. Miles's unwavering devotion remained endearing even amid the chaos. He clasped her hands in his, seeking reassurance. "I promise you, I'll do whatever it takes to ensure you can live the life you want, free from hiding from the council."

"Miles! Fancy seeing you in the deep, dark woods at this hour," Quentin's voice broke in from behind Blythe, disrupting the vulnerable moment. She withdrew her hands from Miles's grip, pivoting to face Quentin, Hera, and Griffin, who had emerged between them and Demetrius's tent. She felt like that teenager back in the House, caught by Ben kissing Miles in the attic. Griffin offered Miles a thumbs-up, his grin mischievous. Hera's arched eyebrow lingered on Blythe, a mix of curiosity and something else in her expression.

"Time for us to receive our marching orders already?" Miles casually positioned himself beside Blythe with his arm draping over her shoulders. A silent standoff brewed between Miles and Quentin, an unspoken rivalry crackling beneath their smiles. Quentin's grin persisted, yet his gaze locked onto Miles. Blythe felt suddenly sick to her stomach. It was an unusual spectacle, an unexpected glimpse of Miles's competitive side that diverged from his usual charm.

"Aye, indeed. But Demetrius would be wantin' your latest update first," Griffin smoothly interjected, seemingly oblivious to the brewing tension. The scene felt akin to an old Western standoff, lacking only the dramatic score and poised pistols.

"Save the romantic rivalry for later, you two," Hera interjected, stepping forward and freeing Blythe from Miles' grasp. "We'll catch up with you shortly."

Blythe's cheeks burned with embarrassment as she was pulled away from Miles. Glancing back, she couldn't discern Quentin's expression, but Miles seemed visibly irked. Swiftly grabbing her bag, Blythe followed Hera to an unoccupied log.

"So... matters of the heart, huh?" Hera's voice held a touch of amusement as they entered the bustling camp's central clearing. Blythe's attention briefly wandered to a group of centaurs engaged in lively conversation, their unique attire and weaponry piquing her interest. She quickly averted her gaze, following Hera to an unoccupied log.

"Something like that," Blythe replied softly.

Hera leaned in a bit, her tone casual. "You know, it might be easier for everyone if you made a choice."

Blythe turned to Hera, genuinely surprised by the comment. "What do you mean?"

Hera twirled a stick she had picked up, her thoughts

clearly on the matter. "Well, between Miles and Quentin, it might be time to pick one. Stringing them both along doesn't seem fair to anyone involved. I mean, pursuing a relationship right now with everything that's going on seems a bit... complicated, don't you think?"

Blythe felt discomfort at Hera's words as if she were being judged unfairly. She struggled to keep her composure and responded firmly, "Why is my love life any of your concern? I'm not pursuing anyone and don't owe explanations to anyone, including you."

Hera's frustration was evident, and she pushed on, her voice tinged with concern. "Because they're my friends, and I care about them. If you're not interested in Miles, it might be time to let him move on."

Blythe's gaze locked onto Hera's, her tone challenging. "Are you in love with Miles, Hera?"

Hera hesitated momentarily, her cheeks reddening slightly before she looked away. "That's not the point. I just want what's best for everyone."

Blythe relented, realizing she might have struck a nerve. "Look, Hera, if you have feelings for Miles, you should pursue them. I'm not competing for his affections. He's a great person, and if you're interested, you should go for it."

Hera's retort was sharp, her frustration apparent as she stood up abruptly. "Your approval isn't necessary, Blythe. You have no say in their lives or mine. Stay out of it. If you don't want them, then let them be." With that, Hera walked away, leaving Blythe bewildered and slightly hurt.

Blythe sighed heavily, masking her confusion by focusing on the campfire before her. It was a welcome distraction from the prying eyes of those around her, and she silently contemplated the tangled web of emotions that seemed to be unfolding.

CHAPTER TWENTY-ONE

Later that evening, Blythe sat alone in her tent, engrossed in the Grimoire of Ancients. Her thoughts raced, torn between her role in the rebellion and her changing emotions. A soft throat clearing broke her concentration, and she looked up to find Hera standing at the entrance.

"May I join you?" Hera's voice carried a touch of vulnerability.

Blythe nodded, closed the ancient book, and gestured for Hera to enter. Hera moved cautiously as if unsure of her footing.

Hera broke the silence with sincerity. "Blythe, I owe you an apology. My emotions got the better of me, and I spoke out of turn, meddling in your relationships with Miles and Quentin. It was wrong."

Blythe considered Hera's words, sensing the tumultuous emotions behind them. She appreciated Hera taking responsibility and respected her open honesty.

"I accept your apology," Blythe replied gently. "We're all navigating our feelings and this situation. It can make us short-tempered. In fact, you were right. I must choose; if I choose neither, I must tell them. If I want others to be open and honest with me, it's about time to start being open and honest."

Hera nodded in agreement. "You're right, Blythe. It's challenging to open up. But life's too short, and I've learned that the hard way. You never know when you might lose the chance to say what's in your heart." She hesitated, then confessed, "You're right about something else. I do have feelings for Miles. I've been struggling to find the right words to tell him."

With tensions eased Blythe considered her next steps. "I know. I need to have those conversations. But it's also crucial to choose the right moment."

"No rush," Hera replied. "Timing isn't everything. Just

speak your truth when you can."

Blythe nodded. "And I think you should know if I were to pursue a romantic relationship with one of them, it wouldn't be Miles. We have too much history. Do you get what I mean?"

Hera looked puzzled, but before Blythe could clarify, their discussion was interrupted by Miles and Quentin's arrival.

"Anyone up for a card game?" Miles beamed, shifting the mood with his enthusiasm. Blythe and Hera exchanged glances before agreeing. After some discussion, Miles and Hera left to fetch drinks and snacks, leaving Blythe and Quentin alone. The lantern's warm glow created a comfortable atmosphere as they engaged in easy silences and light-hearted banter. Beneath the camaraderie, a significant truth weighed on Blythe, urging her to open up to Quentin.

She took a deep breath, her gaze fixed on the lantern's flicker. Her voice trembled with vulnerability but remained resolute. "Quentin, there's something I've been pondering. It involves me, you, and Miles."

After another deep breath, she continued, "After much reflection, I've reached a point where I need to say it aloud. My feelings for Miles... they've changed. I'm no longer in love with him, and pretending doesn't feel right. We have history, and it's just that... history."

Quentin nodded empathy and understanding in his eyes. "That's a brave admission, Blythe. I can only imagine the journey it took to get here."

Blythe nodded, her introspective gaze revealing her inner turmoil. "It's been quite a journey. Miles has been a wonderful friend, and that won't change. But I feel a different pull now."

Sensing the moment's gravity and his opportunity, Quentin moved closer, offering unspoken support. He leaned in, his voice soft. "There's something about this moment, this tent, the lantern, the atmosphere, and you. You're captivating, Blythe."

A blush crept onto Blythe's cheeks, her eyes darting away before meeting Quentin's again. "You're quite the smooth talker,

Quentin. Your way with words is something else."

Quentin's laughter filled the air, his eyes gleaming with charm. "I'm not just playing around, Blythe. There's no time to beat around the bush. You bring light even to the darkest times; being around you is like a reprieve from reality."

Blythe's smile grew, intrigue and happiness dancing in her eyes. "You've got some serious poetic skills, Quentin. But I need to know, is this genuine or just words?"

Quentin's smile softened, his unwavering gaze revealing his sincerity. "It's real, Blythe. Every word. You're magnetic in ways I can't explain. I'm drawn to you more than I thought possible."

Before Blythe could respond, the tent flap lifted, and Miles and Hera returned. Their conversation shifted, and Blythe's confession faded into the background. She tried to read Hera and Miles's faces, but she couldn't tell if they'd talked about anything relating to feelings while they were gone.

"Ready to play?" Miles asked, gathering the cards with a flourish.

As the night wore on, they immersed themselves in the game, laughter, and connection mingling with the opened bottles of wine. Eventually, weariness overtook Blythe, and her eyes fluttered shut as she surrendered to sleep. Later, she stirred to voices outside the tent, and Miles and Quentin exchanged hushed words. She looked around but didn't see Hera. She must have left.

Quentin's voice carried vulnerability and honesty. "Miles, there's something I need to discuss. My feelings for Blythe have reached a point I can't ignore. It's undeniable."

Miles responded with acceptance and longing, his words cutting through the night. "I understand, Quentin. I've been wrestling with my own emotions for her. She means a lot to me as well."

Blythe's heart tugged at the raw honesty, her drowsy mind straining to catch every bit of their conversation, eager to comprehend the intricate web of emotions that bound them all.

Quentin's voice held a sincere weight. "I want you to know, I'd never want to hurt you. Our friendship means everything. If something happened between Blythe and me, I would talk to you first."

Miles, his guard down, met Quentin's sincerity. "I get it. Part of me still feels the same way. Just being around her resurrects those old feelings. I don't want to stand in the way of her happiness, but it's not easy. And then there's Hera. We've talked about my feelings for Hera, but now that Blythe's back, I'm unsure..."

Their voices started to grow fainter, as if they were walking away. Blythe heard Quentin say, "You should probably make a decision and talk to them. Maybe talk to Blythe first?"

"Why?" Miles asked, but then she didn't hear anything else.

Inside her tent, Blythe's heart grappled with a whirlwind of emotions. Their candid conversation painted a complex picture, a web of connections stretched across time and feelings. Amidst the quiet of the night, she sat there, her mind whirling with thoughts.

With the lantern casting a soft, soothing glow, Blythe knew she couldn't avoid confronting her feelings any longer. The path before her was uncertain, but it was time to face her emotions head-on and engage in those crucial conversations with the two men who held significant places in her heart.

CHAPTER TWENTY-TWO

The following day, chatter and clinking utensils cut through Blythe's consciousness like a sharp blade. She groaned and pulled the blanket tighter over her head, feeling utterly miserable. Her head pounded, her mouth felt as dry as sandpaper, and the mere thought of leaving her bed seemed impossible. Staying wrapped in the blankets, avoiding the world felt far more appealing than struggling through her training. She squeezed her eyes shut, hoping that sleep could provide some respite from the agony enveloping her.

"Time to shake off the dreams. Dawn's call awaits!" Blythe reluctantly peeked out from under the covers to find Aenwyn standing inside the tent, exuding a nauseating morning energy. Bright and cheerful, as usual. Infuriatingly so.

"Ugh..." Blythe mumbled, tugging the blanket back over her head and rolling onto her side as if the sheer force of her irritation could make Aenwyn disappear. Maybe she was a mirage. If Blythe ignored her long enough, she might vanish into thin air.

"Ah, so you're not faring much better than the guys, I see." Blythe sensed the cot shift as Aenwyn settled at the edge. "Lucky for you, I've got just the thing for that Veisalgia."

"Vaysal-what?" Blythe's brain was in no mood for unfamiliar terms. "Could you maybe... I'm trying to suffer in dignified silence here," Blythe grumbled, cupping her hand over her exposed ear. Aenwyn's voice was an assault on her delicate senses at this hour.

Aenwyn chuckled, apparently finding Blythe's suffering rather amusing. "Hangover, my dear. You're not on the brink of death. But listen up; you can't spend your day wallowing in bed. You need some training to be useful in the Dark World."

Blythe's attempt to shield herself with her covers

was swiftly thwarted as Aenwyn yanked them away. Blythe retaliated by grabbing her pillow and plucking it on her head. "You remind me of my sister back in the day. She'd avoid the harvest like a plague and stay in bed until the very last moment. Now, behold." Aenwyn snatched the pillow away, prompting Blythe to shoot her an irritated scowl while squinting against the blinding tent light. In Aenwyn's hand was a steaming mug of something that emitted a rather uninviting aroma. Blythe instinctively covered her nose, sitting up a tad too quickly. Thankfully, Aenwyn had the foresight to place an empty bucket nearby, which Blythe made grateful use of, expelling the meager contents of her stomach.

"Drink up," Aenwyn commanded once Blythe was done, and she presented the mug.

Blythe, with her eyes half-closed to shield herself from the sun's assault, accepted the mug from Aenwyn's outstretched hand. She tentatively sipped the hot concoction, feeling the warmth flow down her throat and spread through her belly. It was as if the liquid chased away the headache and the nausea in a sweeping tide. When she opened her eyes, the world was no longer a dagger to her brain. She savored the rest of the oddly-smelling potion, sipping it at her own pace until the mug was emptied.

"Feeling better?" Aenwyn inquired, her concern genuine.

"Yes, what was that stuff?" Blythe's clarity of mind was astounding. It was like the impending catastrophe in her head had been repelled. Also, her ankle's insistent ache seemed to have quieted down compared to the previous day.

"It's a tea brewed from Hygeia root." Aenwyn took the now-empty mug and the bucket that had swiftly turned unappetizing. "I'm glad it did the trick." She started heading toward the tent's exit. "And maybe next time, try not to go overboard. Remember to have some water between drinks, and never do it on an empty stomach. See you around!" With that, she whisked herself out of the tent before Blythe could even offer to clean the bucket. Aenwyn had already vanished into the ether with her bucket of salvation.

Blythe swung her legs off the cot, wincing as she gingerly went to the wash basin to freshen up. Her ankle still throbbed, but it was an improvement over yesterday. After splashing water on her face, she dressed and emerged from her tent into the inviting embrace of the late-morning sunshine.

"The fairy found you too, huh?" Miles strolled over, an impish grin plastered on his face. "You'll be pleased to hear that somehow Hera is immune to hangovers. Lucky her, huh?" He grinned.

Blythe raised an eyebrow. "What's with that look?"

"Look? What look?" Miles didn't respect personal space, taking an extra step closer, pushing beyond the confines of mere camaraderie.

"Miles, back off." She pressed her hand against his chest, signaling him to halt his advance.

"I had a feeling you couldn't resist another touch." He leaned in, his face dangerously close to hers.

"Whoa, whoa, whoa! Another touch? What are you on about?" Blythe scoured her memory, attempting to piece together the previous night's events. Exercising sound judgment under the influence was never her strong suit. A flood of memories from countless occasions when she and Miles had indulged in stolen alcohol from the House raced through her mind.

Miles covered her hand with his own, subtly directing it as he leaned closer. "Perhaps I should give you a reenactment to jog your memory?"

Swiftly, Blythe turned her head, avoiding his attempted kiss, and pulled away.

"Seems a bit premature for that, doesn't it?" Hera's voice chimed from behind Blythe, causing her to start. Miles chuckled, enveloping Blythe at his side, his arm draped casually over her shoulder.

"It's never too early for a little affection, Hera." Blythe caught a fleeting expression on Hera's face— a blend of emotions that defied straightforward interpretation. It vanished as quickly as it emerged. Hera was clearly still holding a grudge.

"Sure thing, Miles." Hera pivoted and retraced her steps. Blythe wriggled free from Miles' grip.

"Miles cut it out. Whatever happened last night, it was probably just drunken nonsense. Don't make a big deal out of it." She said as she rushed out of the tent, intending to apologize to Hera.

"You didn't do anything." Quentin approached from the direction of the campfire and the growing crowd.

"What?" Blythe looked at him, baffled. Hera hadn't gone far and appeared to be busying herself with some logs, but Blythe suspected she was listening in.

"We played cards, then hit the sack in our respective spots. You were asleep before Miles and I left to sleep in our tent. I heard Miles snoring before I passed out." He grinned. "Nice try, Miles." Quentin battled to suppress his amusement as he recounted the tale.

Fuming, Blythe spun around and playfully punched Miles in the arm. "Ass!" She pivoted and headed toward the group huddled around the campfire, leaving Miles and Quentin dissolved in laughter behind her. Hera followed her and exchanged a look that Blythe couldn't quite decipher. Settling together on a log, Blythe contemplated that maybe there was a lesson somewhere about knowing her limits regarding drinking – especially within this crowd.

"You alright?" Blythe inquired, accepting a plate of food from Hera.

"I'm fine. Why?" Hera averted her gaze, her attempt to appear fine, not entirely convincing.

"Really?"

"Yes, really! Maybe you should focus more on figuring out how we'll get through the entrance to the Dark World in the human realm and less on your romantic escapades and my emotional state." She abruptly rose and stormed away before Blythe could formulate a response. Evidently, the grievances from yesterday had yet to fade, and absolution was far from the horizon. In her place, Quentin settled down.

"She's green with envy," he stated straightforwardly, digging into his meal.

"What?" Blythe picked up a piece of bacon and took a bite.

"She's got a thing for Miles... a strong thing." He speared a sausage and popped it into his mouth. "She probably thinks you and he are reigniting some long-lost romance. Miles's display back there wasn't exactly kind, as I've told him that Hera is interested in him."

"Did she miss the part where I pushed him away?" Blythe scowled, her gaze following Hera's path. "I made it clear I'm not interested, and if she is, she should go after him herself instead of projecting onto me."

"It doesn't matter. You two have history, and Hera knows it. She doesn't take kindly to competition... or being told what to do." Quentin's gaze remained fixed on Miles, who was engaged in animated conversation with Griffin and Octo. Gales of laughter erupted from their circle. Blythe tore her attention from them and focused on Quentin.

"Well, I have no intention of lingering around, so she won't have to stress over that." Blythe redirected her focus to her food that had sat forgotten, deliberately tuning out the hubbub of conversations enveloping her. Quentin respected her need for solitude and contemplation and let her be.

CHAPTER TWENTY-THREE

The sun hung resplendent in the sky as Blythe went about her daily routine at the rebel encampment. She had morning training, mid-day washing duties, and afternoon magic lessons. Her diligent cleaning was familiar, but today, something felt different. As she scrubbed a particularly stubborn stained piece of clothing near the edge of the river, her eyes caught sight of something in the underbrush by the edge of the forest.

Startled, Blythe put down her work and moved towards the foliage. She paused, peering closer at the patch of ivy that seemed oddly out of place. Curious, she knelt and began to clear away the overgrowth. Gradually, the outlines of an ornate wooden door emerged, covered in carvings and runes, unlike anything she'd seen before.

Heart pounding with a mix of trepidation and excitement, Blythe pushed against the door. To her amazement, it creaked open, revealing a dimly lit chamber beyond. She stepped inside, her eyes widening as she took in the sight before her.

The chamber was like a treasure trove of magical knowledge. Shelves lined the walls, filled with ancient scrolls, dusty tomes, and intricate artifacts. A low, constant hum emanated from the walls, a pulsing heartbeat of hidden magic. It held a similar feeling to the House.

Blythe's fingers trembled as she reached to touch one of the scrolls. Enchanting illustrations and writings in a script she couldn't decipher filled the pages. She realized she had stumbled upon a repository of arcane wisdom unlike anything she'd ever imagined.

She discovered a pedestal in the chamber's center as she explored further. Upon it sat a crystal orb radiating a soft, ethereal glow. Its surface depicted a swirling, ever-changing pattern as if it held the essence of the cosmos.

Intrigued, Blythe reached out to touch the crystal, and as her fingers made contact, a surge of energy coursed through her. Visions of ancient mages and legendary battles flashed before her eyes. She saw the Magic Houses as a beacon of hope and knowledge in all its glory.

As that sight subsided, Blythe became aware of her surroundings in another vision. She found herself standing in a vast, dimly lit chamber. She recognized it as the chamber where she had been for her trial. In the raised seats around the room were representatives from all races: wizards, elves, dwarves, tree people, fae, merpeople, Warlocks, Centaurs, and more. She somehow recognized that this was the Original Council, a gathering of beings from diverse backgrounds united by their mastery of magic.

Blythe marveled at the sight, feeling a profound sense of history and significance. The council members conversed in hushed tones, their voices carrying the weight of countless decisions that had shaped the course of magic and the world.

However, her fascination was short-lived as she noticed a dark figure looming behind the Council. It was a shadowy presence, its form indistinct but undeniably evil. Except for the wizards, the council members remained unaware of the portentous figure's presence.

Then, something inexplicable happened. Each race that was not a wizard slowly dissolved into the darkness. The elves, the dwarves, and the centaurs faded away along with the other races, leaving only the wizards behind. Panic and confusion rippled through the remaining council members as they realized what was happening, but it was too late.

The scene became impenetrable darkness, swallowing everything, including Blythe. She felt herself drawn into the abyss, her surroundings fading away until there was nothing but darkness.

At that moment, Blythe had a chilling realization. The past held secrets and dangers beyond her imagination, and she had stumbled upon a part of history that may hold the key to taking down the Council.

Gasping, Blythe withdrew her hand from the crystal, her heart pounding. She realized this chamber must connect to the Houses and the Council. These artifacts held the key to unlocking their potential. The Houses may be safe havens while they take on the Council.

She turned to leave, intending to share what she'd seen, but her gaze shifted to a nearby table, where two specific artifacts caught her attention. One was a pendant, intricately carved with symbols and runes. It resonated with a subtle power. The other was a small, unassuming vial filled with a shimmering liquid. She decided to take those for later.

A whisper of doubt crept in as she contemplated the significance of her discovery. She couldn't shake the feeling that someone had deliberately hidden this chamber and wondered why. Could there be a reason Demetrius and the others hadn't revealed its existence? Did they not know about it?

Blythe knew she couldn't keep this revelation to herself. With newfound determination, she left the hidden chamber. She headed back to the heart of the encampment, intent on sharing her discovery with her companions.

CHAPTER TWENTY-FOUR

Blythe couldn't contain her excitement as she returned to the heart of the rebel encampment in the dense woods. Her footsteps had an extra bounce, and her eyes shone with newfound purpose. She had just made an incredible discovery that could change the course of their mission.

Her comrades were engaged in various activities as she approached the gathering area—some sharpened their weapons. In contrast, others strategized for the upcoming mission. Griffin's laughter echoed as he entertained a group with his jokes, momentarily breaking the tension in the air.

Blythe cleared her throat to capture their attention. Heads turned, and the rebel fighters fell silent, their curious gazes fixed upon her. Octo, continuously vigilant, was the first to speak.

"What has you all fired up, Blythe?" he asked, his eyebrows raised inquisitively.

Blythe took a deep breath, her voice filled with excitement. "I've made a discovery that might give us a significant advantage in our mission."

Quentin stepped forward, his eyes filled with curiosity and hope. "What is it, Blythe?"

With a smile, she explained, "I stumbled upon a hidden chamber deep within the trees in the woods. I found ancient scrolls and artifacts inside, but that's not all. Did you all know about this?"

Octo, Hera, Quentin, Griffin, and Demetrius exchanged puzzled glances. The revelation caught them off guard.

Demetrius, ever the inquisitive leader, was the first to respond. "A hidden chamber, you say? No, we did not know such a place. Hera, would you mind going to check it out?"

Hera nodded, accepting the task with her usual determination. "Of course, I'll investigate this hidden chamber."

Blythe gave Hera the directions, and she swiftly went to look. Blythe felt a mix of anticipation and curiosity regarding what Hera might discover in the hidden chamber.

The atmosphere was charged with anticipation as they waited in the rebel camp clearing. Blythe hesitated momentarily, then reached into her pouch and retrieved the pendant and vial. She handed them to Demetrius, who examined them with keen interest, his eyes gleaming excitedly.

"These are remarkable," he said, his voice tinged with excitement as he inspected the Lumina Amulet and Astra Elixir. "The pendant is known as the 'Lumina Amulet.' It's an ancient artifact that can harness and amplify light magic. When we reach the portal in the human world leading to the dark realm, this amulet can temporarily stun our opponents with a blinding flash of light. It might give us the upper hand when we need it most."

Blythe listened intently, realizing the potential of the Lumina Amulet in their upcoming mission. She had inadvertently stumbled upon a treasure trove of magical aids that could make a crucial difference in their fight against the Council.

Demetrius then turned his attention to the vial. "And this," he said, holding it up, "is the 'Astra Elixir.' It's a potion of rare quality. It can temporarily enhance one's magical abilities when consumed, granting increased power and control over their spells."

Blythe nodded, understanding the significance of such a potion in their battle against the Council. The thought of her comrades using the Astra Elixir to bolster their magic filled her with hope.

Demetrius returned the artifacts to Blythe; his gaze filled with determination. "These discoveries are invaluable and have come at a crucial time. We will need every advantage we can get in our mission to breach the portal and confront the Council."

Blythe couldn't help but feel a renewed sense of purpose as she held the Lumina Amulet and Astra Elixir. They were tangible symbols of her contribution to the rebellion's cause, and she was determined to see their mission through to the end.

"That's why I wanted to share it with all of you," she said, her voice unwavering. "We have something extraordinary on our side, and together, we can use it to bring down the Council and restore magic to its rightful place."

Hera returned to the rebel camp clearing, her brow furrowed with disappointment. "I checked the area thoroughly, Blythe, but there's nothing there. It seems your discovery might have been a fluke."

Blythe, undeterred, stood up, determination etched on her face. "I'm certain there's something there. Come with me, both of you."

Hera and Demetrius exchanged glances before following Blythe as she led them to the edge of the clearing, where the dense forest began. They made their way to the riverbank, and Blythe carefully retraced her steps, eventually stopping where she had found the hidden chamber earlier.

Blythe crouched down and began to brush away the undergrowth and ivy that covered the area. As she did, she felt a faint magical presence in the air.

She uncovered the entrance to the hidden chamber—a door made of intricately carved wood, nestled among the roots of a massive tree.

Hera and Demetrius stared in astonishment as Blythe unveiled the door. It was as if ancient magic had concealed the entrance, only to reveal itself to Blythe's touch.

Blythe turned to them with a triumphant smile. "See?"

Demetrius turned to Hera, who shook her head. "No, it wasn't here when I looked. I moved that very ivy."

"Let's test this," Demetrius led them back to the camp and said he would return to the door. Hera and Blythe exchanged looks as they waited. When Demetrius returned, he stated he confirmed his suspicions.

Demetrius nodded, his eyes filled with wonder. "It would appear that the door only reveals itself to you. Whether this is because of your mixed heritage or your status as Keeper of the House of Fas, I don't know. We will have to do some digging to figure that out."

They returned to where Octo, Griffin, and Quentin had sat, waiting.

"Well?" Octo asked, a hint of impatience in his voice.

Demetrius explained their discoveries and continued, "I will research and see what I can find. But until we figure it out, Blythe, please allow me to accompany you inside. There may be valuable information in there that could help us all. "

Griffin, always the jester, said, "Well, ain't ye the chosen one, Blythe?"

Quentin furrowed his brow. "But why would only Blythe be able to find it?"

Blythe shrugged, and Demetrius shook his head before saying, "We don't know. What we do know is that this changes everything. Blythe, you've given us hope and a valuable advantage. We must use this knowledge wisely."

CHAPTER TWENTY-FIVE

Blythe's next two days involved training and preparations - physical in the morning, magical in the afternoon. She wasn't sure which she preferred—getting beaten up by Hera or almost blowing herself up with her magic. But at that moment, she tried not to think about that and focused on what she was doing.

Blythe and Hera stood in the training yard, holding practice swords. Beads of sweat rolled down Blythe's forehead as she eagerly awaited Hera's instructions, mixed with a touch of anxiety. Hera, an experienced warrior, stepped forward, her eyes showing determination and understanding.

"Okay, Blythe, let's move on from the basics," Hera's voice was firm yet encouraging. "Remember, it's all about your footwork and timing. Keep your stance steady, legs apart, and pay attention to your opponent's movements."

Blythe nodded, gathering her determination. She tried to copy Hera's stance, but her legs hesitated and resisted. She shifted her weight, seeking balance while Hera circled her, carefully watching her every move.

"Relax, Blythe. Tension will only slow you down," Hera advised, her tone calming. "Remember to loosen your grip on the sword. Think of it as an extension of your arm, not a burden."

Following Hera's advice, Blythe eased her grip slightly and took a deep breath to calm her racing heart. However, as Hera began her demonstration, Blythe struggled to understand the intricate steps and sequences.

Hera's sword moved gracefully through the air, every movement precise and forceful. Blythe watched in awe, her admiration for Hera's skill deepening.

"Now, it's your turn," Hera said, offering Blythe a patient smile.

Taking a moment, Blythe lifted her sword and tried miming Hera's motion. Her swings were awkward and lacked the finesse of Hera's demonstration. Doubt clouded her mind, making her arms feel heavy.

Hera's gaze softened, showing understanding. "Blythe, remember that mastering this takes time. Immediate perfection isn't the goal; it's about persistence and growth."

Blythe nodded, putting aside her frustration. She refocused on Hera, hoping her determination would help her improve.

Stepping closer, Hera adjusted Blythe's grip on the sword. "Watch me closely," she directed, her voice commanding yet gentle. "Pay attention to the rhythm of combat, the back-and-forth. Anticipate your opponent's moves and look for opportunities to strike."

Blythe absorbed Hera's guidance, studying every detail with unwavering focus. She internalized the lessons to enhance her skills.

As Blythe tentatively resumed her practice, her movements and footwork became more graceful and deliberate. She stumbled at times but quickly regained her balance, refusing to give in to frustration.

Hera's guidance remained unwavering, her patient corrections and encouraging words fueling Blythe's determination. Frustration and challenges arose, but Blythe persevered, determined to prove herself. She understood that setbacks and triumphs marked real progress and was ready to face the journey ahead.

Amid their training, the sun reached its peak, burning brightly in the sky. Blythe's muscles ached, but her determination remained strong. She realized that mastering this skill would require time and effort, which only fueled her resolve. Each stumble and correction brought her closer to becoming the warrior she aspired to be. She was even more grateful when Hera released her from her training for the day.

Amidst the lively atmosphere of the rebel camp, Blythe

had made it to one of her favorite parts of the day - lunch with Hera and Griffin and sometimes Quentin and Miles if they were around. Today, it was just Hera and Griffin. Hera was great to talk to about her more profound thoughts and feelings, while Griffin added levity and fun to the camp's serious nature.

Griffin's bushy beard twitched with every bite, and he couldn't contain his enthusiasm. "By the stars," he exclaimed between mouthfuls, "this stew is a masterpiece! Hera, you've outdone yourself!"

Hera, her expression more stoic but eyes warm, nodded in acknowledgment. "Just doing my part, Griffin. We need our strength for the challenges ahead."

Blythe smiled, feeling a sense of camaraderie with these two remarkable individuals. Griffin's laughter was infectious, and Hera's unwavering dedication to their cause was a source of inspiration. Despite their differences, they were a tight-knit trio, each contributing their unique strengths to the rebel group.

As they savored their meal, their conversation shifted from light-hearted banter to the pressing matters of their shared mission and the looming threat they confronted. The weight of their responsibilities hung in the air, but during such meals, their camaraderie strengthened, and their determination solidified.

Blythe couldn't help but appreciate the unwavering support and companionship of Griffin and Hera. They were her steadfast allies, her cherished friends, and together, they would confront any challenges that dared to cross their path.

Just as she was about to speak, Demetrius, glinting with purpose, approached their table. "Blythe," he said, his voice carrying an air of urgency, "it's time to resume your magic training. Please take me to the hidden chamber."

Blythe nodded, realizing that duty called once more, and with Griffin and Hera by her side, she rose from the table, ready to embark on the next phase of her magical journey. As they walked, Demetrius explained that this would be their last training session before they left camp. The day before, there had been a disaster, leaving the chamber a chaotic mess and nearly injuring Demetrius and herself.

CHAPTER TWENTY-SIX

Her magic lessons with Demetrius were unlike any other. The room, with its walls adorned in shimmering runes and ancient symbols, seemed to resonate with the secrets of a bygone era, and like the House of Fas, this chamber seemed to be able to heal itself. Torches flickered, casting dancing shadows that added an air of mystique to the atmosphere.

Demetrius stood across from Blythe. His eyes, pools of wisdom and curiosity, were fixed upon her. "Now, Blythe," he began, his voice a low, melodious rumble, "we must delve deeper into your magic. There's power in there, but you must harness it lest you harm everyone around you. Your unique lineage makes you exceptional. The tomes I borrowed yesterday gave me some ideas."

Blythe nodded, her anticipation mingling with uncertainty. With the amulet that once bound her powers now lost, her magic had begun to feel unruly and untamed, surging within her like a tempestuous river.

Demetrius continued, "Your mixed blood and the absence of your amulet have revealed a truth, my dear. You might possess a kind of magic stronger than anyone else's. It's the magic of pure potential, of unbridled possibilities." He smiled, "and quite frankly, probably why the Council wants you gone so badly. They must have known. It leads me to wonder if, possibly, Wizardkind themselves could benefit from removing their amulets. Since the Council took mine, I have been trying to tap into my magic with no success. I suspect your mixed heritage gives you an advantage."

As he spoke, Blythe could feel the currents of her magic swirling within her, responding to the resonance of the hidden chamber. It was as though the very room recognized her latent power and whispered secrets only she could understand.

"Let's begin," Demetrius said with a reassuring smile. He extended his hand, and tendrils of energy danced from his fingertips. "Feel your magic, Blythe. Embrace it as an extension of yourself. Let it flow."

Blythe took a deep breath, closing her eyes to center herself. She reached out with her senses, allowing her magic to rise from within. It was different now, wild and untamed like a fierce river threatening to break free of its banks.

As her magic surged, the runes on the chamber walls seemed to shimmer in response, amplifying the energy in the room. Blythe opened her eyes, and they gleamed with an inner light as she began to manipulate the magic around her.

Demetrius watched in awe as she wove intricate energy patterns in the air. It was as though she were conducting a symphony of magic, each note resonating with her unique power.

"Remarkable," Demetrius whispered, his admiration evident. "Your magic, Blythe, is unlike anything I've ever seen. With training and control, you could become a force of reckoning."

A sense of empowerment washed over Blythe as she realized the potential within her. The limitations of her amulet no longer bound her, and her mixed heritage had bestowed upon her a gift of immeasurable strength. For the first time, she no longer hated what she was.

With Demetrius as her guide, Blythe was ready to embark on a journey of discovery, to harness her magic, and to unlock the true extent of her power. Together, they would explore the depths of her unique abilities, forging a path toward a future where her magic could shape the destiny of all magical beings.

Demetrius excused her and attempted to remain behind in the chamber but quickly discovered the room was not having it when he was violently ejected out of the door after Blythe had exited it. He grumbled some curses and left her with a gruff order to handle her chores. His ejection, which resulted in him tumbling head over heels, would have been humorous had it not been for the harsh tone Demetrius had used with her, which startled her. Since she had arrived, he had always been kind towards her, but the look on his face set off alarm bells within her. She walked away and left him to his musings, trying to understand why her instincts were telling her to run.

CHAPTER TWENTY-SEVEN

Under the fading sun, Blythe worked hard to clean up after her training and chores. She used a bucket of water to wash away the dirt and sweat, making her feel useful. She was starting to enjoy these quiet moments in the busy rebel camp, and cleaning up helped her feel like she had a purpose. Her training had been hard but felt useful. She hoped that with all this, she could return to the human world and protect herself from the Council. She considered attempting to keep her role as the Keeper of the House of Fas. Indeed, the House would protect her from the Council there. However, that could mean giving up traveling for the possibility of safety. She wasn't sure she could do that. She was starting to feel more sure of herself and was beginning to make friends among the rebels. Griffin, the funny dwarf, always made her laugh. Bertolf, the werewolf curious about the human world, was like a friend or younger brother she'd known forever. He was constantly peppering her with questions about the human world. Her favorite question so far had been about fast food and whether it meant you had to eat it fast or move quickly to catch it.

Blythe was determined to do her best as the Keeper. The Magic House was likely her only safe home now. She imagined a future where everyone could live together peacefully but worried that may be just a pipe dream.

As Blythe brushed and pulled her hair back out of her face, a gentle tap on her shoulder made her turn; seeing Quentin brought an unexpected warmth to her heart and cheeks. She smiled back at his playful gaze.

"Blythe, how about we momentarily escape the chaos of camp and indulge in a streamside picnic?" Quentin raised a basket. "No need for us to spend another dinner listening to Griffin's overly dramatic Dwarven War stories."

Blythe's fatigue momentarily receded as she pondered Quentin's proposition. The notion of a tranquil break by the stream was a tempting idea. With a slight smile, she carefully placed the bucket and nodded in agreement.

"I found a spot upstream that's just perfect," Quentin declared, his eyes alight with enthusiasm. Blythe's hand naturally gravitated toward Quentin's outstretched one, their fingers intertwining effortlessly. Together, they moved through the camp, their footsteps melding into a gentle cadence that mirrored their hearts' rising anticipation.

As they ventured deeper into the verdant forest, the cacophony of camp life faded behind. The soft melody of the stream beckoned them closer, its tranquil tune setting the stage for their shared expedition. Blythe's fatigue began to lift with each step, replaced by a rekindled vigor and an invigorated sense of curiosity. Being with Quentin made her feel secure and content.

Upon arriving at their chosen spot, Quentin spread a checkered blanket on the grass beside the stream, creating an inviting haven for their picnic. Blythe settled down, attuning her senses to the gentle babble of water and leaves rustling. Nature's soothing symphony enveloped her, cocooning her in a sense of serenity. Sunlight filtered through the forest canopy, casting a dance of patterns upon the earth as though the natural world was celebrating its moment of reprieve. Blythe inhaled the earthy fragrance of the woods, feeling a profound calm infuse her very being.

Side by side, Blythe and Quentin relished the simple feast Quentin had brought. Their laughter blended harmoniously with the stream's mellifluous music, weaving a melodious tapestry that resonated through the woods. Conversations flowed effortlessly, deepening their connection with each shared exchange.

"Blythe," Quentin began, his voice a mere breath, "there's something I've been wanting to do." Blythe met his gaze, her eyes alive with curiosity. "What is it, Quentin?"

Quentin tenderly cradled her face in his hands without hesitation, sending a delightful shiver cascading down her spine. Their eyes locked, an unspoken intensity hanging in the air.

In a graceful motion, Quentin leaned in, and their lips met in a tender, enchanting kiss. Time paused as their mouths converged, a symphony of emotions coursing between them. It was a delicate waltz, charged with expectation and the allure of the unknown. Blythe's heart soared, every nerve electrified by Quentin's touch. Emotions surged within her—a tide of fondness and yearning that left her momentarily breathless. The kiss solidified their bond, merging their essences in a moment of shared longing.

As they gradually drew apart, foreheads still touching, a gentle smile curved on Blythe's lips. The world around them dimmed, leaving only the echo of their intimate moment.

Amid their close embrace, Quentin's voice, tinged with concern, disrupted the tranquility of their tableau. "Blythe, we should return to camp," he murmured, his gaze flickering toward a distant movement. Following his line of sight, Blythe's expression shifted with a trace of unease.

A rustling in the nearby undergrowth caught her attention, triggering a note of caution. Blythe's instincts sharpened, and she slowly disentangled herself from Quentin, her gaze sweeping the surroundings.

"Quentin, something feels off," she murmured, her voice carrying caution and curiosity. They couldn't dismiss the possibility of being watched. With urgency in her gaze, she motioned for Quentin to follow as they retraced their steps toward the camp.

The serene picnic spot by the stream once filled with promise and stolen moments, now held an undercurrent of uncertainty. Blythe's mind raced with possibilities, contemplating who or what might lurk in the shadows. Fear and anticipation pulsed through her heart, shattering the tranquility.

Their senses heightened as they moved cautiously, the tension in the atmosphere thickening with each step. Blythe's training instincts kicked in, her eyes scanning for signs of danger. The nagging feeling that a reason had disrupted their peace remained, urging her to stay vigilant.

The previously tranquil surroundings now seemed shrouded in mystery, as if the forest held untold secrets. Blythe exchanged a wary glance with Quentin, silently acknowledging the need to remain watchful.

They advanced swiftly yet quietly, their footfalls almost silent on the forest floor. The rustling of leaves and faint whispers pricked their ears, intensifying their awareness. Blythe's heart quickened, the rhythm echoing in her ears as she braced for what might lie ahead.

Back at the camp, uncertainty gnawed at Blythe's resolve. Had they been followed? Were they being pursued by agents of the Council or an entirely different threat? Questions flooded her mind, fueled by a mix of apprehension and anticipation.

Approaching the camp's outskirts, the sounds of activity grew noisier—voices, footsteps, and the distant clinking of armor. Blythe and Quentin exchanged a glance, their expressions mirroring caution and determination. The air seemed to hum with tension as Demetrius's voice rang out, announcing the imminent threat from the Council. Blythe's attention snapped to him, her gaze sharpening. The urgency in his words seeped into her bones, sparking a surge of determination. This was the moment they had all been preparing for, the mission that held the key to their ultimate victory.

Griffin, his spirits lifted by a certain level of intoxication, couldn't contain his excitement. He grinned at his comrades with a boisterous whoop, injecting energy into the charged atmosphere. Blythe found herself smiling at his infectious enthusiasm, if only for a moment's relief from the weight of the impending task.

Demetrius continued to list the names of the volunteers. Still, Blythe's gaze shifted to her right, where a figure shrouded in a dark robe materialized seemingly from nowhere. Two more hooded individuals stood behind them, sending a shiver down her spine. Though unsettled, she focused on Demetrius to capture every name called.

Positioned beside Blythe, Octo voiced his impatience, his presence having gone unnoticed until now. His words held a sober seriousness. "We've been plotting and planning for too long," he grumbled, echoing the restlessness within the camp. Blythe nodded in agreement, the sentiment resonating with many of the rebels. The group's muted cheers revealed a mix of relief, and Demetrius unveiled some of their mission's details. Octo's voice melded with subdued enthusiasm as the rebels embraced the upcoming battle with quiet resolve. Blythe marveled at their ability to remain hidden, their every action executed silently to conceal their intentions from prying ears.

Amidst the camp's flurry of preparations, Blythe's eyes scanned the bustling scene, her thoughts briefly consumed by Miles's absence. He hadn't been around yet today. As Blythe fell into step behind Quentin, they merged with the line of rebels waiting to collect their food packs. Concern laced her voice as she turned to Quentin, her words hinting worry.

"Quentin, I've noticed Miles hasn't been around lately. Do you know what happened?"

A flicker of jealousy danced across Quentin's face, though he tried to conceal it behind a smile. "Already miss him, huh?" he remarked, his tone revealing more than he intended. Blythe hurried to clarify, her voice tinged with a touch of defensiveness.

"No, it's not that. I just haven't seen him and wanted to say goodbye before we leave."

Quentin's brows furrowed, momentarily revealing his worry. He glanced back at Blythe before explaining, his voice tinged with regret. "Something unexpected came up, and he didn't meet up with me to come here. I'm sorry, Blythe."

A pang of disappointment echoed within her, yet Blythe understood that unforeseen circumstances could disrupt even the best-laid plans. As they silently followed the line, her mind became preoccupied with the impending journey. When a centaur handed her a food pack, she stepped aside, tracing Quentin's path toward the cluster of sleeping tents.

"Well, I'll catch up with you later," she murmured, veering away from Quentin's trajectory and toward her tent. The fabric of the tent flap beckoned her inside, offering a brief respite from the mounting chaos. "I will count every minute with a pained heart!" Quentin's exaggerated cry reached her ears, and she couldn't help but glance back, witnessing his melodramatic display of heartache. Rolling her eyes, she responded with a playful smirk before turning away and disappearing through the tent's entrance.

Startled, Blythe nearly jumped out of her skin when she saw Miles sitting on her cot, holding her tied-up bedroll. Pressing a hand against her chest, she tried to catch her breath, her surprise and annoyance evident in her hissed words.

"Miles, you scared the shit out of me!"

Miles grinned in response, rising from the cot and placing her bedding down. His playful demeanor shone through as he sauntered toward her. "Do you need a change of clothes?" he asked innocently, his eyes twinkling with mischief. He leaned in for a kiss, but Blythe deftly ducked and veered to the side, skillfully evading his attempt.

"Scared the shit out of me is a human phrase, right?" Miles guessed, a mischievous glint still present in his eyes. Blythe chuckled, finding his guess amusing. "Yes," she replied, "It means you're an ass for startling me like that." She moved to grab the pack waiting at the end of her bed.

Miles stood nearby as she tied her bedroll to the bottom of her bag. "I'm surprised you're not coming with us," curiosity shone in her eyes.

"I can't," Miles replied softly, his voice tinged with sadness. "I wish you wouldn't either."

Confusion furrowed Blythe's brow. "Why? Don't you want the Council gone?"

Miles moved closer to her, his voice lowering as he

revealed his concerns. "This isn't a good idea, Blythe. It's a suicide mission. No one goes into the Dark World and comes out. I'm not entirely convinced that Demetrius did."

Blythe's eyes widened, a mix of surprise and worry crossing her face. "Then why are you involved in all of this? Everyone else seems to idolize him," she countered, matching his lowered volume.

"Well, I don't. And the alternative was to let the rebels take you without me being able to save you from this nonsense," Miles confessed, reaching out and gently taking her hands in his. An air of genuine concern replaced his usually cheerful demeanor.

"Miles, don't worry. I'm just accompanying them until I can find my way in the human world. I have no intention of entering the Dark World," she reassured him, squeezing his hands gently. "And if all goes as planned, I won't even have to go near that portal."

"Do you think they'll just let you go?" Miles moved closer, the distance between them diminishing. His hands felt warm against hers.

"Don't be silly, Miles. I've discussed this with Quentin. He agreed to keep me safe. Do you trust him?" Blythe asked, her eyes searching for reassurance.

"Unfortunately, yes."

"Then relax. I'll be fine. I'll have Quentin inform you that I've made it safely away."

Just as Blythe was about to continue reassuring Miles, a faint sound reached their ears from outside the tent. Miles immediately tensed, his expression turning serious. He sputtered. "I have to go."

Without wasting another moment, he bent down and kissed her on the lips, surprising her once again. Blythe's mind raced, wanting to tell him everything she had been keeping inside.

"Miles, wait..." she started softly, but he swiftly turned her around, positioning himself so his back faced the tent entrance.

"I'll find you," he promised before pulling away and leaving abruptly, leaving Blythe yearning for more time to express herself.

"Miles..." she murmured, her voice trailing off as he disappeared. Standing there, she had a heavy heart and a sense of regret. At that moment, she wished she had told him the truth—that she had developed feelings for Quentin and wanted him and Hera to find happiness together. But the opportunity slipped away, and she was left grappling with her emotions in the solitude of the tent.

CHAPTER TWENTY-EIGHT

The camp brimmed with eager anticipation, drawing every member to the lively fire where Demetrius stood as a steadfast leader. His presence commanded the full attention of those who encircled him. The campfire's dancing flames cast dramatic shadows on their faces, underscoring the moment's gravity.

Among them, the returning werewolves conveyed their reconnaissance findings with urgency. "We've scouted the House," one of them reported, his eyes gleaming in the firelight. "Surprisingly, there's minimal guard presence. It's unnervingly quiet."

Excitement rippled through the group, and Demetrius nodded, emphasizing the moment's importance. "This is our opportunity. But we must remain vigilant. Inform the others we've summoned that our meeting point is the west entrance to the Vallayan Mines."

The werewolves swiftly departed, their purposeful strides reflecting the gravity of their mission. Hope filled the air as rebels gathered around the fire. Blythe stood beside Demetrius, her emotions swirling within her. The prospect of finally moving on from the camp was daunting, and her heart was excited.

Demetrius's voice remained steady and confident. "Tonight, we put our plan into action under darkness. Although we may seem vulnerable, we'll stay alert and prepared."

Quentin stepped forward, his words brimming with unity. "We've come a long way, driven by our unwavering determination. This is where our beliefs translate into action. The human realm beckons, and we won't hesitate."

Their voices merged in cheers and enthusiastic support, uniting them in purpose. As they busied themselves with preparations, Demetrius approached Blythe. His voice carried gratitude and determination. "Blythe, I've entrusted Quentin with those two special items for when we reach the portal in the human world. We appreciate your assistance and promise to keep you safe."

Blythe met his gaze, her determination shining in her eyes. "I hadn't planned to be part of a rebellion, but I'm glad I could somehow assist. And I'm grateful for your help returning me to my life."

Demetrius nodded approvingly and offered a faint smile. "You're a steadfast companion. Your determination inspires all of us. Thank you, Blythe."

Demetrius gave some parting words, and the camp came alive with activity as they broke down tents, gathered packs, and divided into groups. Demetrius gave out instructions to the leaders of each group, and a group swept the area to attempt to remove evidence of their presence there.

As night fell, the camp brimmed with anticipation. Although the path ahead was uncertain, their unity and determination remained unwavering. The campsite gradually quieted as the groups ventured into the unknown, splitting up to travel without drawing attention to themselves. Blythe walked alongside Quentin, with Griffin's reassuring presence close by. Hera, Demetrius, and some of the werewolves formed a protective circle around them.

The wilderness around them was eerily silent, broken only by the faintest rustlings of movement. Shadows seemed to whisper secrets, and Blythe's senses played tricks on her. A rogue vampire lurked nearby, moving stealthily through the night. The group communicated through hushed exchanges, their strategies discussed with shared breaths. Even Quentin and Griffin, who were usually more animated, succumbed to the moment's gravity, their thoughts expressed in quiet contemplation.

Time passed slowly, and Blythe's heart raced with suspense. The night grew heavier as they moved forward in the darkness. Blythe's every step was uncomfortable, her body aching and tired. Her injured ankle throbbed, and exhaustion weighed on her. Despite these challenges, her determination kept her going, a flickering flame against the encroaching darkness.

Blythe's heightened senses picked up every sound in the dark surroundings and paid attention to even the slightest movement. The once comforting silence of the night now felt like an endless void of uncertainty.

She felt out of place, her presence standing out in the stillness. An uneasy feeling gnawed at her, especially when she sensed Xander's disdain. Her intuition warned her to be cautious around him.

Their journey through the woods seemed never-ending, with each step a struggle. The towering trees served as constant reminders of the path ahead, shrouded in darkness. The absence of light disoriented Blythe, and she sometimes stumbled, grateful for Quentin and Griffin's support.

The darkness enveloped her thoughts, leaving her uncertain about her past life. Loyalty and identity felt complicated, and the contrast between her past and present choices was stark. She longed for the comfort and routine of her old life. Yet, the camaraderie and responsibility within the rebel group held undeniable appeal. The prospect of a new chapter intertwined with the magical realm tugged at her spirit.

Her feelings for Miles were a tangle of emotions, intricate and multifaceted. The unspoken truths and the uncharted territory between them carried a profound sense of sorrow. She knew that acknowledging the reality of their situation would be bittersweet, bridging the gap between unrequited love and the friendship they had cultivated. Her conflicted emotions mirrored the dark woods they were traversing.

Amidst her whirlwind of thoughts, Quentin's caring voice provided a comforting anchor. His gentle inquiry cut through her musings, his sincere concern easing her troubled mind. She replied with a fragile facade, concealing the turmoil within. "I'm okay... just a bit sore," she murmured, her voice betraying a weak strength.

Griffin's attempts at humor briefly lightened the mood, but the moment passed quickly. Xander's sudden intrusion, marked by malevolence, was a stark reminder of the ever-present danger. Blythe felt a mix of irritation and intense indignation, her determination unwavering despite the humiliation.

As night gave way to the gentle embrace of dawn, the terrain transformed, giving birth to hills that seemed to rise from nowhere, their rocky forms etched against the sky. The final climb tested their endurance, a challenging trial. Blythe leaned on Quentin, his unwavering support sustaining her as they moved forward. Each step symbolized their unity, a collective spirit propelling them toward the culmination of their mission.

The landscape shifted once again as they approached the Eastern entrance to the Vallayan Mines. The mouth of the mine was an imposing sight, a dark chasm leading into the earth's bowels. Its jagged walls loomed over them like the ancient guardians of some forgotten realm. Massive stone columns flanked the entrance, remnants of the dwarves' craftsmanship, now bereft of the life and activity that had once filled these caverns.

Griffin gave the entrance a hard look, his brow furrowing deeply. "Somethin's amiss," he grumbled, his voice laced with unease. "The dwarves should be here. This place is too quiet for comfort."

Indeed, the absence of the typically bustling dwarven activity was unsettling. The mines were eerily silent except for their footsteps' faint echoes as they ventured deeper into the underground labyrinth.

They walked for what seemed like hours, the darkness growing more oppressive with each step. The tunnel walls were rough-hewn, resulting from centuries of dwarven mining. Faint, flickering torches provided the only light sources, casting long shadows that danced menacingly along the walls.

Their journey led them deeper into the heart of the mountains, heading toward the Western entrance, where they would meet the rest of the rebels and consolidate their forces before launching their assault on the portal that connected the dark world to the realm of magic.

As they descended into the mines, the air grew colder and more oppressive, a tangible weight pressing down on them. The tunnels seemed to stretch endlessly into the earth, twisting and turning in a complex maze that spoke of generations of excavation.

A low, guttural growl suddenly reverberated through the tunnel, sending shivers down their spines. The sound was unmistakable—a warning from the depths of the darkness that they were not alone.

Quentin raised a hand, signaling for silence. The group halted, their breaths held in fearful anticipation. The growl grew, reverberating through the mines, and the ground trembled beneath their feet.

And then, emerging from the shadows, a monstrous figure loomed—a gigantic troll, its grotesque features illuminated by the flickering torchlight. Its gnarled skin and piercing eyes spoke of a malevolence born from the depths of the dark world.

With a deafening roar, the troll charged forward, its massive fists swinging toward them. The rebels reacted swiftly, drawing weapons and summoning magic as they braced for the ferocious assault of the creature lurking in the depths of the Vallayan Mines.

Paralyzed with fear, Blythe watched in terror as the colossal troll lunged forward, its monstrous form an impending nightmare. Her heart pounded in her chest, a cacophony of fear and dread overwhelming her senses.

With lightning speed, Quentin notched an arrow and let it fly, the projectile finding its mark and embedding itself in the troll's thick hide. Hera and Erya moved in tandem, their blades flashing in the dim torchlight as they engaged the creature in close combat. Griffin swung his massive battle ax with incredible force, cleaving through the air as he aimed for the troll's vulnerable legs.

Octo, the trident-wielding warrior, leaped into action, his weapon slicing through the air in a graceful arc. Demetrius, their stalwart leader, met the troll head-on, his sword clashing against the creature's gnarled, club-like arm.

The rebels fought valiantly, their coordinated efforts a mesmerizing display of skill and unity. The cavern resounded with the clash of steel, the group's battle cries, and the troll's enraged roars. They fought with calculated strikes, each movement precise as they danced on the precipice of danger.

Blythe deeply admired her companions, their unwavering resolve, and their fierce determination. They were a force to reckon with, an indomitable spirit that refused to bow to the darkness.

But as the seconds passed, it became painfully clear that they were not winning this battle. The troll's immense strength and regenerative abilities made it a formidable opponent, and its roars grew even more ferocious as it fought off the rebels.

Blythe knew she couldn't stand idly by any longer. Her hands trembled as she reached for the magic she had been honing in her training. She had used it before, but it seemed elusive in this moment of desperation as if the darkness conspired to keep it from her.

She closed her eyes, blocking out the chaos around her, and delved deep within herself. Her thoughts connected with the dormant energy within her, a flickering ember that needed only a breath to ignite.

With a surge of determination, Blythe finally found the magic that had always been a part of her, waiting to awaken. She channeled her newfound power, focusing her intent on a single, desperate act.

Summoning every ounce of energy, she formed a ball of

radiant light, her hands trembling as she held it aloft. She hurled the luminous sphere at the troll with all her strength, aiming for its eyes.

The ball of light exploded upon impact, blinding the creature and causing it to roar in agony. The troll's enraged roar thundered through the cavernous tunnel. The rebels seized the opportunity presented by the troll's momentary distraction and launched a coordinated attack. Swords clashed, arrows flew, and magic crackled as the group fought to subdue their formidable foe.

Blythe's heart raced as she watched her companions engage in the battle. Her small contribution seemed insignificant compared to their skilled maneuvers and well-practiced combat techniques. But she refused to let doubt consume her. She took a deep breath, channeling the magic within her, and conjured another orb of light, more significant and radiant this time.

With unwavering determination, Blythe hurled the luminous sphere toward the troll again. The orb exploded upon impact, enveloping the troll in a brilliant cascade of light. The creature let out an agonized howl, its massive body convulsing as the magical energy surged.

Emboldened by her modest success, Blythe pressed onward, her fear giving way to a resolute determination. She conjured swirling gusts of wind around the troll, aiming to disorient and impede its movements. The breeze whipped around, buffeting the creature and causing it to struggle to maintain balance.

Drawing strength from the impact of her magic, Blythe pushed herself even harder. She focused her thoughts, envisioning a shield of shimmering energy enveloping her companions, shielding them from the troll's unrelenting onslaught. The guard materialized, offering a brief reprieve for her allies.

As the battle raged on, Blythe delved deeper into her magical abilities, pushing the boundaries of her power. Tendrils of earth emerged from beneath the ground, ensnaring the troll's legs and briefly immobilizing it. Her spells were unpolished and raw, yet they effectively bought her companions precious moments.

Her magic wavered sometimes, resulting in misdirected bursts of energy and prematurely fizzling spells. However, Blythe refused to succumb to discouragement. She pressed onward, adapting and learning in the crucible of battle. Her determination fueled her desire to shield her comrades and make a meaningful impact.

The battle's intensity swelled the clash of weapons and the troll's roars reverberating through the cavern. Blythe's magic surged and flared, casting an ethereal radiance upon her face. She culminated her efforts with a final burst of power, a brilliant surge of energy that engulfed the troll, momentarily blinding it and forcing it to recoil.

Seizing the opportunity, Griffin lunged forward, his blade gleaming as he struck a decisive blow to the troll's leg. The creature's balance faltered, and crashed to the ground with a resounding thud. The rebels redoubled their efforts, striking with precision and unity.

Blythe's heart swelled with relief and awe as she watched her comrades fight alongside her. Their camaraderie and determination were a testament to the strength of their bond. Despite the odds, they stood united against the monstrous adversary.

Breathing heavily, Blythe observed as her companions seized the opportunity, launching renewed and vigorous attacks against the vulnerable troll. Their collective efforts eventually overwhelmed the creature, bringing it crashing to the ground. Finally, with a final strike from Demetrius's blade, the creature let out a last, guttural cry before falling still.

As the dust settled and the echoes of battle receded, Blythe stood amid the aftermath, her body trembling with exhaustion and awe. The weary group, comprising Blythe, Demetrius, Quentin, Griffin, Hera, and others, convened in a dimly illuminated chamber deep within the dwarven mines. Their expressions mirrored a mix of fatigue and concern as they endeavored to comprehend the unfolding events.

The tunnel fell silent, the echoes of battle dissipating into the shadows. The rebels lowered their weapons, chests heaving with exertion. Blythe's hands trembled as she let her magic recede, the orb of light fading away. She looked around at her companions, their faces illuminated by exhaustion and triumph.

Hera approached Blythe, a rare softness in her gaze. "Well done. You held your ground and contributed to the fight. That's more than most could have done."

Blythe's lips curved into a tired but proud smile. The adrenaline still coursed through her veins, and her ankle throbbed with renewed pain, but she felt a profound sense of belonging. She was a part of something greater than herself, a group of individuals who had faced danger together and emerged victorious.

As the rebels regrouped and tended to their wounds, Blythe's gaze flickered to the tunnel ahead. Griffin's voice cut through the air, tinged with anger and frustration. "I want ta make it clear, I had no inklin' of the dwarves abandonin' this mine. This here's a right peculiar situation, and it's got me mighty worried 'bout what might've gone down."

Blythe's eyes narrowed, her mind working through the implications. "The sudden absence of the dwarves and the reappearance of the trolls cannot be mere coincidence. I can't shake the feeling that this might be a trap orchestrated by the council."

Demetrius crossed his arms, his tone resolute. "The council has shown that they're willing to employ such tactics. They'll stop at nothing to eliminate any opposition to their rule. However, we haven’t had any intel to indicate that they knew where we were going."

Quentin stepped forward, his gaze intense. "Even so, we mustn't let our guard down. If the council released that troll as part of a trap, they may know our journey and the warriors waiting for us on the other side."

Hera's eyes widened in realization. "They aim to weaken us, divide our forces, and prevent our alliance from becoming a true threat to their power."

Griffin nodded firmly, determination evident in his voice. "We dwarves ain't gonna let 'em get away with it! Our mission's got a heap o' weight on its shoulders now. We'll keep on goin', get to our allies, and give 'em a good heads-up 'bout the council's dirty tricks."

Blythe's injured ankle throbbed, but her resolve remained unshaken. "Time is of the essence. We can't afford any delays. If the council was aware enough to plant a troll here, they might be lying in wait at the House."

The group exchanged resolute glances, their unity unwavering in adversity. They understood that their path forward would hold peril and uncertainty. Yet, they were prepared to confront whatever challenges lay ahead.

Quentin placed a reassuring hand on Blythe's shoulder, his voice brimming with confidence. "Blythe, while we may not have all the answers, your burgeoning magical abilities could be our key to deciphering the council's plots. Your role has become even more crucial."

After a breath, Blythe's voice was resolute yet tinged with concern. "I understand the importance of this rebellion and the struggle against the council, but my primary objective remains to return to the human world. I hadn't intended to become so deeply enmeshed in this."

Quentin nodded, his gaze unwavering. "We know. We are prioritizing your safety to make sure you reach the human world unscathed."

Hera stepped forward, her determination evident. "Blythe, we're all in this together, and your well-being is paramount to us. We won't expose you to undue risks. Our foremost concern is reaching the human world, and we're committed to safeguarding you."

Blythe felt gratitude wash over her as her concerns were acknowledged and respected. During the turmoil, she found solace in the unwavering support of her companions.

Demetrius placed a reassuring hand on Blythe's shoulder, his tone sincere. "Our journey continues, but we'll take every measure to ensure your safety, Blythe. Your presence is invaluable to our cause, and we'll prioritize your welfare."

Knowing that her safety was foremost in their minds, Blythe felt a renewed sense of purpose. While her ultimate goal remained the journey to the human world, she couldn't ignore the growing bond she shared with her companions and their mission. As they resumed their trek through the treacherous mines, Blythe kept her focus on the path ahead, resolved to safeguard herself and facilitate the secure passage of her companions.

CHAPTER TWENTY-NINE

A gentle hand shook her shoulder, rousing her from her slumber. "Wake up, Kitten. It's time to head to the house." As Blythe's eyes fluttered open, she realized the darkness around her had given way to a starlit night. She was slightly disoriented until she remembered they had emerged into the early dawn after leaving the mines. Slowly sitting up, she took in her surroundings, the silhouettes of her companions forming a gathering around her.

"How long was I asleep?" she inquired, rubbing her eyes to dispel the remnants of drowsiness.

"A good while," he began, his tone laced with concern, "I was starting to get concerned, but then I remembered the intense training you've been through lately, not to mention our recent battle." He cast a fleeting glance behind him, scanning the surroundings for potential threats before his gaze returned to her. "Regardless, we need to get moving." His hand extended, offering her support as she rose to her feet. Her ankle still ached, but it felt better than when they had first entered the mines. Griffin had insisted she ride in one of the carts after the battle to give her ankle a break. Quentin assisted her in adjusting her pack and then handed her a block of sustenance. "Have something to eat," he urged gently, concern evident in his eyes.

As Blythe's senses fully adjusted, she observed the figures encircling her. Through the darkness, the distinct forms of elves, dwarves, valkyries, halflings, merpeople, and other fantastical beings became discernible. Their presence exuded determination and unity, underscoring the importance of their shared mission.

Beside her, Quentin offered a comforting smile. "We've gathered reinforcements, Blythe. Warriors from various realms have joined our cause. They're here to ensure our journey to the house is a success. They believe in us and our mission."

A surge of gratitude and inspiration swept over Blythe as she surveyed the diverse array of warriors. This was no longer just a small band of rebels; it had evolved into a potent coalition driven by a collective purpose. Each member brought their unique strengths and skills to the forefront, united in their quest for freedom.

Demetrius stepped forward, his voice projected a blend of conviction and thankfulness. "Tonight, we embark on a path that will test our mettle, unity, and unwavering commitment. With these brave allies by our side, we stand a stronger chance of triumph. Together, we shall reclaim the House and secure a brighter future. This marks our initial stride towards liberty."

Anticipation hung in the air as the assembly prepared to move. Torches ignited, casting dancing shadows across determined faces. The soft clinking of armor and hushed strategizing intermingled in the night. Blythe could sense the collective determination flowing through the ranks, an unspoken pledge to reclaim their rightful place.

Confidence surged within Blythe. While her magic skills were still budding and her familiarity with warfare was limited, she had witnessed the tenacity and resilience of those around her. She had found her niche among them, a vital cog in the grand mechanism.

"From this juncture onward, we shall divide. Half of us will advance toward the House, while the remaining half will proceed to the Mireglow Fen Bogs. We will take control of the portal there. We will have won one portal between the human realm and the Dark World, one between the Dark World and the Magic Realm, and with the House, one between the Magic Realm and the Human realm. We will then regroup with our friends from the Dark Realm and proceed from there." Demetrius commanded his voice a firm beacon of authority. "I will lead the contingent going to the bogs, Quentin; you shall lead the group bound for the house." Quentin acknowledged the assignment with a nod.

Armed with purpose and kindled hope, Blythe took her place among the ranks, poised to march alongside the diverse army assembled for this pivotal juncture. The journey ahead was fraught with challenges and uncertainty, yet their collective strength fortified them. The path to the house beckoned, arduous and fraught with peril, but with their combined fortitude, they were ready to confront any obstacles.

Blythe was ready to go when a gust of wind caught her attention from her left. She turned to see Xavier, or whom she assumed was Xavier, based on how quickly he'd arrived, and wore a cloak completely enshrouding his figure. As usual, his demeanor was cold and hostile. He leaned in, his voice urgent and filled with disdain. "Blythe, listen carefully because I'm not going to repeat myself. I'm only telling you this because I'm certain the betrayal isn't yours. Not all rebels can be trusted."

Taken aback by Xander's hostility and what he said, Blythe furrowed her brows. "What's happening, Xander? Aren't we all fighting for the same cause?" Her voice carried genuine concern.

Xander's expression hardened, and he scanned their surroundings, cautious and watchful. "I've kept my senses sharp, tuned into the whispers that flow through the camp. I've got a gut feeling that someone in our midst is double-crossing us, leaking vital information to the Council, or being disingenuous about their interest in bringing peace and equality. There's a traitor among us but I'm uncertain what their goal is."

Dread settled heavily in Blythe's stomach as she absorbed the implications of Xander's revelation. The idea of betrayal undermining their efforts and risking lives sent a chilling shiver down her spine. Leaning closer to Xander, her voice barely above a whisper, she voiced her concern. "Who, Xander? Who might be behind this?"

Xander's gaze bore into her, his voice a low murmur. "I can't be certain yet, but my instincts suggest it could be someone close to you or trying to get closer. Trust no one."

Shock and suspicion filled Blythe's eyes as she grappled

with the gravity of Xander's words. She had trusted the rebellion, believing in their united stand against the Council's tyranny. She should have learned from all the lies she'd been dealing with recently. Now, faced with betrayal and lies again, she understood trust had to be earned, and so far, no one had it. Except for maybe Quentin, her trust in him was unstable.

"You need to be cautious, Blythe," Xander cautioned firmly. "Stay vigilant, question everyone's motives, and don't place unwavering trust in anyone until we uncover the truth. Basically, stop acting without thinking. Our enemy could seamlessly blend in with the rebellion, masquerading as one of us." He paused, "The rebellion itself could not be what it seems."

Blythe felt his words like a punch in her gut. What else could the rebellion be after? Quentin and the others seemed determined to obtain equality and freedom. They had everything to lose if this didn't succeed. She started questioning her plan to bail once they reached the human realm. What if something happened to Miles or Quentin because someone was being disingenuous? She couldn't forgive herself if that happened.

Determination surged within Blythe as she absorbed this new information. She wouldn't let a traitor jeopardize their cause. She would remain vigilant, expose the traitor, and safeguard the mission's integrity and the lives of those striving for a brighter future.

Blythe nodded in agreement and locked eyes with Xander, cementing their unspoken pact. They would stay watchful, untangle the traitor's web, and protect their friends from lurking betrayal.

As Blythe's mind swirled with thoughts of deception and treachery, doubt crept into her heart, shaking her belief in the unity of the rebellion. Xander's words couldn't be dismissed; the stakes were too high.

"Xander, what about the upcoming mission to the House? Do you think it's a setup?" Blythe asked, her voice filled with worry.

Xander nodded solemnly. "I fear it might be an ambush. The Council could be onto us. Stay sharp and watch your back."

Blythe's heart raced, the weight of Xander's warning heavy on her shoulders. The rebellion teetered on the edge of danger, and her trust in her fellow rebels was now clouded by doubt.

"Thank you for sharing this with me, Xander," Blythe murmured, gratitude mixed with concern in her voice. "I'll proceed cautiously and ensure this mission doesn't falter."

Xander acknowledged her with a curt nod before vanishing into the shadows, leaving Blythe to grapple with the newfound unease that enveloped her. His words hung in the air like a haunting melody, a stark reminder that their quest for liberation was riddled with uncertainty and concealed threats. With unwavering determination, she would navigate this treacherous path, fully aware that the lives at stake and the success of their cause depended on her vigilance.

CHAPTER THIRTY

As they entered the enveloping night, Blythe was lost in worried thoughts. The path ahead was uncertain, leaving her torn between her initial plan of going to the group and her newfound sense of responsibility. She couldn't bear the thought of harm coming to her new friends, and the mere possibility of a traitor among them sent a chill down her spine. It was also disturbing to think that maybe one of them was the traitor.

With every step, doubt gnawed at her, making her wonder if Xander, with his harsh demeanor, might be the actual traitor, attempting to sow distrust and lead them astray. It was a disconcerting thought; she couldn't ignore the nagging suspicion.

Walking alongside her comrades, Blythe examined the peculiar food block Quentin had given her, intrigued by its scent. Curiosity piqued, she took a cautious bite, savoring its savory, ever-changing flavors. She couldn't help but inquire, her voice filled with fascination, "What is this, Quentin?"

Quentin, by her side, offered a warm smile. "It's travel food, an elven specialty. It adapts flavor to your craving and provides essential nutrients for our journey."

Blythe continued eating, occasionally glancing at the shadowy figure leading their group, likely one of the vampires, given their more diminutive stature than Xander. Griffin engaged Quentin in a hushed conversation on the other side.

Underfoot, the ground felt softer than the mines, and even in the darkness, Blythe noticed faint patches of light in the distance, possibly indicating dwellings atop hills. Quentin's voice reached her ears, hushed and cautious. "We're approaching our destination."

With a renewed sense of purpose, Blythe finished her meal, her ankle still throbbing from the discomfort endured during the journey. She yearned for the comfort of a warm bath, candles, and a good book, a stark contrast to their current tumultuous journey.

Amidst her doubts, Blythe turned to Quentin, voicing her concerns. "Do you truly believe this plan is foolproof? What if it's a trap?" Anxiety cast a shadow over her confidence.

Quentin's voice held firm reassurance. "Our intelligence network has been reliable. It has never led us astray." However, Blythe couldn't help but consider the possibility that Quentin might be the traitor. Would he even tell her if their mission was a trap?

An elf approached her, walking alongside a familiar face from the previous night. The elf's name eluded her memory, but his presence exuded reliability. "We have discreet channels for gathering information," he explained. "Our network of spies has proven dependable so far."

Skepticism colored Blythe's mutterings. "There's always a first time for everything."

The terrain shifted underfoot, with the group adjusting to up and downhill stretches. They matched Blythe's pace, aware of their collective fatigue but driven by the anticipation of reaching their goal.

As Blythe's weariness and unease became evident, Quentin drew closer, their arms brushing lightly, sending an unusual tingle through her. The sensation intrigued her, leaving her wondering if it was a Fae peculiarity or simply a result of their proximity. Fascinated by their connection, she pushed the thoughts aside, but the unease lingered.

Griffin interjected, breaking the brief silence. "When we get to the House, we'll get some rest, but it can't be for too long. We can't risk them discovering our plans and reinforcing the portal entrance here. We'd be in trouble if that happened."

Hera, walking a few steps behind, added her perspective. "Strength is crucial, but if they outnumber us significantly, we'll face a formidable challenge."

Blythe's confusion found a voice. "If the wizards treat non-witches and non-wizards so poorly, why haven't the people risen against them now?"

The elf, still nameless in her memory, offered an explanation. "Elves prefer diplomacy over direct conflict. We believe in seeking alternative solutions through reason and dialogue. However, some have realized that the Council doesn't respond to such approaches. We suspect a darker force is at work."

Griffin grumbled skeptically. "Sounds like a lot of superstition to me. Some folks just can't fathom that wizards might be that malicious. After all, they ain't Warlocks or nothing."

Blythe's thoughts turned to the Warlocks they aimed to rescue. "Hold on, aren't we trying to aid the Warlocks?"

"We are," Quentin explained, his voice a mix of understanding and determination. "Warlocks draw their magic from a darker source than Witches and Wizards. They possess undeniable power, precisely why the Council sought their eradication. Just because their magic source is darker doesn't mean they are evil. It is just what they are."

Before Blythe could respond, a sudden hiss cut through the air, silencing her. Cloaked in dark attire, Xander loomed over her, demanding her attention. "We've arrived at the driveway."

Blythe shifted her gaze and bathed in moonlight; the dirt path unfolded ahead, flanked by trees. Xander's displeasure was evident in his tone, making Blythe anxious. She glanced at Quentin, and her anxiety reflected in his eyes. Sensing her unease, he squeezed her hand reassuringly.

"I'll be right behind you," he murmured in her ear, his breath sending a shiver down her spine. Part of her hesitated to let go of his touch, but as Xander advanced, she knew lingering wouldn't be well-received. Reluctantly, she quickened her steps, prompting Xander to halt momentarily.

They made their way up the driveway, with the rest of the group moving silently. But Blythe's every footfall seemed to disturb twigs and rustle leaves, much to Xander's evident annoyance. The embarrassment and frustration gnawed at her as she berated herself for not being able to walk silently, a skill she had never needed before. Ordinary people didn't worry about such things unless, of course, they aimed to startle someone. But their context allowed no room for leniency.

The ascent up the driveway felt never-ending, but thoughts of a warm bath, a steaming cup of tea, and much-needed rest drove Blythe forward with increased urgency. Upon entering the clearing where the House stood, two figures seemingly appeared out of thin air, joining Xander at her side, blocking her path. Quentin stepped forward.

Glowing orbs of light materialized near the House, each emitting a distinct hue, revealing the figures responsible for their creation. Approximately 20 figures stood there, their presence illuminated by the radiant orbs. Blythe sensed her group drawing closer to the vampires, seeking security.

Quentin's voice, sharp and commanding, pierced the silence. "Identify yourselves!"

The figures advanced cautiously, prompting hisses from the vampires that halted their progress. Blythe strained to hear a voice from the shadows. "It's me, Xander," a familiar voice said, prompting her to step forward instinctively, only to be held back by Quentin, his grip firm on her arm.

"It could be a trap," he warned in a hushed tone.

Respecting his caution, Blythe remained partially concealed within the safety of her group. She squinted, focusing on the figure that stepped into the light, revealing himself as Miles. The glow from his orb provided a clearer view, confirming his identity. Quentin loosened his grip, allowing Blythe to approach.

"Who are these individuals with you, Miles?" she inquired cautiously, venturing slightly out of the protective cluster, mindful of the need for caution.

Beside her, Quentin couldn't hide his astonishment. The tension was palpable. "Miles, what's going on? I thought you were on our side."

"In a way, I still am. We share the goal of ousting the Council from power, but we believe there's a better way than resorting to full-blown conflict. We aim to unite all races peacefully and demand change. If every race stands against the Council, they will have no choice but to step aside. Our vision is for a new council, representative of every race," Miles responded calmly, determination coloring his words. "We convinced the Valkyrie hanging out around here to go away. You're welcome." Griffin's discontent was audible.

"You're dreaming! Most Dwarves won't ever turn against the Council. They're indifferent unless the Council's actions directly impact 'em. Only those who see the Council's true intentions are ready to rise," Griffin countered, his voice charged with frustration and unwavering belief.

"The fae won't join you either," Quentin interjected skeptically. "They have their own priorities, like safeguarding their pure bloodlines and preserving their way of life. Not everything the Council does is viewed as malevolent by them. Your group is misguided in thinking otherwise."

Ignoring the objections around him, Miles focused his attention on Blythe. "Come with us, Blythe. We can provide protection while we work toward a solution. Quentin, it surprises me to find you siding with the rebels, given your role as a legal representative."

"Our laws are outdated, Miles. Many of them hinder us from taking the actions you propose. Just gathering representatives from different races without a council member present can be construed as plotting against them," Quentin replied, his tone laced with sadness.

Conflicted, Blythe contemplated her choices. Joining Miles's faction offered the promise of a peaceful solution, yet her recent experiences had revealed the Council's cruelty firsthand. And she couldn't shake the memory of the suffering Warlocks. She needed time to weigh her options, time that she knew they couldn't afford. The night was wearing on, and their mission was at a critical juncture.

Just as the tension in the air seemed unbearable, Griffin spoke up, his voice laden with sarcasm. "Seems we're missing someone from this little confrontation, don't you think?"

Miles, nonchalantly as ever, replied, "Oh, Ben? He's probably drowning his sorrows in fairy liquor right about now."

The comment about Ben's absence hung in the air, adding more discomfort to the situation. The group remained on edge, uncertain of their next move.

However, the uneasy silence was shattered by an unexpected turn of events. A heated argument erupted between members of both groups. Accusations were thrown, and tempers flared. It became apparent that neither side was willing to back down or find common ground.

Blythe, Quentin, and their group exchanged worried glances. The tension had reached a breaking point, and a physical confrontation seemed imminent. With a heavy heart, Blythe realized they couldn't afford to waste more time on this dispute. She turned to Quentin, who nodded in agreement.

"Enough!" she declared, her voice cutting through the chaos. "We have a mission, and this bickering won't get us there. Miles, if you believe in your peaceful approach, pursue it. We won't stop you. But we have our own path to follow."

Miles and his group exchanged one final, disappointed glance before turning to leave, their presence fading into the night. Blythe, Quentin, and their remaining allies, their resolve strengthened by the confrontation, turned their attention toward the looming House.

"We can't let anything else deter us," Quentin said, determination evident in his voice.

With a collective nod, they pushed forward, determined to confront the challenges within the House. Blythe hoped that was what Xander had been worried about, but something in her gut told her it wasn't. The memory of the looming darkness behind the Council she had seen in that vision came to the forefront of her mind. Something wasn't right, but she couldn't put her finger on it.

Hopefully, the House could help.

CHAPTER THIRTY-ONE

The group swiftly gathered in a cramped room, transforming it into their improvised planning hub. Quentin assumed the leadership role, guiding Blythe through the intricacies of their next move—the cave's location concealed within the Poconos. Blythe absorbed the details attentively, her intimate knowledge of the area evident as she proposed swift travel options: car or bus. She stressed that walking was too time-consuming for their urgent mission.

Griffin interjected, pragmatically voicing concerns about vehicle availability. Blythe's eyes swept the room as her mind churned through potential solutions. "Last I checked, we had two cars for travelers," she began, "but here's the challenge: Does anyone here possess the skills and a valid license to drive them?" A momentary hush engulfed the group, every member's gaze shifting, each waiting for someone to step forward with the required qualifications.

Quentin leaned in, his presence intensifying. "You know how to drive, don't you?" he asked, sitting beside her, their proximity injecting a subtle tension.

"Yes, I do," Blythe admitted, "but cramming everyone into a single car won't work, and attempting to rent a larger vehicle might draw unwanted attention. If the authorities are searching for me, any movement on my part becomes a risk. Even going to the bus station could be perilous," she explained, settling back onto the couch and surveying the group. Griffin had found a spot in a wing-backed chair while she and Quentin occupied the sofa by the window. The rest of the group either stood or sat nearby. Hera lingered by the door, Bertolf casually leaned against the fireplace, and two slender figures resembling elves lounged on a chaise lounge, conversing with a man named Marlan and a woman named Venus.

"So... how challenging could driving really be?" the female elf inquired, her voice tinged with hope. "Could you teach one of us?"

Blythe took a moment to consider the proposal. "In theory, yes. But what if we get pulled over?"

"We'd manage," the male elf assured. "Quentin possesses a unique talent for persuasion."

Quentin's grin widened. "It's one of my many talents."

Blythe nodded, accepting their unconventional plan. "Alright then. Who's willing to take on the task?"

"I will," a voice finally rumbled after a prolonged silence. All eyes turned toward the young werewolf, momentarily hushing the room.

"Very well," Quentin took charge, seizing control of the situation. "Blythe, would you be so kind as to give Bertolf a driving lesson before we settle in for the night?" Blythe rose from her seat with a resigned sigh, heading for the door, Bertolf following closely. She couldn't help but notice the eerie absence of the usual creaking floorboards beneath Bertolf's feet, momentarily distracting her. She found the car keys on the hallway table, unlocked the blue Toyota hybrid in the driveway, and gestured for Bertolf to take the driver's seat.

"Before you get in," she began, her voice tinged with nervousness, "take a look at the pedals on the floor." Her finger pointed to each one. "The right is the gas, and the left is the brake. You use your right foot for both. That circular button to the right of the steering wheel," she indicated, "is the start button." Stepping back, she circled around to the passenger side and climbed in. "The first thing you always do is buckle up," she demonstrated, fastening her seatbelt, and he followed suit.

"Now, put your right foot on the brake," she instructed, watching as he followed her guidance. "Good. Now, press the button." He complied, and she nodded in approval. "Great. This is your gear shift," she explained, pointing to the lever in the center console. She ensured he understood their functions by going through each setting—drive, park, neutral, one, and two.

Soon enough, they were backing down the driveway and onto the road. Her car was nowhere in sight, and the road stretched before them, empty and inviting. Bertolf handled the vehicle with unexpected competence, displaying a skill that belied his novice status. Despite the occasional jerky stops and hesitant starts, they navigated the road for half an hour before turning back and returning to the house.

Entering the house, they found Griffin and Quentin in the sitting room, enjoying their drinks. The rest of the group dispersed, seeking rest for the upcoming day. A sense of calm had settled over the house, the atmosphere interrupted only by Quentin and Griffin's playful banter. Griffin's flushed face indicated his indulgence in the liquor cabinet. At the same time, Quentin appeared to have chosen a more measured approach to his drinking.

"Bertolf!" Griffin's boisterous voice called out a bit too loudly. "How are ya, Wolfie?" Rising from his seat, he enveloped Bertolf in a bear hug that seemed to leave the hirsute man uncomfortable. Bertolf stood frozen, his expression reserved, waiting for the embrace to end. Bypassing the duo, Blythe settled into a seat beside Quentin.

"Blythe?" Quentin's arm encircled her, offering reassurance. He spoke softly, concern in his voice.

She briefly closed her eyes, weariness evident in her response. "I'm fine, just a bit tired."

"We could retire for the night," he suggested in a hushed tone. Meanwhile, Griffin had bestowed Bertolf with a drink, and the storyteller was engrossed in a lively tale. Yet Bertolf's attention seemed more focused on Blythe and Quentin than Griffin's narrative.

"Yeah, that sounds like a good plan," she agreed, her ankle's dull ache serving as a persistent reminder of her injury. "I just need to tend to my ankle." Carefully rising from her seat, she began crossing the room. Quentin followed her, stepping into the hallway alongside her. Before she could object, Quentin swept her off her feet, eliciting a surprised gasp from her before she realized that Quentin was securely holding her in his arms. With one arm supporting her legs and the other her back, he drew her close to him.

"No need for you to strain your ankle climbing the stairs," he said playfully, gracefully ascending the steps with her in his arms.

"I can walk perfectly fine, you know," she half-protested, her fatigue setting in as her head rested against his shoulder.

"I'm aware of that, kitten," he responded, kissing her forehead tenderly as they reached the top landing. "So, which way?"

"The first door on the right," she answered, savoring the comfort of his embrace. The door swung open as they approached her bedroom, prompting Quentin to chuckle. He carried her into the room, gently placing her on the edge of her bed.

"Thank you," she murmured softly, her voice reflecting her fatigue. She leaned over to remove her boots, letting them drop to the floor with a satisfying thud. Quentin excused himself with a smile, disappearing into the bathroom. The sound of running water filled the air, indicating he was preparing a bath for her. Moments later, he returned, finding her standing on her bare feet.

"I thought you might want a bath," he said, crossing the room toward her. With one hand behind her back and the other cupping her face, he tilted her chin, sharing a tender kiss on her lips. The kiss was fleeting, leaving her momentarily breathless. Stepping back, he headed toward the bedroom door. "Go ahead and enjoy your bath. I'll be back." His reassuring smile lingered as he exited the room. Her gaze fell upon a small pile of clothing at the end of the bed—her pajamas. Even after all this time, the familiarity of this house was comforting and surprising. She gathered the clothes and entered the bathroom, ensuring the door was locked behind her.

Without hesitation, she shed her clothing and carefully removed the bandage from her ankle before stepping into the steaming hot water. The bubbles enveloped her, carrying the soothing scent of lilacs. Quentin had thoughtfully added a bubble bath to enhance her experience. She sank deeper into the water, letting the warmth seep into her tired muscles, gradually melting away the tension. Leaning her head back against the curved edge of the claw-foot tub, she closed her eyes, surrendering herself to a realm of tranquility. Eventually, the water shut off automatically, signaling the end of her bath.

Slowly, she emerged from the tub's comfort, finding that the water had retained its heat throughout her entire soak—a luxurious indulgence rarely encountered in the human world. She dried herself off, her gaze catching her reflection in the bathroom mirror. Then, she noticed the bruises scattered like shadows across her upper body—an undeniable testament to the intense training she had undergone. Looking down, she examined the minor and more extensive contusions adorned her skin. These silent marks told her story more vividly than words ever could. Slipping into a comfortable tank top and pajama bottoms, she took the time to brush her hair and teeth before finally stepping out of the bathroom.

Quentin was seated on the edge of her bed, closest to the bathroom. His damp hair clung slightly to his forehead, and he wore sweatpants. The definition of his chest and arms was on full display, a sight that she couldn't help but appreciate, even in her exhausted state. Pushing aside the thought, she greeted him with a tired but genuine smile.

"Hey," his grin was warm and welcoming.

"Hi," she replied, crossing the room to the other side of the bed. Retrieving a small jar of salve and a roll of bandages from her pack on the floor, she settled on the edge of the bed and propped her injured foot up on the mattress. Gently, she began applying the salve to her ankle, relieved to see that the bruising had already started to fade with the treatment. Quentin shifted on the bed, his touch light as he traced the edge of a bruise on her shoulder, sending a shiver down her spine. With the wrapping complete, she turned to face him, offering a small but appreciative smile.

"What's that grin for?" he asked playfully, stepping closer. Blythe instinctively raised her hand to halt his approach, her fingers brushing against the solid planes of his chest. She pulled her hand away quickly, embarrassment warming her cheeks.

"I... I'm not sure... I know what you're thinking, and I'm just not quite ready for..." She stumbled over her words, her heart racing as her thoughts jumbled together. He reached out and caught her hand, his touch gentle yet firm, preventing her from pulling away completely.

"Don't fret, kitten. Tomorrow promises a long day," Quentin reassured her, his gaze locking onto hers, brimming with longing. "And believe me, the desires are strong." A blush tinted her cheeks at his words.

"However, I've been awake for two days straight." With his spare hand, he drew her closer, an irresistible magnetic force. His scent mingled with aftershave and soap, and she found herself appreciating the rugged outline of his jaw and the allure of his lips. Their mouths met before she could fully grasp the situation, igniting an intense fervor within her. Her arm instinctively circled his neck while her other hand pressed gently against his chest, savoring the robust sensation beneath her fingertips. His arm slipped behind her back, his other hand caressing the curve of her neck.

He lifted and lowered her onto the bed in an instant, his lips briefly parting from hers before descending with renewed passion. He straddled her, his weight carefully distributed, yet the kiss remained fervent. Reluctantly breaking the kiss, he traced a trail of fiery kisses along her jawline, each touch setting her skin ablaze. One arm was anchored by her head, and his other hand explored the contours of her side.

As abruptly as it had begun, he pulled back, rolling onto his side and resting beside her. Both of them were breathless, chests heaving with intensity. She lay there, studying his features, endeavoring to catch her breath and quiet her racing heart. Her mind raced with a whirlwind of emotions, a mixture of desire and uncertainty. The room seemed to pulse with the shared intensity of their moment, the air laden with anticipation.

Quentin turned toward her, his gaze soft and searching. "Blythe, I didn't mean to push—"

She silenced him with a finger on his lips, her eyes locking onto his. "I wanted this," she admitted, her voice barely above a whisper. "I want this, Quentin."

A smile tugged at the corner of his lips, and he leaned in to kiss her forehead gently. "I want it too," he confessed, his voice filled with emotion that resonated with her.

They lay together in silence, wrapped in each other's presence, the weight of their unspoken desires hanging in the air. The room was bathed in the soft glow of moonlight filtering through the curtains, casting a serene aura over their shared moment.

Quentin's fingers traced idle patterns on her arm as they drifted into a peaceful slumber. The events of the day, the journey, and the revelations had taken their toll on both of them. With their hearts and minds entwined, they surrendered to the embrace of sleep, finding solace in each other's arms as the night deepened.

CHAPTER THIRTY-TWO

"Good morning," Quentin's face was closed as her eyes fluttered open. He kissed her gently and unhurried. A knock on the door startled them apart. She swiftly covered Quentin's mouth before he could speak.

"Just a moment!" she called, quickly leaving the bed. Surprisingly and thankfully, her ankle felt fine. Maybe the House's bath had done more than she thought it could. Glancing back, she saw Quentin's amused look. Cracking the door open, she positioned herself to block the visitor's view. It was Griffin, grumbling a morning greeting and letting her know it was time to get moving.

"Thanks, Griffin. I'll join you downstairs shortly," she replied, closing the door quickly. Turning, she found Quentin heading for the bathroom.

"Not ready to face the world?" he teased. "A bit of secrecy adds thrill. I wonder where else we could sneak in some clandestine rendezvous?" Annoyed, she considered throwing something at him, spotting a pillow at the foot of the bed. But before she could grab it, Quentin had disappeared into the bathroom, laughing. Despite his irritating remarks, an instinctual part of her yearned to follow him and explore the possibilities. She resisted and, instead, opened the window to let in the cool breeze.

Leaning against the windowsill, she gazed outside. Birds sang, and the sky had a few fluffy clouds. Stepping away, she closed the window and turned to see Quentin emerging from the bathroom. He was wearing jeans, no shirt, and no socks. He tossed clothes onto the bed.

"Now, come here, Kitten," he beckoned with a mischievous grin. She moved out of his reach, but he caught her around the waist from behind, his lips at the base of her neck.

"Alright, alright!" She managed to free herself from Quentin's grasp and headed toward the bathroom, snatching a pile of clothing. She pointed a warning finger at him as she closed the bathroom door.

Shortly after, she descended the stairs, fully dressed and refreshed. They gathered in the dining room, where a bountiful breakfast spread awaited. Quentin and Griffin were engrossed in conversation. Bertolf's intense gaze followed her. She hesitated but eventually took a seat. They laughed as Griffin shared stories of drunken escapades.

After breakfast, they gathered their supplies. Blythe handed Bertolf the Prius keys. Griffin, Hera, and Quentin piled into one car while the others took the second. She gave Bertolf some last-minute instructions before they set off.

As they drove, Quentin fiddled with the radio. A blast of static startled them. Blythe quickly turned it off.

"Maybe we'll skip the radio," she suggested gently.

"What the hell was that god-awful noise?" Griffin growled from the back seat. Hera remained stoic. Packs were scattered around them, with more in the trunks.

"That was radio static," she explained, breaking the silence. "It happens with bad reception." A moment of quiet followed.

"So, it's like those jolts you get from shuffling on a carpet in socks?" Griffin asked, seeking a relatable analogy. She acknowledged the challenge of explaining the concept accurately.

Blythe retrieved her phone, plugged it in, and queued up her playlist with the volume down. The car filled with '90s music. Quentin seemed fascinated by the passing vehicles, and Griffin was unusually quiet, occasionally pointing out cars.

After a little over two hours of driving, they reached mountains and dense forests. They parked outside a small town and prepared to continue on foot. Blythe turned to Quentin.

"Where do you go from here?" she asked, her eyes locked onto his.

"Demetrius gave me this map," he replied, producing it from his pocket. "We continue on foot."

"Good. I've brought you this far, as promised," Blythe stated, stepping back as the others got ready.

"You can't," Hera interjected. "It's not safe for you in this world yet."

"I'll be alright here. I'll go back to the House and wait there," Blythe reassured her.

"Blythe..." Quentin began, but she silenced him with a shake of her head.

"No, you don't need me. I'm not fully trained in my magical abilities and utterly unfamiliar with the Dark World and the Magic World. I've done what I could to assist. Now it's up to you guys." Blythe's awareness of the other members observing their exchange made her feel exposed.

Quentin sighed, and her attention was drawn to Griffin, who was inching away, clutching a needle. A wave of dizziness washed over her, blurring her vision. Her legs wobbled, and Quentin promptly caught her, offering sturdy support as her consciousness teetered.

"I'm sorry, Kitten," he murmured softly, the world gradually fading to black as she surrendered to the embrace of unconsciousness.

CHAPTER THIRTY-THREE

Gradually, Blythe's senses reawakened, her eyes fluttering open as she winced against the harsh assault of sunlight. Bound and gagged, she lay on the ground, her view askew, revealing the rugged landscape of rocks, a babbling stream, and a looming cavern entrance. Slowly, her vision cleared, and a tumultuous battle unfurled before her. Magic crackled in the air, clashes of weapons resounded, and anguished cries pierced the atmosphere. Her struggles against the restraints got her nowhere, stoking her frustration. Doubts about the trustworthiness of anyone in the Magic World swirled within her, explicitly aimed at Griffin and Quentin. Still, all the others had allowed her to be abducted, too. So they were no better.

Blythe, squinting through the brightness, focused on the frenzied figures within the melee. A gleaming figure clad in armor engaged in a fierce duel with another brandishing a long staff. Their movements rapidly blurred as they crossed the stream, each refusing to yield. Eventually, the armored warrior gained the upper hand, delivering a fatal blow to their opponent's chest. Blythe's muffled scream was stifled by the gag pressing against her mouth.

The victorious figure withdrew their sword, leaving their fallen adversary to be claimed by the current. It was Hera.

Blythe's shock deepened, her attention drawn to a robust, dark-skinned man locked in a grappling match with a lithe, agile opponent—Quentin. Employing a blend of strength and surprising agility, Quentin held his ground. At the same time, Hera approached the skirmish from behind, swiftly severing their foe's head. The detached cranium tumbled, and the lifeless form crumpled, akin to a puppet with its strings cut.

Nausea churned within Blythe's gut as more combatants fell, reducing their numbers to a mere eight. Some paused to cleanse themselves in the stream. In contrast, others congregated around her, reclaiming their packs and preparing for the next move. Quentin crouched nearby, washing his bloodstained hands, his somber expression shifting when he caught sight of her awakening gaze. She endeavored to direct a glare his way, but the gag and bindings stifled her efforts. He approached cautiously, extending a hand to brush her cheek. Blythe recoiled as much as her constraints allowed, prompting him to retract his touch.

"I'm genuinely sorry, kitten. I had orders," Quentin explained, Hera, standing sentinel behind him as she gathered her belongings. "If I hadn't, someone else would've. I had to ensure your safety and well-being."

Blythe's retort was muffled by the gag. "I know," Quentin sighed, lifting her from the ground and cradling her as he had the previous night. He strode across the stream, her body squirming in defiance.

"Marlan, Venus, the two of you will stay behind, alongside a few Warlocks, to safeguard this portal. We can't allow the darkness to infiltrate this realm, regardless of our doings in the Magic World," Quentin commanded, addressing two figures who set down their packs near the cave entrance. "Rest must wait. We're in the dark about Miles and his crew's fate, and the threat of traitors looms. We press on." The group assembled before the cavern's yawning abyss. Blythe's gaze beseeched Quentin wordlessly. He leaned down, planting a gentle kiss on her forehead. "I'll release you once we're inside."

She wriggled and strained against her bonds as Quentin advanced, but her resistance proved futile. Peering into the cave's shadowy depths, she discerned four figures emerging—one pair resembling ordinary men. At the same time, the other two women possessed an eerie, grayish complexion and eyes that glowed like radiant slits.

"Identify yourself," Quentin commanded, directing his words at the largest of the quartet.

"I am Palus, and these are my comrades," the man introduced himself, a formal tilt accompanying the gesture.

Quentin mirrored the acknowledgment.

"I'm Quentin. Demetrius has dispatched us to traverse the Dark World and aid your escape to the Magic World. Our counterparts in the Magic World will lend support from that side of the Mireglow Fen Bogs," Quentin elaborated, engaging in a swift dialogue with Palus before leading the group deeper into the cave.

As they delved into the gloom, a smoldering anger coursed through Blythe. How could Quentin have orchestrated this betrayal? With each step, the cave's darkness intensified, reducing visibility to a mere few feet. The others' footfalls blended into the cave's dripping cadence, strangely devoid of the expected bat noises. Quentin's hushed words barely permeated the cave's steady rhythm as he whispered, "I apologize for this whole situation." Blythe emitted an incredulous noise in response. "I'll explain everything once we're past the portal."

"Look," Griffin's voice pierced the silence beside Quentin, jolting Blythe from her thoughts. She hadn't even detected his presence until then. "I see the light."

"Red light," Hera's whisper brushed the air from the opposite side of Quentin.

"That's our target," Quentin affirmed. Their pace quickened as the luminance expanded, but so did Blythe's trepidation. The crimson radiance ahead felt like a danger she hadn't bargained for. Her attempts to break free from her restraints met Quentin's unyielding hold, thwarting any escape endeavor. Trapped and suffocated by helplessness, her frustration churned within her.

As they neared the source of the light, it dimmed intermittently as figures crossed its path—likely their comrades who had preceded them. Quentin's pace slackened, the uncertainty of the situation forcing the group into a hesitant pause, with Blythe still clutched by Quentin's grip.

"Stay vigilant," Quentin's voice brushed the air, a barely audible whisper. "They could be demons. The Warlocks assured Demetrius of security, but we can't take their word for granted."

Pressing onward, the cave's interior brightened, the reddish hue penetrating its depths. The advancing figures retreated cautiously, their wariness tangible. Finally, the group emerged at the threshold of a cavern, similar in appearance to the outside but bathed in an eerie red illumination, casting the surroundings in an uncanny twilight glow despite the visible sun. Blythe's attention shifted to the figures ahead, now clearly visible. Four distinct individuals awaited—one with blonde hair, another with flowing blue locks, one with closely shorn hair, and a woman bearing long, curly black tresses. It was the latter who stepped forward to greet Griffin and Hera. All four shared the distinctive gray skin of the Warlocks they'd encountered before, their appearance blurring the lines between humans, witches, and wizards. Blythe pondered whether this was their original appearance or a product of their time in the Dark World.

"You must be Demetrius's crew. We were beginning to worry that you might not arrive," the woman greeted, extending her hand toward Hera, a gesture reciprocated with a firm shake.

"By the beards of the ancients, we got through easier than we thought with the Lumina Amulet!" Griffin exclaimed. Blythe noticed a fleeting expression on the Warlocks' faces, though it disappeared quickly. Doubts about handing over the artifacts crept into her mind.

"We four shall guide you through the Dark World, leading you to the opposite portal. But be forewarned, the journey is perilous. Caution must guide our every step, for even in this realm, adversaries await. Some relish the quarry cast into this abyss by the council," she warned, a shadow passing over her features. "The council's dominion has lasted far too long. It is time we bring an end to their rule."

Quentin carefully placed Blythe on the ground, removing the gag from her mouth. She erupted in anger. "How could you, Quentin Hendrix! Kidnapping me like this? You had no authority! I fulfilled my end of the bargain. I was supposed to be free. To go back home!" Quentin untangled the ropes around her wrists, but as she raised her hand to strike him, he deftly captured her wrists, preventing the blow.

"Blythe, your anger is justified, but remember, we're in the Dark World now. This isn't the time or place," Quentin reasoned while Griffin efficiently worked to untie her ankles. Stepping away, Griffin evaded her kick, granting her freedom with calculated caution.

"Have you two finished arguing about your love life? We've got a mission to complete," Hera interrupted, making her presence known next to Blythe. "You can sort out your issues with Quentin and the rest of us after we've done what we came here to do. Right now, let's concentrate on the job." Blythe tried to leave through the portal but was blocked by the four Warlocks.

"Apologies, miss," one spoke, remorse underscoring his words. "You can't return through. You're entwined in this now. Make the best of it."

Blythe's gaze pierced their defense before shifting to the waiting group. Her missing backpack caught her attention – a consequence of having to carry her alongside her supplies. Yet, her primary concern remained her festering indignation.

"Fine," she snapped tersely. "Let's just get this done." Quentin ventured forward, but she halted him with an upraised hand, gesturing for him to keep his distance. Purposeful strides directed her towards the four Warlocks, shadowing their steps, and the group continued their trek. While the terrain resembled the Human World, Blythe couldn't ignore the oddity in the stream's composition.

"Don't drink from the water," Melya, the voice of earlier caution, advised as they walked side by side. "The demons have tainted many of the freshwater sources with their blood. We have methods to purify it, but it's a constant struggle." Despite Melya's extended hand, Blythe ignored the gesture, her anger unrelenting. Undeterred, Melya persisted, her voice retaining its untroubled cadence. "I'm Melya, by the way. I'm guessing you're Blythe?" Blythe's surprise briefly lifted her silence.

"Yeah, I am," she replied curtly.

"We don't need to talk if you don't want to," Melya acknowledged.

They continued, their footsteps echoing amidst the renewed chatter swirling among the group—a medley of exchanged information and stories from both realms.

"I figure it's fair I provide a little context. All right?" Melya finally broke the silence. Blythe's lips remained sealed. "You're Demetrius's niece, aren't you?" The inquiry caught Blythe off guard, her gaze meeting Melya's. "He was aware of why he was punished. He knew your name and had speculated you might end up here one day." Melya's smile radiated warmth.

"I really don't need to talk," Blythe muttered, her reluctance palpable.

"I get it. But sometimes, on a tough day, having someone try to lift your spirits can be kind even if you're not receptive. At least, that's how I see it," Melya's laughter danced in the air.

"Ah, lover squabbles, they can be so overly dramatic," Griffin joked from ahead.

"He's not—" Blythe started, her volume slightly too elevated, momentarily halting the surrounding discussions.

Melya chuckled, "Okay, not your boyfriend. Got it."

Silence once more settled in their midst, punctuated by revived dialogues. Quentin slid to Melya's other side.

"We need to talk," he asserted.

"I'm not talking to you. I'm here engaged in an enlightening exchange with the delightful Melya. I'll converse and socialize with her and the Warlocks until they inevitably deceive me, just like everyone else," Blythe countered, her eyes fixed ahead, refusing to direct her gaze toward Quentin.

"Alright then," Melya interjected with her playful cadence intact. "So, what's your take on the council?"

"Not much, honestly... I've gathered that it once had a diverse makeup. Still, now it's exclusively witches and wizards," Blythe replied, her gaze drifting across the landscape as they ascended a densely forested hill. "And they seem to be a bunch of jerks."

"Two out of three ain't bad... We've had suspicions that the council is a mere puppet. The elder Warlocks were accumulating evidence before we were exiled to this forsaken realm. My mother, who held my position prior, was slain by a gang of orcs," Melya's posture carried a heavy burden of grief, her eyes betraying the shimmer of unshed tears as she recounted the harrowing past. She fell into silence, her emotions palpable, before resuming with a fragile smile. "But you know what they say, right? 'Warlocks don't die; they just go missing in the Dark World.'"

Blythe's heart ached for Melya, and while her anger towards Quentin still festered, the unfamiliar sentiment of camaraderie stirred within her. "I'm sorry about your mother."

"Thank you," Melya's gratitude was heartfelt. "And I understand your frustration with him."

Melya's gaze held a glint of wisdom as she continued, "Blythe, in a place like the Dark World, unity among our group is crucial. Sometimes, people's actions and words may have motives behind them that we don't understand until we listen and watch. Trust me, we're all here for a reason and must make the best of this situation. Hearing Quentin out might bring some clarity."

Blythe clenched her fists, her anger still simmering, but Melya's words had made an impact. After contemplating, she finally conceded, "Alright, I'll hear him out."

"I'm sorry that I betrayed your trust. I couldn't just let you leave us, Blythe," Quentin began, his brows etched with sincere concern.

"More like you wouldn't let me. I don't want to hear excuses from you, Quentin!" Blythe snapped. Her frustration grew, and she even wished she could express her anger more forcefully, like a wild cat that could literally bite his head off.

"Fae tend to forge potent bonds... Demetrius requested that I ensure you remain with us. Initially, I contemplated betraying him and helping you go free from us. But it became clear that if I didn't do it, someone else would, and I needed to make sure you were well taken care of. Blythe, I care deeply about you and couldn't sit back and watch you possibly get hurt," Quentin confessed, his gaze unwavering.

"Well, tough luck for you because as soon as I can, I'm gone, and I've got zero interest in any of this, especially not you," Blythe retorted, folding her arms tightly. A wall of silence returned.

Abruptly, Melya halted, extending her arms to signal both Blythe and Quentin to stop.

"We've got company," Melya declared, her cerulean hair catching the subdued light.

"What are we dealing with?" Quentin inquired, scanning the vicinity, his perception failing to match the Warlocks' insights. Blythe noted the puzzled expressions etched on their companions' faces. Hera poised herself, sword at the ready, primed for any threat.

"Ghouls," the blond Warlock confirmed, positioning herself on Blythe's opposite side.

"They're not alone," the shaven-head Warlock added, taking his place at Quentin's flank.

"Dark elves, too," Melya contributed. Following a brief pause, she appended, "Plus demons."

"Orcs," Bertolf growled, making his presence known a short distance behind Blythe.

"How can you tell?" Blythe inquired, her curiosity piqued. While aware of the Warlocks' mystical abilities, Bertolf's distinct origins from another realm intrigued her.

"I can smell them," Bertolf snarled, his senses keenly attuned to the impending peril.

"Get ready for a fight!" Quentin commanded. Blythe shifted her focus to the forest ahead, just in time to witness shadowy figures emerging from the cover of trees. Events unfurled in a whirlwind, almost dizzyingly swift for her comprehension.

Blythe's attention shifted to her right. Melya deftly wove light strands between her palms, crafting an orb that merged crimson and obsidian shades. The other Warlocks synchronized their spells—summoning a sphere, conjuring an imposing spear, and one even kneeling to enact a ritual on the ground. Blythe realized her lack of weaponry, armed only with two spells that might prove helpful. She felt a step behind as the others surged ahead, plunging into the fray with determination.

Melya's light erupted, fragmenting into a constellation of eight smaller spheres colliding with unseen assailants, illuminating them like vibrant Christmas lights. The other Warlocks swiftly dispatched their targets. Griffin, Bertolf, and the original expedition members grappled with tangible foes—lithe beings resembling elves, propelled by unyielding aggression.

"One more wave from behind!" a Warlock's voice rang out. Blythe turned to witness a group of six figures converging on them. The non-combatants repositioned, forming a vigilant defensive circle with backs pressed together, ready to repel the impending threat.

"Hold on!" a voice cut through the tension. "We figured you might need a hand, considering your daring mission. Apologies for our delayed entrance."

"Miles?" Hera's voice rang out as Blythe scanned the approaching figures.

"It could be a trap..." someone cautioned, casting a shadow of doubt.

"Wait!" Blythe interjected, her gaze locked on the approaching figure. A mix of skepticism and determination played across her features. "Prove you're who you claim to be."

"Fair enough," he conceded, pausing briefly to recollect. A sly grin emerged. "Oh, I remember now! Our first encounter was when we were about six. You were supposed to be confined to your room because of Dorian... your father wanted to keep your existence a secret. Yet, my curiosity always got the better of me. I sneaked upstairs. Surprisingly, your door was left open, so I wandered in. There you were—a beautiful sight. Given your striking looks, I couldn't resist asking if you were fae." He chuckled. "And do you remember your response? You asked if I were a dwarf because of my short stature."

A smile tugged at Blythe's lips, a brief respite amid the gathering darkness.

"Memories aside, we can reminisce after this skirmish!" Hera rallied the group. They turned as one to confront the impending onslaught. Miles approached Blythe, his focus on her rather than the fray.

"I'm sorry for not telling you the truth, Blythe," his familiar azure eyes offered comfort in the bleak surroundings.

"Honesty seems scarce lately... but there's no time for this conversation now," she replied, returning to the encroaching foes.

"Later then?" Miles asked, his hands poised for action.

"Yes," Blythe affirmed, determination etched in her gaze.

"Very well... now it's time to deal with these darklings!" Miles declared. His stance held for an instant before a gleaming white spear materialized in his grasp. With practiced precision, the spear soared over their comrades before piercing the chest of a dark elf, who crumpled as the weapon dissolved into the air.

In the chaotic clash of battle, dizziness threatened to overwhelm Blythe. Suddenly, Griffin appeared by her side, thrusting a short sword into her hand. "Take this, lass! Don't just stand there. Fight for your life!" His urgency spurred her into action as Miles and Hera positioned themselves nearby, shielding her from the onslaught of attacks. The situation's intensity gripped her, and she could feel the weight of their defense hanging by a thread.

A grotesque creature lunged at her, and fear surged through her veins. Instinct took over as she moved to parry the attack, but her footing faltered, and she stumbled. Just as the creature's blade loomed over her, a powerful impact knocked it aside. Eyes tightly shut, she braced for the hit, only to find herself untouched beneath the lifeless body of the creature that had moments ago been a threat. Her own spear had saved her, an unexpected ally.

Gripping her spear with determination, she regained her balance and swiftly pivoted, facing an approaching adversary head-on. Adrenaline fueled her movements as she swung her sword, meeting the creature's advance with fierce resolve. The blade found its mark, slicing through flesh before she deftly withdrew it. Surprisingly, she repeated the motion, her actions flowing smoothly despite her lack of formal training. How was she pulling this off with such agility?

Facing another opponent, she evaded a sweeping ax agilely and retaliated with a quick slash to its exposed side. A pained shriek filled the air, yet the creature pressed on, its ferocity undiminished. She sidestepped just in time, narrowly avoiding the deadly arc of the ax, her torn shirt bearing witness to the near miss.

In an instant, a luminous spear pierced the creature, causing it to dissolve into nothingness. Miles appeared at her side, a grin playing on his lips. She returned the smile, their unspoken camaraderie bolstering her determination. Side by side, they stood against the relentless tide of enemies, each movement a testament to their shared resolve. Fear had faded, replaced by a surge of newfound courage that propelled her deeper into the fray.

Yet, during her fight, a sudden impact sent shockwaves through her senses, and darkness descended. Her consciousness teetered on the edge of oblivion, the sounds of battle a distant echo. As her vision faded to black, the cacophony of conflict remained, a stark contrast to the featureless void enveloping her —a boundless expanse devoid of walls, floor, and ceiling, where nothing existed except impenetrable darkness.

CHAPTER THIRTY-FOUR

"Hello?!" Blythe's voice sliced through the air but vanished into the silence surrounding her. A chilling laughter emerged, reminiscent of eerie movie voices, its tones deep and menacing.

"Hello, dearie," the voice sneered, its words slithering into her mind. "Care to let me borrow your body for a while?"

"Uh... a firm 'no' to that!" Blythe's sword swung with determination, only to meet empty space. The voice's laughter echoed again, a twisted symphony in the darkness.

"Sorry, consent's not on my agenda. Now, be a good girl, and hush!" A jarring blow struck her head, stars dancing before her eyes. Struggling to regain her balance, she fought the disorienting onslaught. Invisible hands seemed to press her down, melding her with the ground. She thrashed, clawing at the unseen restraints, her struggles futile.

"Help!" Her voice strained, tears mingling with desperation. "Miles! Quentin! Hera! Griffin!" Her pleas dissolved, sinking into the void. Battling the invisible assailant, Blythe felt her strength ebbing away. The voice's laughter swelled as phantom hands pushed her deeper into the abyss.

Finally, she lay on the ground, sword clutched tightly, her sobs the only testament to her ordeal.

Blythe's consciousness languished in an all-encompassing void where darkness was a tangible entity. Boundaries melted, space and time lost in the black expanse. Isolation trapped her in her mind, a disconnect from the outside world.

Straining, she yearned for sound, but a deafening silence engulfed her. Battle cries were absent, replaced by the eerie laughter reverberating like a haunting melody. Her spine tingled with primal fear, an instinctual response to the malevolence that encased her.

Attempts to move met resistance; invisible chains held her in place. Quicksand-like sensations pulled her down, her struggles in vain. She was a spectator, a reluctant passenger in her own body, trapped on this ominous journey.

Laughter transformed into a voice dripping with malevolence. "How amusing to watch you squirm, Blythe," the voice taunted, dripping with contempt. "Resisting, yet utterly within my grasp."

Blythe's thoughts raced, desperate to reclaim control, to shatter this malevolent hold. Her voice strained, futilely attempting to summon strength, yet her pleas vanished into the void. Mockery laced the voice's response, reveling in her vulnerability.

As minutes stretched into eternity, Blythe's spirit flagged, despair's weight threatening to engulf her. Tears welled, mourning stolen moments and yearning for a lost life. Yet, from within despair's depths, a spark of determination ignited. She refused to succumb.

Summoning willpower, she fixated on memories of loved ones, their faces igniting a defiant fire within her. Resilience surged, her spirit defiantly radiant amidst encroaching shadows. The voice recoiled, sensing her newfound strength.

Defiant to the core, Blythe rallied the fragments of her shattered self. She mustered her deepest wellsprings of courage and unwavering love for her dear companions, channeling them into a single, unyielding thought: "I am Blythe, and darkness will not overcome me."

A blinding surge of energy tore through her, shattering the chains of captivity. The darkness wavered, vanishing like mist under the morning sun. Blythe's consciousness reintegrated with her body, her mind reclaiming its dominion.

Gone was the oppressive weight, replaced by the rush of life coursing through her veins. The frigid grip subsided as her arm lowered, her gaze meeting Melya's face.

"Hey there," Melya chimed, a cheerful greeting. "Good to

have you back in the land of the living."

"Blythe!" Quentin appeared over Melya's shoulder, with Miles on her other side.

"Is it really her?" Miles inquired, concern etched into his features.

"Oh yes... The demon's influence has waned," Melya exhaled, her relief tangible as her shoulders relaxed and her stance eased. Her eyes conveyed reassurance, affirming the significance of the moment. She extended her hand to Blythe, the heat of her touch searing through Blythe's palm. With a yelp, Blythe pulled back. "Sorry, dear. Your senses will recalibrate in a few moments," Melya explained, creating distance to allow Blythe space. Gradually, her balance returned, and her senses reacclimatized to normalcy. Surveying the battlefield, she noticed the abating chaos. Quentin re-engaged with Hera, helping fend off a looming foe reminiscent of the earlier adversaries—before what?

Blythe's brow knits in a soft expression of confusion. She scanned her surroundings, piecing together fragmented memories of her possession. As she tried to comprehend, Melya shifted her focus. Purposeful and fluid, she knelt beside the fallen, eyes critically assessing.

"Demon took hold of your body," Miles murmured. Blythe brushed off her hands and retrieved her sword from where it had fallen. Miles recounted the eerie events. "Your eyes rolled back, and—I kid you not—you floated above the ground. Like that movie, 'The Exorcism of Emily Rose,' remember?"

"Ah, yes," Blythe recalled, a shiver running down her spine as memories of the spine-chilling film resurfaced.

"Exactly," Miles affirmed, a smile touching his lips. "It was eerie, and Melya was concerned if the demon would be able to use your magic. We'd be in some serious trouble. But I'm glad you're back."

"Likewise," Blythe replied, reciprocating the smile.

"Time to move," Quentin interjected. Melya and Miles helped her up and they resumed their trek.

Pressing forward, they navigated treacherous terrain, their determination mingling with exhaustion. Seeking sanctuary, a place for respite and strategy, they faced a rugged path.

Winding through a dense forest, unease settled over them. Leaves rustled, distant growls hinting at lurking threats. Blythe's instincts flared, signaling the group to halt. Huddled, eyes darting, tension thickened.

A horde of menacing figures emerged from the shadows —an amalgam of demons, orcs, and trolls. Grotesque forms and gleaming malevolence signaled an ambush.

With a battle cry, dark creatures surged forth. Steel met claw, and magic clashed with might. The air crackled as combatants danced in a symphony of survival, chaos reigning supreme.

A novice in hand-to-hand combat and magic, Blythe found herself thrust into the heart of the battle against the menacing horde of demons, orcs, and trolls. Her grip on the sword tightened, her hands trembling under the unfamiliar weight. Within her, a wellspring of magic remained untamed, its potential uncharted.

With cautious steps, Blythe engaged her adversaries. Her sword swings lacked the finesse of a seasoned warrior, yet her eyes blazed with unwavering determination. Her attacks were driven by sheer willpower, each swing a testament to her refusal to succumb to inexperience.

CHAPTER THIRTY-FIVE

Blythe's attempts at using magic were unpredictable. She struggled to produce spells during the chaotic battle, and her sword swings lacked the finesse of a seasoned warrior. But giving up wasn't an option; determination pushed her forward, guiding her through the tumultuous fray.

Amidst the battle's frenzy, Blythe adapted on the fly, evolving her approach with each encounter. Her initial hesitation gave way to newfound confidence as she navigated the chaos.

Miles, a seasoned mage, took on the role of her battle mentor. Together, they forged a formidable partnership, unleashing her latent magical potential with his guidance.

Progress unfolded steadily but surely. Blythe's skills improved with each defeated adversary, enabling her to pinpoint vulnerabilities and channel her magic more effectively.

While her swordsmanship and magic remained works in progress, her unwavering determination pushed her onward, undaunted by her limited experience.

Quentin, a master archer, joined her side, using his keen eyes to identify enemy weak points, every arrow finding its mark. She set aside her animosity towards him and together, they became an unstoppable duo.

Amid the battlefield's cacophony—clashing metal, demonic growls, and thunderous troll roars—Blythe's senses sharpened, adrenaline keeping her laser-focused.

Then, an earth-shattering roar rattled the ground, sending panic coursing through Blythe as her companions vanished in the turmoil.

Blythe continued to fight her way through the horde, desperately searching for her allies, hoping they could regroup.

As time passed, her desperation grew. She called out for

her friends, her voice filled with worry. Yet, she remained focused on her immediate surroundings, trusting that destiny would reunite them.

The battle reached a crescendo, and the once chaotic battlefield grew quiet. Bodies littered the scarred terrain and filled the air with a sense of dread.

Guided by unwavering belief, Blythe moved with determination, searching for Miles among the aftermath. Her voice echoed with his name as she moved through the debris and fallen enemies.

Her hope dwindled with each passing moment. Warlocks tended to their wounded while Griffin and Quentin shared a moment of reassurance. Hera, covered in blood and filth, cared for Marlan and Venus. But Miles was nowhere to be seen.

Blythe's frantic search became more desperate, her voice filled with urgency. The battlefield revealed no trace of Miles, and her heart grew heavy with worry.

She moved through the battlefield, the scent of smoke stinging her eyes. Fear gripped her as she continued her search, her steps growing heavier with each passing moment.

Then, she spotted a motionless figure among the carnage. It was Miles. His face was pale, and blood stained the ground around him. He appeared lifeless.

Tears welled in Blythe's eyes as she rushed toward him, the world around her fading away. Everything grew eerily quiet as she reached his side.

Kneeling beside him, Blythe's horror deepened. Miles lay motionless, his armor telling the story of a valiant struggle. But now, he was still a fallen hero.

Grief overwhelmed Blythe as she mourned his loss. She clutched his cold cheek, her tears blurring her vision. Memories of their time together flooded her mind, forever tainted by this tragedy.

She pleaded with him, her voice choked with sorrow, but Miles remained lifeless. Time seemed to stand still as Blythe's world shattered.

She let out a heart-wrenching cry, her sobs echoing across the battlefield. Her cries of grief filled the air as she began the painful journey of mourning her lost love.

"Why did you have to come here..." Her words were filled with regret and longing as she gently caressed his forehead. "You could have been safe..." She lamented the hopes they had for a future together.

"I love you..." Her voice quivered as she expressed her deep affection, tears streaming down her face. Blythe's fingers trembled as she held Miles's lifeless hand. Her world had shattered into a thousand pieces, and grief threatened to consume her.

Time seemed to stand still as she clung to his still form, her heart heavy with sorrow. The battle raged around her, but she was oblivious to the chaos.

A faint voice broke through her despair, and Blythe opened her eyes to see Miles's fading gaze. His words were weak but carried a weight that etched into her soul.

"Blythe," Miles coughed, his voice strained and raspy. "You're... special," he gasped for breath, each word a labor. "Wanted... you... love Hera," his breathing became erratic, struggling to continue. "Good times, right?"

Blythe's vision blurred through teary eyes. "Yes," she whispered, her voice quivering. "We did."

"Happiness... both," he whispered, a fleeting smile touching his lips. "Tell Hera…" A fleeting smile touched his lips, a moment of peace within the chaos. His eyes closed, his hand slipping from hers, his flame extinguished forever.

Grief and love mingled as Blythe nodded, her voice barely a whisper. "I promise, Miles. She'll know."

Tears streamed down Blythe's face as she gently touched Miles's cold cheek, her fingers quivering. Memories of their shared laughter and stolen moments flooded her mind, now forever tainted by loss.

"Miles... No, please, no," she pleaded, her words lost in the anguish of her grief. She clung to him, desperately hoping for any sign of warmth or life. But it was futile; the light in his eyes had faded, leaving only emptiness.

Time felt suspended as Blythe remained there, her world shattered. The sounds of battle echoed around her, a harsh reminder of the cruel reality that had taken Miles. Grief enveloped her, its icy grip threatening to drown her.

With the weight of loss bearing down on her, Blythe's anguish erupted into a gut-wrenching wail, her cries piercing the battlefield and reaching the heavens. Each sob wracked her body, a lament for a love cut tragically short.

"Why did you have to come here..." Her words were filled with regret and yearning as she tenderly traced her fingers across his forehead, caressing him with affection and sorrow. "You could have been safe..." Her voice held the echoes of unspoken hopes, a shattered future.

"I love you..." Her voice cracked, a trembling sob releasing the weight of her being. Emotions resonated in her words, an unspoken longing. Tears welled once more as she hoped her declaration could bridge the gap between them, transcending barriers. Her forehead met his, seeking solace even in pain.

Someone's fingers gently touched her shoulder, but Blythe recoiled, not ready to be torn from Miles. Griffin's voice broke through, gently reminding her, "Blythe, lass, we must go..."

"I can't leave him..." she sobbed, her grip on Miles's hand tightening. Yet Griffin and the others persisted, urging her away, driven by the urgency of survival.

"No..." she cried, her heart shattering further as they pulled her from Miles. She sorrowfully gazed at him, etching his form into her memory.

Amid her grief, a sound drew her attention. Nearby, Hera stood, mirroring Blythe's pain. Covered in blood and filth, with her sword embedded in the mud, Hera's agony was palpable. Their eyes met, silently conveying their shared loss.

"He's gone, love," Griffin's voice conveyed the painful truth. Another sob escaped Blythe, the finality of Miles's absence echoing. Hera's gaze locked with Blythe's, a mix of anger and sorrow overshadowing their connection.

"I couldn't..." Blythe gasped, her fingers curling into fists as if grasping her helplessness. Her voice quivered, each word revealing her inability to save him. Tear-glistened eyes met Hera's, seeking forgiveness.

Hera's tear-streaked face mirrored the roiling emotions within Blythe, silently sharing their sorrow and regret. Hera's gaze remained fixed on Miles, her expression a blend of grief and unwavering determination. With deliberate yet pained movements, she meticulously wiped her sword clean with a cloth. The rhythmic motion symbolized closure and the steadfast commitment to persevere. As the blade found its sheath, a sense of finality hung in the air, an unspoken vow to honor the fallen and carry the battle forward.

Turning back, Hera walked toward the gathering group, seeking solace in their collective anguish. Blythe's eyes tracked Hera's path, watching as Bertolf and Marlan lent their support—a united stance against the ravages of war. Slowly, Blythe hoisted herself up. Bertolf and Marlan released her gently, their gazes brimming with empathy as they rejoined the others.

Casting a final glance at her childhood love, Blythe's heart weighed heavy with loss. She pivoted and began her departure. A backward glance allowed her gaze to sweep the desolate battlefield one last time, desperately trying to imprint the scene in her memory. Amidst the wreckage and debris, a glimmer caught her attention—a shard of metal.

She hesitated, her gaze fixing on a nearby object. A glimmer in the dim light revealed Miles's cherished talisman, a pocket watch. Time seemed to stand still as she knelt, gently retrieving it, her fingers trembling with a mixture of sorrow and reverence.

The pocket watch possessed a substantial weight, its familiar heft a poignant reminder of their shared connection. Blythe's thumb traced over the engraved initials, the intricate design capturing Miles's essence. This trinket encapsulated their love, a silent keepsake of his being, now left behind as a testament to his existence.

As she held the pocket watch, a sudden realization struck her. It was more than just a memento; it was Miles's magic anchor. It had bound his magic to him. Tears welled once more as she clutched the pocket watch close to her heart, finding solace in this tangible link to Miles and understanding the responsibility that came with it. It became a precious relic, a piece of him to hold onto as she embarked on the uncertain road ahead, now a reminder of their love and a source of his magic that she would safeguard.

Summoning a deep breath, Blythe stood, her resolve rekindled. Miles would tell her to keep going, to honor his memory by championing their shared beliefs. As she merged with the group, the pocket watch cradled against her chest, she bore Miles's essence—a steadfast reminder of their love and the fortitude he had instilled within her.

CHAPTER THIRTY-SIX

Leaving the harrowing battlefield behind, a solemn hush enveloped the group, every footfall heavy with the gravity of their losses. Blythe's gaze remained fixed on the distant horizon, her heart aching for Miles. She couldn't look at Hera, for her grief was reflected in her face. She also avoided Quentin because he was the last person she wanted to deal with. Time itself seemed to warp as they pressed on, each step a testament to their unwavering resolve and the flickering ember of hope that guided them.

The path ahead stretched out, an arduous journey punctuated by intermittent pauses for rest and sustenance. Seeking refuge, they found temporary solace within the embrace of dense forests, seeking shelter beneath ancient trees that whispered tales of age-old wisdom. But their respite could never be prolonged, for the battle against the encroaching darkness showed no signs of relenting. This unrelenting tide pushed against them without mercy.

Days became blurry, marked by skirmishes and clashes with unyielding adversaries. Swords clashed in a symphony of determination and unity, each swing and strike a testament to their shared purpose.

Their path took them deeper into the shadows, where Blythe encountered an array of malevolent creatures that would have seemed unimaginable in a different time. Each entity imprinted itself upon her memory, a haunting image of their grotesque forms that would forever linger in her mind.

Dybbuks, restless spirits given form, materialized as ethereal apparitions wreathed in a sinister aura. Their tattered robes billowed like specters, and their translucent countenances twisted with anguish. Eyes devoid of light gleamed with an otherworldly glint, and their hollow whispers reverberated deep within the soul.

Banshees, harbingers of doom, were ethereal beings cloaked in sorrow and mourning. Their ghostly forms exuded an eerie luminescence, their flowing garments as insubstantial as the morning mist. Their mournful wails pierced the air, a chilling echo of the grief that pervaded the realms of the departed.

Zombies, embodiments of the undead, were macabre figures of decay and rot. They staggered forward with a relentless hunger for the living, their decomposing flesh hanging from skeletal frames. Their lifeless eyes burned with an insidious craving, their movements driven by an eternal thirst for flesh.

Goblins, twisted and malicious, scurried through the darkness with an unsettling nimbleness. Hunchbacked and adorned with sickly, mottled skin, they bore an air of treacherous cunning. Pointed ears and malicious grins marked them as purveyors of malevolent trickery.

Ogres, towering and brutish, emanated raw power with their colossal frames. Ugliness was a trait they shared, their rough skin marred by warts and boils. Hideous faces bore mouths filled with jagged teeth, forever stained by the blood of their victims. Their presence exuded a potent force, their strength poised to crush anything that dared cross their path.

Through these encounters, Blythe gained an intimate understanding of the horrors concealed in the shadows. With its unique and nightmarish visage, each entity served as a stark reminder of the darkness that threatened to engulf their world.

Amidst spilled blood and inflicted wounds, they pushed forward, unswayed by the trials that beset them. With each battle, Blythe's proficiency grew, her once uncertain hands now exuding newfound confidence as they wielded swords and channeled her burgeoning magical abilities. She symbolized unwavering resolve, transforming her grief into a wellspring of fierce determination. Her fight was a tribute to her fallen loved ones and a testament to the promise of a brighter future.

After an eternity of enduring trials, they finally reached

their destination—an ominous portal concealed amidst the treacherous terrain of a murky bog. Griffin commented that it looked just like the Mireglow Fen Bogs, but somehow darker. The air crackled with an unsettling energy, raising the hairs on the back of their necks. The group stood assembled around the portal, their feet sinking ankle-deep into the clinging muck as though the bog resisted releasing them.

Beside Blythe stood Bertolf, his massive wolf form imposing and formidable. The weight of the impending confrontation bore down on her, causing her body to tremble with a blend of anxiety and fear.

"So... we're moving forward with this now," her fingers toyed with the edge of her sleeve, her gaze shifting between each group member. Her soft murmur in the tense atmosphere held the delicate equilibrium between uncertainty and determination as if she wrestled with the decision even as the words left her lips.

"Yep," Quentin's shoulders sagged slightly as he exhaled the affirmation, his gaze traversing the group with a fusion of acceptance and resolve. His fingers drummed a restless beat against his thigh, the tension in his posture betraying the urgency of their circumstances. His succinct response hung in the air, amplifying the weight of their situation. Blythe winced at his words, a mélange of emotions swirling within her. A part of her, laden with guilt, secretly wished it had been Quentin lying lifeless instead of Miles. Yet, in her depths, she understood that losing Quentin would have been equally shattering, regardless of the pain he had caused her. Revelation settled upon her, illuminating the battlefield's ability to distort emotions and unveil the intricate nature of human connections.

"We need to advance now," Quentin ordered, his stance unwavering, his gaze surveying the group for compliance. A similar directive echoed from behind, propelling their comrades forward, akin to an unyielding force closing in on its quarry.

CHAPTER THIRTY-SEVEN

The group allowed the surge of enraged Warlocks to rush past them, their faces contorted with wrath as they brandished weapons forged from the vivid luminescence they harnessed. Blythe felt a firm grasp on her wrist, arresting her forward movement. She turned to find Quentin at her side, his eyes blending apprehension and care.

Drawing close, his words brushed against her ear, a hushed murmur meant for her alone. His warm and reassuring breath kissed her cheek, "It might be safer if you hung back." She furrowed her brow, pulling her wrist from his hold, unwilling to be dictated by his counsel.

"You don't control me, Quentin Hendrix," she countered, her tone infused with defiance. "I determine my own path." With that declaration, she pivoted on her heel and hastened alongside her fellow warriors, resolute to confront whatever lay ahead.

A fierce skirmish ignited as Blythe and her companions fought alongside the Warlocks. They forged a united front in unison, pressing onward with unwavering resolve to breach the portal and venture to the other side. The clash of weapons and the sizzle of magic filled the air, birthing a symphony of chaos and desperation.

Blythe's sword sliced through the air, deflecting incoming strikes and launching swift, calculated counterblows. Her muscles strained with each movement, yet adrenaline coursed through her veins, propelling her every action. Alongside her, her companions fought with equal fervor, their combined efforts coalescing into a barrier of strength and determination.

The Warlocks harnessed their arcane abilities, casting spells that rent through the ranks of their adversaries. Fireballs erupted, engulfing enemy combatants in scalding infernos. At the same time, lightning bolts crackled with deadly precision, striking down foes with searing electricity.

Blythe's magic surged within her, a turbulent energy storm that yearned for release. She wielded it with newfound mastery, conjuring protective barriers and unleashing devastating blasts of arcane force. The magic coursed through her veins, an extension of her will. With each incantation, she felt herself drawing closer to a power she had never imagined.

A deafening roar pierced the air, drowning out the cacophony of battle. Blythe turned to see Bertolf, the massive wolf at her side, leaping into the fray with a primal ferocity. His fangs gleamed in the dim light, and his muscular form struck fear into the hearts of their adversaries. With every swipe of his claws and snap of his jaws, he ruthlessly dispatched their enemies.

Blythe marveled at the sight, a mixture of awe and gratitude swelling. Bertolf had been an unexpected ally, his loyalty and strength a testament to the bonds forged in the crucible of conflict. She knew that his presence was not only a boon to their cause but a reminder that even in the darkest times, allies could be found in the most unlikely places.

As the battle raged on, Blythe's thoughts raced, her newfound power surging through her like a tempest. She could feel it building, a potent force that threatened to overwhelm her. With each passing moment, it grew stronger, its origin and purpose shrouded in mystery.

And then, it happened.

A surge of power unlike anything she had ever experienced, coursed through her being. It was as if a dam had burst within her, releasing a torrent of raw energy. The air around her seemed to ripple with her newfound might, and a shockwave emanated from her, sending foes staggering back.

Blythe's eyes widened with astonishment as she realized the extent of her newfound abilities. She could feel the magic within her, an untapped well of potential that had been awakened in the crucible of battle. It flowed through her like a river, and at that moment, she knew that she had been irrevocably changed.

The portal before them flickered and wavered, its insidious presence faltering under the onslaught of their combined efforts. With a final, concerted push, they breached its threshold, hurtling into the unknown with a collective resolve that transcended fear.

As the portal enveloped them, Blythe couldn't help but wonder about the source of her newfound power and the mysteries that awaited them on the other side. One thing was sure—she was no longer the same person who had embarked on this journey. She had been forged in the crucible of conflict, her spirit tempered by the trials of battle, and she was ready to face whatever lay ahead with unwavering determination.

The world around them shifted in the darkness of the portal's embrace, and Blythe knew that their true journey was just beginning.

Emerging from the portal, the group was thrust into a nightmarish tableau. The air reeked of smoldering embers, the cacophony of clashing blades drowning out all other sounds. Lizard-like creatures, claws glinting ominously and tails poised like lethal weapons, bore down upon them, their malevolent eyes glittering with cruel intent.

Amid the chaos, the rebel forces and Warlocks, locked in a desperate struggle with the reptilian foes, were gradually yielding ground. Desperation clung to the atmosphere like a suffocating shroud as the collective might of their adversaries threatened to consume them.

Blythe's heart raced in her chest as she surveyed the harrowing scene. The rebels and Warlocks fought valiantly, but their valiant efforts were futile despite overwhelming odds. The ebb and flow of the battle now favored their enemies, and with every passing heartbeat, their plight grew increasingly dire.

In the heat of the relentless fray, Quentin, breaking away from the combat for a fleeting moment, urgently beckoned Blythe to take cover behind a lifeless tree. His eyes bore into hers, the urgency reflected in his gaze. He withdrew a vial filled with a shimmering, arcane elixir from a pouch at his side. With a fervent plea, he implored, "Blythe, take this." The vial she had discovered in the enigmatic room lay in his outstretched hand. "Demetrius unearthed the incantation—'Ignis Aeternum.' If you say it after ingesting this elixir, you'll unlock the power of the Astra Elixir. I know you may harbor anger and distrust toward me, and I'm the last person you'd willingly rely on. But please understand that this may be our only chance to survive this ordeal."

Quentin's words held a stark truth. Trusting him was a daunting prospect that weighed heavily on Blythe's mind. Her hesitation lingered, but amid the chaos and bloodshed, there was a stark clarity in the crucible of this battle. She couldn't deny the gravity of their situation, and she couldn't deny that she had already lost too much.

With a determined resolve, Blythe uncorked the vial and consumed its contents. An electric surge of magic coursed through her being, igniting her senses and infusing her with an otherworldly vitality. Her eyes blazed with newfound power as she stepped away from the tree's shelter, her sword poised and a free hand extended toward an approaching horde of lizard people.

Summoning her newfound magic, she chanted the incantation with unwavering conviction. A luminous burst of energy erupted from her fingertips, colliding with the oncoming reptilian adversaries. The arcane blast sent them hurtling through the air, their agonized contortions a testament to the searing pain coursing through their scaled bodies.

In the blink of an eye, the tide of battle shifted as if the very fabric of the conflict had been rewoven. Inspired by Blythe's astounding display of power, the rebels and Warlocks rallied, surging forward and pushing the lizard people back. What had seemed imminent defeat now transformed into a desperate retreat for the once-victorious foes.

Blythe continued to wield her newfound magic with precision and skill, each spell she cast propelling the enemy forces further into disarray. Her companions fought alongside her, their spirits reignited by the dazzling spectacle of her might.

Amidst the chaos, triumphant cries and defiant roars filled the air as the rebels and Warlocks pursued their retreating adversaries. Blythe's heart swelled with pride as she witnessed her comrades pressing forward, their resolve rekindled by the glimmering ember of hope.

In the tumultuous battlefield, Blythe understood their journey was far from over. But armed with her newfound power and fortified by the unwavering determination of her allies, she was now more resolute than ever to confront whatever challenges lay ahead.

CHAPTER THIRTY-EIGHT

Warlocks and rebels erupted in cheers, their jubilation reverberating through the air. Magical displays soared overhead, painting the sky with vibrant hues. Embraces, kisses, and joyous expressions ignited among the diverse races, spreading rapidly. In this fleeting moment, they bathed in victory's euphoria, savoring long-denied freedom. Love and hope prevailed over battle scars, uniting them in rare harmony.

Blythe's gaze swept the scene, witnessing unbridled affection and camaraderie. Melya's intense embrace of a stranger stirred mixed emotions. Griffin and Octo's brotherly bond, evident in laughter and cheers, evoked a twinge of longing for an absent someone. Fallen adversaries—Troglodytes, Warlocks, witches, elves, dwarves—marked the toll of battle. Amidst it all, she contemplated Miles' words, pondering alternative paths to avert such loss.

"Blythe." Startled, she spun, her sword meeting Quentin's blade. His battle-worn face, smeared with blood and dirt, bore testament to the price they'd all paid. His injured arm hung limply, his left hand firmly gripping his sword to skillfully lower hers. "Easy there, Kitten. It's just me."

The sword dropped, and Blythe rushed into Quentin's waiting arms, tears streaming down her face. Emotions suppressed since Miles' death were released in trembles. Quentin held her close, his cheek against her head, offering solace.

"It's okay, Kitten," he whispered, gently stroking her back. Safety enveloped her momentarily, but Blythe pulled away, resolved to return.

"Hera... where is she?" Her eyes scanned the crowd, searching for her loyal friend.

"I saw her a few moments ago. She's okay," Quentin reassured, but Blythe shook her head, unabated worry.

"She's not... she loved Miles... I need to find her." Resolute, she set off, ensuring Quentin followed at a distance. Hera walked ahead alone. Blythe quickened her pace, intercepting Hera. Hera's attempts to turn away were met with Blythe's unwavering determination. Pulling Hera into a tight embrace, resistance melted as Hera succumbed to grief, tears streaming down her dirt-streaked face.

"Oh, Hera..." Blythe whispered, compassion in her touch. Hera's mix of grief and determination tried to regain control.

"I'm fine, Blythe," Hera insisted, her words hollow. "Go back to Quentin, leave me be." She moved to walk away, but Blythe jogged, blocking her path. Arms wrapped around Hera again, unwilling to let her face pain alone.

Blythe felt Hera tremble, and seeing Quentin nearby, his tears flowing, she realized he, too, had lost a dear friend.

"I know you loved him," Blythe said softly, empathy in her gaze. "And he loved you too." Hera's eyes welled, her lips trembling.

"No, listen to me. Miles told me before he passed... He didn't love me the way he used to. Not anymore. I believe... he just hadn't been ready to admit how he felt about you, and he realized it too late."

Hera's eyes glistened, her voice trembling. "Why are you telling me this?" Raw vulnerability colored her words. "What difference does it make now?" Grief etched her features, her lips quivering.

"He's gone," Blythe said, looking off into the distance.

"You deserve the truth, Hera." Blythe gently brushed a strand of hair from Hera's tear-stained face. "We all do. I think it's time we uncover the truth." Hera shook her head, pulling away and taking a deep breath, gathering strength against the tidal wave of emotions.

"He's gone. That's the truth. But our fight isn't over. The Council still lives... and they will pay." Hera resumed her determined stride. "Camp shouldn't be far from here. It's time for us to regroup."

Blythe stepped beside Hera, a heavy blend of loss and determination weighing on her heart. Side by side, they walked, their bond strengthened by shared grief and the unwavering resolve to deliver justice to those who had orchestrated their suffering.

The next few hours revolved around rounding up the injured, assigning patrols for the portal, and strategizing. Blythe, intentionally excluded from those discussions, occupied herself with wound care, cooking, and anything else that would help her elude Quentin. Despite her attempts, she had failed to approach Demetrius, who seemed immersed in talks with Warlock leaders and delegates from other races. Blythe couldn't even get close enough to overhear their conversations.

She managed to avoid Quentin's presence for nearly a week. Wondering if he was deliberately granting her space or if her evasion skills were exceptionally honed, she concluded that he was intentionally keeping his distance.

Around a week after the battle of Mireglow Fen, as it would later be known, Blythe found herself seated around a campfire in her small encampment. Hera, Griffin, Melya, Bertolf, and several others with tents nearby were gathered, finishing their meal.

"Good evening!" Blythe glanced up, spotting Demetrius, Quentin, and an unfamiliar, pale-faced Warlock entering the clearing. Quentin smiled and winked at her, but she swiftly redirected her focus to Demetrius, feigning obliviousness to Quentin's gesture. No, Quentin, she thought, I haven't forgiven you.

"Good evening," a few voices chorused from the group.

Demetrius introduced the unfamiliar Warlock. "For those unfamiliar, this is Zelos Dredmor. We've been discussing our future plans. Before we make our way to the capital, we want to convey our gratitude for your bravery and hard work. We're in the process of assembling forces for our final assault. Zelos has some insights to share about Warlock knowledge and strategies."

"Thank you, Demetrius." Zelos stepped forward, a rare smile gracing his face. "As you may already know, the Warlocks have held deep resentment against the Council long before those on this side of the portals. You might not be aware of our belief that one of our own betrayed us and colluded with the Council. Over a century ago, a few sought power and authority when we were banished to the Dark World. We attempted to police ourselves, but one individual managed to evade us. He went by Precious the Eternal, claiming to have unlocked the secret to eternal life. Our ancestors were skeptical, but before they were cast into exile, we had reason to suspect that he not only attained immortality but also infiltrated the Council, manipulating it to his advantage."

Whispers rippled through the group—a mixture of skepticism and concern. Blythe's mind churned, contemplating the veracity of Zelos' claims. Was he attempting to manipulate minds with deceit, or did his words bear sincerity? She withheld judgment, demanding more clarity. Gray-skinned council members hadn't registered in her memory.

"We've decided that to crush the Council and Prexius, we must gather a formidable force. A portion of the Warlocks, Elves, and Werewolves will stand guard at the portal. The rest of us leave in two days to march on the capital. Those opting out can depart tomorrow at dawn. Good night." Zelos and Demetrius exited the scene. Having positioned himself across from Blythe, Quentin shadowed her during the conversation. She sensed his gaze as she shook her head and headed to her tent.

As anticipated, she detected Quentin trailing behind her. "Blythe, we need to talk."

She shook her head, pivoting to confront him. "We don't 'need' to talk. You want to. I don't." Her steps resumed, only to feel Quentin's grip on her left wrist.

Swiftly whirling around, her wrist deftly yanked him forward. With a fluid motion, she pivoted on her left foot and drove her knee into his side. Caught off-guard, Quentin released her wrist with a grunt of pain. She retreated, assuming a defensive stance. "Do. Not. Touch. Me. Again!"

Quentin's surprise was palpable, but Blythe's pride surged. Hera's hand-to-hand combat lessons had been well-taken, evident in her swift defense. Quentin nursed his side, a wry smile playing on his lips. "Look at you... graduated from a kitten to a full-blown Tiger."

Blythe's glare spoke volumes. "I'm not amused, Quentin. I'm serious. You have NO right to touch me without my permission."

"Okay." Quentin raised his hands, stepping back. "I won't touch you." Blythe snorted. "No, I mean it. You're right. It's time for the truth to come out, so I needed to talk to you."

"Five minutes. Go." She crossed her arms, standing her ground, her gaze unyielding.

"Though explaining my actions is important, it's not my primary concern now." He scanned their surroundings to ensure privacy. Few were within earshot, and those present were engaged in separate conversations. His eyes locked with hers once more. "The Warlocks and Demetrius are deceiving us."

"About what?"

"Their goal extends beyond dismantling the Council. They also intend to shatter the boundaries between worlds." He assessed their surroundings again before returning to her gaze. "We must halt them."

"What on earth are you talking about?" Blythe's brow furrowed. "Why would Demetrius want to unleash Dark World malevolence into our realm and the human world?"

"That's the dilemma... I'm uncertain if that's truly their aim." Quentin shifted restlessly. "I've worked tirelessly to secure my standing within the rebellion... I never anticipated something like this. I wasn't meant to overhear it. I was delivering information to Demetrius and circled around his tent. The usual guards were absent. Some Warlocks were nearby, but they were preoccupied with Demetrius's guards. The only explanation is they didn't want eavesdroppers." He shook his head. "I don't grasp everything, but we must intervene."

"How do you know this is the truth?" Blythe whispered, drawing closer to him to ensure their conversation remained confidential.

"I heard it... but certainty eludes me. I can't linger behind when others depart without rousing suspicion. I've discussed this with Hera and Griffin. They've agreed to feign departure but covertly monitor the portal guards. Yet, I require a valid pretext for them to separate from the group, lest it appear contrived."

"Which is where I come in, I assume?"

"I didn't wish to involve you, but Griffin proposed the notion. He understands I would never allow you to wander alone, and I'm prepared to take any measures to safeguard you. Naturally, he suggested dispatching them to ensure your welfare."

"So, you're asking me to leave." She arched an eyebrow, her skepticism palpable.

"Yes and no... It's common knowledge that you yearn to return home. Thus, if you opt out of the battle, it won't raise eyebrows."

Blythe's fingers tapped an anxious rhythm on her thigh, her unwavering gaze locked onto Quentin's. "So... hypothetically, if I agree, and we confirm the portal guards have deserted their posts... what's our next move?" Her forehead creased in profound contemplation, a blend of doubt and apprehension flickering in her eyes. She leaned forward slightly, her body taut with anticipation as she awaited Quentin's response. "How do we avoid being overrun by demons cascading into our world?" A quiver of unease tinged her voice, mirroring the worry on her face. "What's the strategy for containment?" Frustration tinged her tone, her eyes narrowing in a challenging stare. "Quentin, I don't see how this scheme offers a solution!"

Quentin's brow furrowed, acknowledging the gravity of her concerns. "Ellira will await your trio's return, ensuring your safety to me, for verification. Once confirmed, we can endeavor to thwart the Warlocks. Regrettably, lacking substantive proof, we'll struggle to convince Demetrius of their intentions."

"But demons could inundate our realm... they might even have infiltrated the Human World if your account holds truth."

"I'm aware..." Quentin's frown deepened. "This is the best approach I could devise, Blythe. If indeed it's the reality, we confront a monumental predicament." Blythe sighed, the enormity of the situation bearing down on her.

"Fine... I'll do it... and if it turns out you're wrong, I'll have the liberty to return home, correct?"

"Yes. You have my pledge." Quentin managed a sincere smile. "Should I be mistaken, go home. I understand your desire to distance yourself from me, but after all is resolved, I will seek you out and explain my actions."

Her skepticism lingered, but Blythe nodded. "Alright then... I'll go prepare... unless you're considering tailing me again?"

Quentin shook his head. "No." A warmer smile graced his lips this time. "Take care, Blythe." With a slight bow, he turned and departed, leaving her alone to grapple with her thoughts.

CHAPTER THIRTY-NINE

The next day, Blythe departed from camp at dawn, following Griffin's described path. The sun bathed the surroundings in radiance, and the chorus of birdsong replaced the echoes of the Dark World's desolation. With each step, the scent of marshes yielded to the fragrant embrace of blooming flowers. Blythe's gait lightened, a fleeting semblance of joy momentarily eclipsing the shadows of her trials and losses. Nonetheless, her body bore the marks of battles fought and days of travel, coupled with the rigorous training Hera had put her through.

Her journey continued, punctuated by two pauses for meals, the sun's descent signaling the time to establish her temporary camp. As twilight painted the sky, Blythe discovered a tranquil glade within the woods, where she pitched her tent. Her familiarity with camp life allowed her to gather firewood and ignite a flame using Griffin's flintstone. The crackling blaze cast a warm embrace against the encroaching night.

Patience accompanied her as she anticipated Griffin and Hera's arrival. While waiting, she hummed a soft melody, her voice filling the solitude with an intimate serenade. Long had she yearned for autonomy and an escape from the others' constant presence, yet at this moment, she found herself missing Griffin's playful banter and Hera's unwavering companionship. Even Quentin's irrepressible energy held a certain allure. Stirrings in the shadows drew her focus, and she conjured a luminescent orb to illuminate the surroundings.

Emerging from obscurity, a robust figure materialized —Griffin. With an exaggerated bow, he entered the clearing, performing a theatrical flourish. Hera followed, her expression less enthused. Their unspoken dynamic suggested that Griffin had likely uttered a comment that hadn't resonated well with her. Blythe's relief at their arrival was unmistakable, her face lighting up.

"Greetings, noble maiden!" Griffin announced dramatically, punctuating his words with another ostentatious bow. Hera rolled her eyes, walking past him and settling beside Blythe. "Hey," she greeted Blythe, her tone more subdued. "How was your solitary jaunt?"

"Surprisingly uneventful," Blythe replied, a hint of a smile touching her lips.

"Fantastic!" Hera enthused, producing a food block and taking a bite. "Let's hope Quentin's off the mark, and we can all return to our desired pursuits."

"Ah, but should Quentin's forecast hold true, think of the epic tale we must recount!" Griffin interjected with ebullience, joining them on the ground and beginning his meal.

"I'll pass on that adventure," Hera mumbled.

"Seconded." Blythe nodded. "I'm more than ready to return to my world, and... well, I'm not entirely certain what I want to do once I'm there. What about you?"

"One can never have too many thrilling escapades on the battlefield!" Griffin declared with gusto, promptly finishing one food block and reaching for another. Blythe couldn't help but marvel at his prodigious appetite.

"You're welcome to all of mine." Blythe chuckled. "So, our task here is to await confirmation that the rest have set out for the capital. But what are we supposed to do in the meantime?"

"If memory serves, you've yet to complete your training," Hera observed, a playful glimmer in her eyes. Blythe let out an exaggerated groan, dramatically flopping back onto the ground and gazing skyward. Griffin and Hera shared a laugh.

"You certainly surprised Quentin when you were training with him yesterday," Griffin added, his laughter contagious. "He never saw it coming."

"Yes, but you left your side wide open," Hera chastised. "Quentin might not have hurt you, but I could've easily cracked your ribs."

"Ah, but if it were ye, the outcome would've been a whole lot different!" Griffin grinned. Blythe reluctantly agreed.

Griffin erupted in laughter and produced a flask. Blythe offered a grateful smile, aware of his fondness for spirits, but politely declined. After a prior run-in with a particularly unpleasant hangover, she had no intention of experiencing the full brunt of alcohol's effects again, especially without the magical assistance of the fairies.

Griffin laughed heartily and took a swig. "Ah, my dear, if only I had more time, I'd turn ye into a proper drinker!"

"Or you'd end up destroying my liver." Laughter resonated between Blythe and Griffin while Hera shook her head in mock disapproval.

Throughout the night, they rotated shifts to keep watch, ensuring everyone received a reasonable amount of rest. Blythe's slumber was interrupted by Hera, who immediately launched her into an intense training regimen before granting her reprieve to eat from the rabbits Griffin had managed to catch. In the cycle of training, Griffin and Hera took turns sparring with Blythe while the others foraged and prepared food. Breaks were allocated during mealtimes, for cleanup, and when darkness enshrouded the camp, signaling a halt to the training. When Blythe finally settled into her sleeping roll, her body ached from the strain.

The following morning, they rose early and embarked on their journey in silence, each secretly yearning that Quentin's assessment had been awry and they wouldn't encounter any malevolent entities on their way back to the portal. Tension clung to the air as their footsteps carried them forward. Blythe tightened her grip on her short sword, Hera readied her longsword, and Griffin held his trusty axe. Blythe couldn't help but notice her improved stealthiness, a testament to Hera's guidance.

Throughout the day, they progressed, punctuating their march with occasional pauses for sustenance and rest before pressing on. As the sun dipped toward the horizon, they arrived at the base camp, greeted by an unsettling stillness. Remnants of the army's presence were etched into the landscape: scorched circles and patches of withered grass. Undeterred, they pushed onward, their pace steady as they traversed the landscape, heading toward the marshes. Their momentum was suddenly shattered by a sound that jerked them to a halt, weapons poised and ready.

Emerging from the shroud of the trees, a formidable figure advanced calmly toward them. Blythe conjured a soft ball of light, illuminating their visitor without blinding themselves. It was unmistakably Bertolf, his hirsute form immediately recognizable.

"Bertolf," Blythe sighed in relief, easing her grip on her sword.

"Best not to lower your guard just yet," Bertolf intoned grimly. "Quentin was right. This forest is on the brink of an invasion."

"How did you discern that?" Hera inquired.

"Werewolves possess acute hearing," he replied nonchalantly. "Summon the dragon. Xander isn't far. I apprised him of our covert mission. He's rallied several vampires who will do their utmost to hold back the assailants. Although vampires are more inclined to protect nocturnal creatures, they share little interest in the likes of you."

"Very well," Blythe nodded, her gaze lifting skyward. "Ellira!" she called softly, recalling Quentin's advice on the dragon's keen senses. Almost on cue, a piercing screech pierced the air, emanating from their left.

"The dragon?" Griffin's voice carried a note of skepticism.

"No, ghouls," Bertolf's growl responded. The sound of mighty wings reached their ears, and Blythe's gaze lifted to witness Ellira descending gracefully towards them. The dragon touched down, and Hera promptly seized Blythe's wrist, guiding her toward the majestic creature.

"Quickly!" Hera whispered urgently. With practiced coordination, Blythe and Hera assisted Griffin onto the dragon's back before Hera herself mounted. They arranged themselves with Griffin at the front, followed by Blythe and Hera securing the rear.

"Go!" Bertolf's command rang out as he delivered a firm slap to the dragon's flank.

"What about you?!" Blythe's concern for the werewolf's well-being was palpable.

"I'll manage," he grunted before pivoting and melting into the forest as Ellira lifted off the ground.

Blythe's eyes darted skyward, tracking the advancing ghouls with worry and apprehension. She turned to Hera, brows furrowing with concern. "Will the ghouls be able to reach us up here?"

"I'm uncertain," Hera replied. As the dragon ascended swiftly, the terrain below receded from view. Sinister shapes began to materialize among the trees, an unsettling echo of the Dark World's horrors. Ellira emitted a threatening growl, diverting Blythe's attention from the ground.

"Look!" Griffin's sudden exclamation broke through the tension, his arm pointing urgently as Ellira veered sharply in response. Blythe followed his indication, narrowing her gaze to discern the silhouettes of additional miniature airborne figures against the darkening sky.

"Gargoyles," Hera breathed, her voice barely audible as the words slipped from her lips. The three clung tenaciously to Ellira's scales, their fingers digging into the rough texture as the dragon surged forward, wings battling against the rushing currents. Blythe's stomach churned with unease, brows furrowing as the encroaching darkness threatened to engulf them.

The wind roared in Blythe's ears as the pursuing gargoyles maintained their relentless chase. Their wings beat with a thunderous resonance, gusts of air buffeting against Blythe as they swooped dangerously close. Clinging tightly to Ellira, she sensed the dragon's determination to outmaneuver their pursuers.

Hera unleashed a mighty swing of her sword, deterring the closest gargoyle and compelling it to retreat momentarily.

Resourceful as ever, Griffin hurled small alchemical fire vials, igniting brief bursts of flames that disrupted the relentless pursuit.

Yet the gargoyles pressed on, their determination unyielding. Their numbers seemed to swell, their ranks multiplying as more joined the relentless chase. It was an unrelenting struggle, a desperate race against the encroaching darkness.

Ellira let out a resounding roar, a fierce blend of anger and determination, her wings propelling them higher into the night sky. Blythe's heart raced within her chest as they ascended, yearning to gain sufficient altitude to elude the clutches of their relentless pursuers.

Minutes stretched into an eternity as their heart-pounding flight persisted. The gargoyles, driven by primal instinct, mirrored their every movement, steadfast in their resolve to prevent their quarry's escape. Blythe's muscles screamed with exhaustion, her body aching from the ceaseless exertion.

Just when it seemed they might succumb to the unrelenting pursuit, a break in the overcast sky unveiled a faint glimmer of moonlight. Sensing a fleeting chance, Ellira adjusted her wings and propelled herself forward, summoning one last surge of strength, leaving the pursuing gargoyles behind.

Gasping for breath, Blythe stole a glance backward, watching as the gargoyles dwindled into specks on the horizon. Relief flooded through her, mingling with a profound reverence for the remarkable connection she had forged with Ellira and the unwavering courage of her companions.

As the threat waned, the tension that had gripped the air slowly dissipated. Blythe looked down upon the sprawling panorama below, a blend of wonder and gratitude filling her heart. They had narrowly escaped the clutches of death, and she resolved to honor the lives lost by steadfastly confronting the impending darkness that loomed ahead.

The flight continued, but a renewed sense of hope

bloomed within them. They pressed onward, fortified by the strength they found in one another. Together, they would confront the challenges ahead and fight to safeguard their worlds from the encroaching threat of darkness.

"If evil has been unleashed into the Magic World, it might also be spreading to the Human World," Blythe whispered, her eyes widening as the gravity of her realization settled in. Her fists clenched at her sides, her body tense with urgency. She closed her eyes, suppressing the tears that threatened to escape. The thought of darkness consuming her home filled her with dread. The prospect of losing everyone she cared for was too much to bear. Amid her despair, she silently prayed for a glimmer of hope to guide them.

As Ellira soared through the clouds, the trio shivered in the cold wind. The sun had long set, leaving only scattered lights below, distant beacons of houses and cities. Blythe's mind conjured an unsettling image of darkness spreading from the Dark World, smothering those lights like a suffocating shroud, snuffing out lives within.

An inexplicable intuition led Ellira toward a small clearing, forcefully parting the trees before landing with remarkable gentleness. The clearing lay shrouded in darkness, an enigmatic void devoid of visible presence. Overcast clouds veiled the moon and stars, casting an eerie ambiance. Blythe sensed Hera dismount, and in her attempt to follow suit, she stumbled to the ground, wincing as her body made contact with the earth. On the other side of Ellira, she heard Griffin's landing thud. Slowly, she pushed herself up, using the dragon's flank for support.

"Good girl," a voice called out, resonating through the shadows. Blythe's heart skipped a beat as Quentin emerged, a faint smile playing on his lips.

"You were right," Hera exhaled, her shoulders sagging as if a weight had been lifted. Blythe noticed her companions' apparent calm in the darkness, restraining the urge to conjure light.

"It went as ye expected," Griffin added, moving away from the dragon's impressive form. "We barely escaped... Bertolf stayed behind."

"I'm not surprised," Quentin replied, his concern evident. "Well, that confirms it."

"Confirms what?" Blythe's brows furrowed, her eyes widening with fear. Her fingers fidgeted anxiously, and she took a step back involuntarily. The color drained from her face, and her breath quickened as her mind raced through grim scenarios. "If the Dark World has spread here, who's to say it hasn't opened to the Human World too? Innocent humans could be dying right now!" Her hands trembled, her body poised for action, ready to confront the impending threat.

"Shh..." Quentin hushed her gently. "They knew I was waiting for Ellira to bring you, but not why. We can't let them know we're aware."

"But what do we do now?" Hera's brows furrowed, her eyes searching for answers, a mix of desperation and determination etching her features.

"I don't have all the answers yet, but our troubles are far from over," Quentin sighed. "We must act along, establish camp, and tread carefully. Warlocks are cunning and skilled manipulators." Quentin paused, his words brimming with caution. "Blythe, maybe you could provide some light now. It's time to move on."

"I can't!" Blythe's hands clenched into fists, her eyes brimming with tears. "I can't pretend I don't know innocent lives are being taken or are at risk of being taken!" Emotions surged within her, a blend of agony and determination evident in her posture and expression.

"You have to," Hera stepped forward, her grip firm on Blythe's hand. "Pretend you're furious. You're allowed to be furious, knowing what they're doing... Be angry that Quentin coerced you to return. Let them think that's why you're upset. They'll understand Quentin's motivation. Fae are deeply protective of their mates."

"Wait... what?" Blythe stammered.

"Now ye've gone and done it," Griffin muttered under his breath.

"That's enough... we can discuss this later. Light, Blythe?" Quentin's voice held a trace of annoyance. Blythe struggled momentarily to gather her thoughts, then traced the light rune on her hand, conjuring a soft ball of radiance that enveloped them in a gentle glow.

"Alright... let's go," Quentin declared, turning to lead them into the woods. Blythe followed, struck by the irony of the situation. Her journey into this world had begun with secrecy and deceit. Now, she willingly walked into this treacherous charade, fully aware yet unable to expose the truth to others. It felt like she had come full circle, trapped within an inescapable loop. Leaving this place was no longer her desire; she couldn't depart until both worlds were secure until she had cast the malevolence back to its rightful realm.

Her safety had become less critical, as her main focus was driving away the encroaching darkness and uncovering the mystery hinted at by Hera's cryptic mention of the Fae and their strong connection to their chosen companions. However, given their current urgent challenges, this revelation would have to wait.

As they entered the shadows, their destinies intertwined and their determination guiding them forward, it was clear that more challenges lay ahead and more secrets would be revealed. In this way, the story was just beginning, and its intrigue continued to capture their attention.

The End. For now.

ABOUT THE AUTHOR

S.j. Winter

S.J. Winter, a dedicated wife and mother, finds inspiration in the simple joys of life. Balancing her roles as a loving spouse and devoted parent, she has embarked on a journey of self-discovery through literature, photography, and adventure.

Beyond her creative pursuits, S.J. Winter is an avid traveler who cherishes the opportunity to explore diverse cultures and landscapes. These adventures have enriched her life with unique experiences and a broader perspective.

With a heart full of gratitude for life's blessings and a spirit eager to embrace new challenges, S.J. continues to pursue her passions and create meaningful connections with people from all walks of life. She hopes to inspire and uplift those she encounters on her journey through her words, her lens, and her actions.

BOOKS IN THIS SERIES

Legacy of Shadows

Legacy Of Shadows: Deception's Gambit

Look out for the next thrilling chapter in the epic saga! In the sequel to 'Legacy of Shadows: Keeper's Rebellion,' join Blythe, Quentin, and their brave companions as they confront an even more significant challenge. The cruel Council's grip on power tightens, and the Rebellion leader's sinister plans threaten to unleash unspeakable evil upon the world. Stay tuned as the rebels face trials of courage, wit, and strength and embark on a heart-pounding journey to dismantle the oppressive regime and restore balance to the realms. With danger lurking at every turn, can they triumph against all odds? Don't miss the next installment, where the fate of their worlds hangs in the balance.

www.ingramcontent.com/pod-product-compliance
Lightning Source LLC
LaVergne TN
LVHW050622100826
845148LV00011B/1688
9798218248901